Emily was acutely a[...] At last, she heard him w[...] silence, which seemed very long, before she caught a quiet splash and knew that he had gone into the pool.

Emily felt a brief glow of satisfaction. He had succumbed to this small indulgence. He wasn't immune. She heard water ripple against rock, the sound of swimming. Unbidden, her imagination began to build a picture. It grew more and more detailed, filling her senses until she was conscious of nothing but the liquid sounds behind her and the images in her mind. Her cheeks reddened. Had he done this when she was in the water?

Without realizing it, she had inched around on the rock. She was perpendicular to the cliff now. Shocked, she started to turn back. But splashing stopped her. Emily bent her head, letting her damp hair hang down along her face. Twisting her head slightly, she sneaked a look at the pool.

Richard had just climbed out. He stood at the edge, shedding water like dripping gold. His body was dappled with shadow from the overhanging trees, and it was gloriously formed—broad shoulders, lean muscled arms and legs, a deep chest that narrowed to . . .

He raised his head and caught her looking.

BANTAM BOOKS BY JANE ASHFORD

BRIDE,
TO
BE

JANE,
ASHFORD

BANTAM  BOOKS

New York Toronto London
Sydney Auckland

BRIDE TO BE

A Bantam Fanfare Book / August 1999

FANFARE and the portrayal of a boxed "ff" are trademarks of
Bantam Books, a division of Random House, Inc.

ISBN 0-553-57774-3

Published simultaneously in the United States and Canada

Bantam Books are published by Bantam Books, a division of Random House, Inc. Its trademark, consisting of the words "Bantam
Books" and the portrayal of a rooster, is Registered in U.S. Patent
and Trademark Office and in other countries. Marca Registrada.
Bantam Books, 1540 Broadway, New York, New York 10036.

PRINTED IN THE UNITED STATES OF AMERICA

WCD   0 9 8 7 6 5 4 3 2 1

BRIDE
TO
BE

ONE

E MILY CRANE WALKED briskly along the path that rambled through the property behind her house. On either side, meadow grass bent under shimmers of morning dew. The line of ancient willows that marked the course of the brook rustled against a crystalline blue sky. The sound of water bubbling over rocks came to her ears. It was an idyllic early spring scene; and she savored it, and her solitude, to the full. Her companions had gone on ahead. She could enjoy a brief respite from the continual upheavals of her home.

This morning, she had finally realized that her parents enjoyed chaos. Indeed, they seemed to thrive on it. When bailiffs pounded on the door, or another landlord threw them out, or the sight of a half-clothed model in the studio caused the cook and maidservant to give notice, they ranted and railed and bemoaned their fate. But they did it with such gusto, Emily thought. Why had she never noticed that before?

Once, when she was fifteen, she had asked her mother how she could bear the endless alarms and disruptions. Her mother had considered the question with bright interest and then decided that it must be a reaction to her upbringing. Emily's parents had been born into noble families—"the stifling atmosphere of upper-class convention," as her mother put it. Emily wondered what it would be like to be surrounded by a large family, never to wonder where one would be living this time next year, or whether the boiler might explode, or whether some disreputable friend of her father's would be hauled off to jail in the middle of dinner.

She loved her parents dearly, but she didn't share their artistic temperament. Paints and canvas didn't console her for every setback. And the itinerant life was beginning to wear on her. She was almost twenty years old; where would she be when she was twenty-five, or thirty? Still helping her family cope with daily disasters? Lately, she had been dreaming of a more settled existence—of tranquillity and even, perhaps, a touch of the conventional.

How outraged her father would be by such thoughts! Smiling, Emily parted the curtain of trailing willow branches and stepped through. Wouldn't it be pleasant if she had played in this spot as a child? If she had scores of happy memories of this secret hide-away? In fact, she had forgotten most of the places she had lived as a child. There had been so many.

A movement on the other side of the stream caught her eye. Two rough-looking men were dragging a third along the ground, tugging him toward the spot where the brook widened into a small pond. When one of the men stepped aside for a moment, she saw that the victim's hands were tied.

Emily grimaced. She had wanted only a quiet walk. In a life full of the unusual and unexpected, she had asked for just a few minutes peace. Was it so much? Evidently it was, replied a dry mental voice. And was she going to allow a helpless man to be drowned? For that was clearly what the two attackers intended.

She sighed. It must be her fate to resolve other people's difficulties. She had been doing it for her parents for so long that she had begun to attract other victims of circumstance. It was a lowering reflection.

Emerging from the willow branches, Emily started across the stream on a line of stepping-stones. "David! Jonathan!" she called.

Her escorts came running.

"What are you doing there?" she cried to the men. She didn't feel a trace of fear. She had been confronting various adversaries since she was thirteen. Indeed, the mob in Essex who had wanted to tar and feather her father had been much fiercer looking than these two disheveled individuals.

Startled, the two men let go of their burden and straightened. Then, seeing David and Jonathan racing toward them, they took to their heels.

They were heading for the road that ran along the back of the property, she saw. Confident that they wouldn't be back, she went to examine the man lying on the bank of the pond. His ankles were tied as well as his wrists, and he had been knocked on the head. A bruise was swelling at his temple. Emily sighed again. Did other young ladies, out for a soothing stroll, encounter such difficulties? She didn't think so. Perhaps her parents somehow *attracted* trouble.

She looked down at the bound man. He had an impressive physique. It was no wonder it had taken two ruffians to subdue him. His skin was bronzed, and his brown hair streaked gold by the sun. His hands were callused, but he didn't wear the clothes or quite have the look of a laborer. Even unconscious, his straight brows and chiseled features held a proud fierceness. Her father would paint him as a Roman legionary, Emily thought. Or, no, a gladiator. It was oddly easy to imagine this man in a brief tunic, his arms and legs gleaming with oil, his . . . Emily shook her head, startled at the immediacy of the picture and her uncharacteristic flight of imagination.

David and Jonathan came running back. "Have you chased them off?" asked Emily. "Good."

After giving the matter careful consideration, Emily untied the ropes that bound the man. She went to soak her handkerchief in the pond and then applied it to his bruised temple. The chilled cloth elicited a groan, and she moved back out of reach as the man drew in a deeper breath.

He opened his eyes, and blinked at the formidable pair of fangs poised inches from his face. With a speed that was truly startling, he jerked away and reached for Jonathan's throat in one fluid movement.

"Jonathan!" cried Emily.

The dog hadn't needed the admonition. He had already retreated from the look in the man's eyes. "Sit," said Emily.

The man stared at her blankly. Slowly, he sat up, biting back a groan. He put his hands to his head. When they encountered her embroidered linen handkerchief, he removed it and stared as if he'd never seen such a thing before in his life. Then he looked around at the pond, meadows, willow trees as if they too were strange and disorientating.

Had the attack addled his wits? Emily remembered the time her father had brained the local squire with a vase he had been using in a still life. That poor man had been incoherent for quite half an hour. Of course, with the squire it was mostly fury. And then they had had to move again and . . .

The man turned his head and then swayed dizzily. He squinted up into the sunlight and, looking at her, blinked.

"Are you all right?" Emily said. "You've had a knock on the head."

He put a hand to his temple, and winced.

"I believe you were attacked on the road," she added helpfully. "But we scared them off."

Sinking back, the man blinked again as if to clear blurred vision. He surveyed her more closely. "You?"

Emily snapped her fingers. Immediately, she was flanked by two gigantic Irish wolfhounds, nearly three feet at the shoulder and fiercely alert. Her father didn't let her go walking without them. She watched with some amusement as they regarded the man and each gave a soft growl. "David," she said, gesturing left, then right. "And Jonathan."

"I see." He looked well aware that those jaws would shatter bone.

"Why were those men trying to throw you in the pond?"

He looked at the water behind him. "What?"

"They had tied you up." She indicated the ropes lying in a tangle beside him. "And they were dragging you to the pond. They meant to drown you, I think."

He cradled his head as if it ached. "They must have been footpads. I was riding toward London when they . . ." He frowned. "One of them jumped from the hedge and started to pull me from my horse. I was fighting him off when the other came out of nowhere and hit me." He fingered the bruise on his head. "He must have had a cudgel."

"Common thieves wouldn't tie you and drag you across a field," she pointed out.

The man shrugged. "Perhaps they were angry that I had nothing to steal." He frowned again. "Except my horse. It's gone, I suppose." He looked around as if the animal might magically appear.

"They might have kicked you for that, or taken your clothes, but they wouldn't have bothered with more."

"You are an expert on footpads?" With an obvious effort, the man made it to his feet.

The top of her head barely reached his shoulder, Emily noticed. He really was quite large. And impressive, somehow, despite his condition.

"I appear to owe you a debt," he added. "You

have my thanks. I won't trouble you further." He turned away and then stopped, swaying and putting out a hand to catch his balance as he staggered.

Emily slipped under his arm and steadied him. "You probably shouldn't move."

"I am not going to lie here in the grass. I must find my horse."

"You can't even walk."

"Of course I can." But when he tried to push her away, he almost tumbled to the ground again.

Emily looked up at him, the latest in a seemingly endless line of dilemmas that she had had to solve. "You had better come to the house. We'll send for the doctor."

"I don't need a doctor."

"Yes, you do."

The man managed with some difficulty to gaze down at her, tucked under his arm. "You are a very odd young woman."

It always came to that, Emily thought wistfully. Everyone she met—particularly every young man she met—found her dauntingly eccentric. It was her parents' fault, with the life they had given her.

"You seem to take highway robbery quite in your stride," he added.

And so would he, if he had spent just about all his life moving from one emergency to another. Her father had a weakness for rogues. Over the years, he had befriended a variety of beguiling confidence men, at least one of whom made his living by highway robbery.

"Yet you have the face of a Botticelli angel," he said.

Emily looked up at him, meeting his intelligent hazel eyes from a distance shorter than she had ever experienced before—a rather unsettling distance, if the truth be told. Her eventful life had not included many compliments or the attentions of attractive young men. Her father's freewheeling ways most emphatically did not extend to his only daughter. He never allowed her to be alone with a man, let alone plastered against one's side holding him upright. Papa was going to be apoplectic if he found out. She needed to get her charge home and safely out of her arms. "Come along," she said, giving him a slight push.

He took a step, and stumbled. She wrapped her arm around his ribs to give him more support. With a naturalness that surprised her, his arm draped itself over her shoulders. The warmth of his body against her side was disturbing. "Move," she said, pushing him slightly again.

"I can walk," he declared, stepping away from her. But to his obvious frustration, vertigo returned, and he reeled.

"Why can't you be reasonable?"

"Reasonable? There is nothing reasonable about this situation. Any reasonable young woman would be sunk in a fit of the vapors by this time, wringing her hands and praying for aid."

"Would she?" Emily let her hands fall to her sides and frowned. Could this really be how a gently reared girl would behave? "That wouldn't be particularly helpful," she had to point out.

"No," he agreed, fixing a fascinated gaze upon her. "Who are you?"

It was a very good question, Emily thought. She often asked it of herself. "My name is Emily Crane." She waited, and when he said nothing, added, "And yours?"

"I beg your pardon. I am Richard Sheldon."

"Well, Mr. Sheldon, if you really wish me to have a fit of the vapors . . ."

"I don't," he put in hastily.

"Good. You will be spared a disappointment." She approached him once again. "We must go to my house."

She put her arm around his waist. His arm settled over her shoulders once again. "Come," said Emily, pressing closer to urge him forward. Richard stiffened a little and nearly toppled both of them to the ground. "Are you going to faint?"

"No," he snapped.

Pressed together, they made their way slowly across the meadow, the massive dogs gamboling at Emily's heels like puppies. Fortunately, the stepping-stones in the stream were large and flat, and they got across without mishap. Now and then, Richard would lurch unexpectedly as dizziness caught him. Each time, she supported him, and each time he stifled a curse.

The journey was beginning to seem endless when he said, "We are going to the house of . . . ?"

"My parents. We are nearly there."

And with any luck, they would evade her father, she thought as she helped their unexpected visitor across the last bit of meadow. The Honorable Alasdair Crane might be outrageous. He might wear Turkish robes and stand before his easel barefoot. He might threaten the local vicar with a cauliflower. He might send his Irish wolfhounds to the post office with a parcel. But his daughter was supposed to be a model of propriety. And this did *not* include dragging large virile strangers home from country walks.

Emily stole a look at his face through her lashes. He seemed to radiate heat. Perhaps the blow had given him a fever? But that didn't explain why fitting her head into the hollow of his shoulder was so disconcertingly pleasant. Nor why she was so intensely conscious of his hand on her arm.

Although Emily's experience of humanity was far broader than that of most young ladies, she had never encountered anyone like Richard Sheldon. His voice and bearing had an aristocratic polish, but his clothes and hands were not even those of a gentleman. He had come within an inch of throttling Jonathan, and in that moment he had been—ferocious. Yet he spoke to her with civility.

Emily shook her head as they stepped up onto the weedy flagstone terrace that ran along the back of their current house. It didn't make sense. She couldn't figure him out.

Perhaps it would be easier when she no longer had her arm around him. His proximity was distracting. He was so large, looming over her, and the scent of leather and soap and . . . man were so heady.

The French doors that led inside were propped open, which was fortunate because one of them was loose on its hinges and continually threatening to fall. Now if only she could get Mr. Sheldon seated in their shabby drawing room before her father discovered his arrival. . . .

But here Emily's luck ran out. Her father appeared in the archway opposite before they had taken two steps into the house.

"What the devil is this?" he shouted. "Get your hands off my daughter, you blackguard!"

He surged forward with his hand raised to strike, obviously forgetting that he held a loaded paintbrush. "Father!" Emily cried. "This man was attacked on the road. He's hurt."

Knowing that the words wouldn't penetrate at once, she pivoted somewhat clumsily and dropped Richard Sheldon into an armchair.

"Footpads," she added loudly. "In broad daylight."

"Eh?" Her father came to an abrupt stop before them. "What? Footpads?"

"Yes," said Emily. "They knocked him on the head and stole his horse. I found him in the meadow, ah, er, crawling toward the house for help."

A stifled exclamation escaped Richard, and Emily sent him a silent command to be quiet. Simple explanations worked best with her father.

"Crawling?" he repeated.

Emily nodded, gazing innocently up at him.

The hand holding the paintbrush dropped, leaving a streak of brilliant crimson along his pants leg.

"I was *not*—" began Richard.

"Isn't it a terrible thing?" put in Emily quickly. "Do you think we should inform the magistrate?"

"That jumped up country squire?" exploded her father. "He wouldn't know a footpad from his own backside. Of all the dim-witted, bad-tempered, ragmannered blusterers . . ."

Satisfied with her diversion, Emily let her father's ranting run its course. She threw Richard Sheldon a fierce glance, signaling that he should keep quiet.

"We should send for the doctor," Emily said when her father at last fell silent. "Mr. Sheldon has suffered a severe blow to the head."

Her father stared at their guest suspiciously. His eyes narrowed. His dark brows drew together. "Olivia!" he bellowed.

Wherever they lived, each of her parents always had a workroom. In this house, they were at opposite ends, which Emily found far more restful than some arrangements she had been forced to endure. But in this case it meant that her father had to shout at the top of his lungs, before he gained her mother's attention.

"I was painting the petal of a golden poppy," she said reproachfully as she entered the drawing room. "You startled me and made me spoil it, Alasdair."

"Emily's brought this fellow home with her," he explained, in the same aggrieved tones he used when one of the dogs dragged in a half-dead rabbit. "Says he must have the doctor."

The Honorable Olivia Crane raised slim red-gold brows and surveyed her unexpected guest. There was no question about where her daughter got her looks, Richard thought. They were both petite women; red-gold hair, a pointed chin, arched brows and a wide, serene forehead, eyes of heavenly blue. No wonder he had thought of Botticelli.

As Emily repeated the story she had concocted to her mother, Richard looked about him. It was certainly an odd family. They spoke and moved like members of the nobility, yet their clothes and sur-roundings were bohemian. The mistress of the house had a smear of yellow paint on her cheek. The master carried a paintbrush as if it were part of his hand. Richard wondered if he was related to the earl of Radford, who was also a Crane. Now that he thought about it, there was a resemblance. Indeed, his host looked a great deal like the old earl's two sons, whom Richard had often seen in London drawing rooms.

A memory intruded. There were actually three sons, but the third was some sort of black sheep. He had heard the story—what was it?—something about a painter's studio and a nobleman's daughter caught posing nude.

"Good God!" Richard exclaimed, his eyes irre-sistibly drawn to Emily's mother. "You're Shelbury's lost daughter." The flaming hair of Marquess Shelbury's line was unmistakable. This eccentric pair had caused one of the great society scandals of the 1790s.

Olivia Crane's brows rose again. "My father knows perfectly well where I am," she answered with-out embarrassment. "I'm not the least bit 'lost.' "

Something like a growl escaped her husband.

Richard flushed. For a man famed for his conver-sational skills, he had been remarkably clumsy. It was another measure of how much had been left behind in the last eleven months.

"Just the opposite," asserted Alasdair Crane.

"I found myself in my art," his wife agreed. "And, of course, I found Alasdair." They exchanged a smile that seemed more suited to the wild young lovers who had fled for the border than a middle-aged married couple with a grown daughter.

"We should send for the doctor," said Emily.

Richard turned to gaze at her. Once again, she looked unperturbed. She obviously knew her parents' scandalous story and was thoroughly accustomed to their behavior. It must have been fascinating to grow up in such a household. "I'm feeling much better. I don't need the doctor."

"You can't even walk," protested Emily.

"Yes, I can." To prove it, he stood. The dizziness was still there, but it was receding. He took an experimental step. "You see?" He raised his eyes to find all three Cranes staring at him.

Emily looked slightly dazed. Her mother seemed suddenly thoughtful. The Honorable Alasdair appeared rapt. "Samson," he murmured dreamily. "Chained to the pillars, straining to bring the temple down."

"I beg your pardon?" replied Richard.

"A tunic?" was the incomprehensible response. "No, no. A breechclout."

The two Crane women blinked. Emily's cheeks flushed a delicate pink.

"I could invent the hair," continued her father. "It would take weeks to grow it out." He grasped Richard's forearm. "Just come with me. I must make sketches. . . ."

"Father!" cried Emily.

"Alasdair," admonished her mother at the same moment.

He turned to gaze at them as if he had forgotten

their presence. His grip on Richard's arm remained tight.

"You cannot paint him, Father," added Emily. "He is a stranger, a traveler. You cannot just . . ."

"He would be very glad to pose," answered Alasdair, in a tone that suggested he was used to getting his way.

"No, he wouldn't!"

Emily looked distressed, and her mother irritated. It was all very awkward. And he hadn't the least desire to become an artist's model. "If you would just lend me a horse . . ." he began.

"I will if you pose," said Alasdair, looking crafty.

"Nonsense," said his wife.

"Lively" didn't begin to describe the discussion that ensued. It ranged from high dudgeon to broken pathos and back again. After a while, Richard realized that the Cranes were enjoying themselves far too much to come to any conclusion. It was better than many plays he'd seen, Richard thought, suppressing a smile at a particularly clever exchange.

Emily plucked at his sleeve. She didn't seem to find the argument amusing. "Come," she said, urging him out into the hallway.

Her parents' dispute had upset her, Richard concluded. The kindest thing was to ignore the shouting. "If I could borrow a mount," he said.

Emily frowned. "Are you sure you can ride?"

"Quite sure. I'm fully recovered."

Although she looked doubtful, she led him out to the stables and ordered the groom to saddle a horse.

"I'll be sure you get it back. And I must thank you again for—"

"Must you?"

She wanted to get rid of him, Richard decided. She was embarrassed because he'd witnessed the family dispute.

The groom brought out a good-looking bay, and Richard prepared to mount. It was rather a pity that he would never see her again. After his unwanted adventure of the last year, it was clear that nothing about his old life would be right, including the women who had been part of it. Emily Crane might be just the sort of girl he could admire now—free and forthright, with a mind of her own, not bound by senseless convention. The memory of her slender body against his came back with warm vividness.

He put it aside. He had a great many things to accomplish. He had already lost eleven months—or twenty-nine years, some might say—of his life. He had to get on with it. "Good-bye," he said. "Thank you once again."

Emily raised a hand in farewell, then turned back toward the house. Richard hesitated a final instant before directing the horse out through the gate.

It was no wonder he had been eager to get away, Emily thought as she made her way to her bedchamber. Her parents' voices still echoed from the drawing room. He must have thought they were all demented. People generally did.

She was truly tired of it. It wasn't the moving, the tantrums, the upsets, so much as the loneliness. Her parents had each other, and that would always be enough for them. She had her parents, but it wasn't the same. She wanted what they had—a consuming love, marriage to a man who matched her in every particular, a companion to share the rest of her life. It would be different from her parents' life, of course, a bit more stable, even conventional. Emily smiled slightly. But she longed for the same compelling bond.

Impossible. She would never fall in love. There was no one to fall in love *with*. On her rare encounters with a young man, he was appalled by her bizarre household, just as Richard Sheldon had been today. Everyone just assumed that she was like her parents.

No, she was doomed to a single life. She would have to find some useful profession, make her own way. But as usual, at this point in the reasoning process, she was stopped. Her education had been spotty, so she couldn't be a teacher or a governess. She despised sewing and fancywork. She had no talent for acting, even supposing her father would allow her to go on the stage. Perhaps she would set up as a highwayman. It was one thing her life had suited her for. Her father had taught her to shoot a pistol. She had a fine seat on horseback. And who would suspect a woman of taking to the High Toby? There was nothing else for it. She would sustain her old age by highway robbery.

IN THE DRAWING ROOM, the quarrel ended, as they always did, with an embrace. "Come upstairs," murmured Alasdair, stroking his wife's paint-streaked cheek.

"In a moment." Olivia raised her limpid blue eyes to his. "We must talk about Emily."

"What? By Jove!" He scanned the room. "Where has that blackguard taken her?"

"I imagine that *she* has taken *him* to the stables and lent him a horse. Emily is such a practical girl. But that is not the point."

"Not the point! She comes in with her arm around some vagabond, practically glued to his side, and—"

"*That* is the point. Emily must be put in the way of meeting some suitable men. She cannot stay with us forever."

Alasdair scowled, his black brows bristling. "Suitable?" he growled.

"Emily does not share our passion for art," Olivia pointed out. "She has no wish to devote her life to it."

His shoulders drooped a little as he conceded this.

"And I must admit that I don't know if I would do so if I did not have you to share that life."

This earned her another embrace, and it was some time before she was able to continue.

"My sister would introduce Emily to society," she said then. "If I asked her to do so."

"You want to send my daughter to the house of a duchess? What the devil would she do there?"

Olivia looked suddenly haughty. "Do you imagine she wouldn't fit in?"

"I *imagine* she's far too good for 'em." Alasdair shook his head. "And Julia'll fill her head with all sorts of nonsense."

"Emily is a very sensible girl. We have done all we can to give her a proper perspective on what is important in life."

"*You* have," replied her husband admiringly.

"You are a wonderful example of a man following his true passions."

The look that passed between them then was incendiary. Further talk was unthinkable, but Olivia was well aware as they retired to their bedchamber that the issue was decided. She had learned to manage Alasdair three weeks after she met the fiery young artist all those years ago. And how much else she had learned, she thought, just before all thought was swept away.

Two

ICHARD SAT in the taproom of the Blue
Dragon nursing his pint of ale and listening to a pair
of shopkeepers at the next table vilify the duke of
Wellington. Londoners were a fickle lot. They had
worshiped the man as a hero not long since, but now
that the war was over and the duke was involved in
politics, he had become fair game.

He shouldn't be here. He ought to be in quite a
different part of town, taking up the obligations and
responsibilities that had brought him home. The attack on the road was the least of the obstacles he had
overcome to reach London again. But now that he
was here, he found himself delaying. From the mo-

ment he contacted his mother, there would be no turning back.

It was inexcusable to leave his mother thinking that he was dead, asserted a stern inner voice.

He acknowledged it with a nod. But he didn't rise to hurry to her house in the heart of fashionable May-fair. The problem was, he was no longer the son who had embarked on a voyage to the West Indies. That Richard Sheldon, Baron Warrington, had been a pink of the *ton*, a wit, a habitué of White's and Almack's. And he had expired in the first few days after the ship foundered off South America and a longboat had deposited him on a stretch of unexplored coast. The baron had not been prepared to scrabble for grubs to survive, thought Richard wryly, or to fashion a spear and kill his own food. In a very real sense, he had succumbed to the rigors of the wild. The man who had returned was someone else entirely.

But who?

That was a question he couldn't answer. He felt less like a single person than a bundle of fragments. There was the old Warrington—heedless, improvi-dent, sardonic. Looking back, Richard didn't like him much. He had been overindulged by a widowed mother, he saw now. And then he had lived off his stepfather's bounty without a scrap of gratitude or any appreciation of the older man's virtues. Indeed, he had thought him a prating old stick. When Sir Wal-ter Fielding died unexpectedly, the old Warrington's first thought had been of money, and how he would continue to live in high style. He had actually been surprised, Richard remembered with wonder now, that his stepfather had left him only a token legacy to add to his ruined patrimony. What else had he expected? Sir Walter had made it clear enough that he disapproved of his mode of life.

And so he had gone off in a fit of the sulks, Richard thought, abandoning his mother in her grief, behaving as badly as he possibly could. No one would miss that Richard—least of all himself.

But in England there was little call for the skills of a jungle savage. The Richard born out of sheer need to survive had no place in this city, in this tavern. He could kill with his bare hands, endure plagues of leeches, fade invisibly into a screen of foliage. With a thin smile, Richard sipped his ale. No, that Richard had served his purpose and must now take his leave.

And then there was the silent, determined man who had paid his passage home by working the sails of a merchant ship. He had had just one goal in life— to reach England—and now it was achieved. He didn't appear to have suggestions about the future.

On the docks in Cartagena, there had been ships departing for Barcelona and Shanghai and Boston. That Richard had toyed with the idea of hiring himself out on one of those and disappearing for good. A disorderly chorus of inner voices had dissuaded him. Duty called. Warrington deplored the hardships of a common sailor's life. The man who had fought his way out of the jungle resisted such confinement.

And so, he had come home.

Richard grimaced as he lifted his tankard once again. He was damned if he knew *who* had come home. In Southampton, he had encountered the shipping agent who originally booked his passage. The man had been astounded to see him, of course.

He was barely recognizable, even to himself, Richard thought. Just now, he felt more like a committee than a man.

Would his mother be happy to see the son who had returned? She'd reared him to become a darling of the *haut ton*, and her pride in his success had been vast. What would she think of the rough-handed man who came back from the dead?

She would expect him to revive his former self as quickly as possible. That was the dilemma that kept him in his chair. Not that he would do so. The cut of a coat or the latest gossip held absolutely no interest for him now. But what was he going to do?

Life spread out before him, a blank slate. Once he had assured his mother of his continued existence, he would have to find some occupation, some task that would use his skills and not drive him mad, as his former pursuits were likely to do.

He might try to discover if anything could be salvaged from the wreck of the Warrington estates, which his father had nearly managed to waste before his death. Richard, succeeding to the title at the tender age of six, had rarely spared a thought for his tumbledown patrimony. His mother's remarriage had ensured his comfort and he hadn't cared for anything else.

What an insufferable puppy he had been. He had never willingly moved a muscle to help anyone, and he hadn't cared a snap of his manicured fingers for his heritage or posterity. He would have to make a push to save his estates, though frankly, he wasn't drawn to land management. But it was a step toward finding a Richard Sheldon he could tolerate. He had been stripped down to the bare essentials of humanity. He had survived. He would build, step by step, on that. Perhaps, along the way, he could find a pursuit that consumed him.

It occurred to him that Alasdair Crane had exactly that. The man's passion for painting, and for his wife, had been striking. Crane had known what he wanted, and he had taken it. All the strictures of society had not been enough to stop him. That was what he wanted—that certainty, that savor. And perhaps, someone to share it; a . . . a kindred spirit.

Richard blinked, surprised at where his thoughts had led him. Even in his lonely fight to escape the jungle he had not indulged in such philosophical ruminations. He sighed. Every person he knew would think he had gone mad. No one would begin to understand such ambitions.

Emily Crane might, stated this new, rather disconcerting inner voice. She had been reared by parents who set their chosen work above society. She would know precisely what he meant. Memories of her red-gold hair, her delicate face and form pressed close against his own, lingered, even haunted his dreams. What if he rode back there now? Would she welcome him?

Shaking off these recollections, he drained the tankard and set it down. First, he had to see his mother and assure her of his safety and good health. After that . . . he would see.

AS HE STROLLED toward his mother's townhouse in the fading light of a fine spring day, Richard's mood was far from mellow. A visit to his bankers had been annoying. They had treated him like an idiot. And though he acknowledged that he had usually behaved like an arrogant young fool in the past, their condescension had filled him with rage he could barely contain. He had become far too used to strangling any entity that opposed him. London wasn't that sort of jungle.

In truth, it had been unsettling. Had he lost his ability to deal with people? An unfamiliar emotion crept over Richard then—a distrust of himself and his own impulses.

He had reached his mother's door. This wouldn't do. He was a civilized man—overcivilized many had said before his departure. The last eleven months hadn't destroyed that entirely. Perhaps he no longer knew just who he was, but he hadn't spun completely out of control. He could manage the conflicting forces that beset him. After a brief internal struggle, Richard pulled on the mask of his former persona, raised his hand, and rapped on the oak panels.

The door was opened by a footman he didn't know. The man surveyed Richard's clothes with rising insolence and said, "Yes?"

Richard pushed past him and into the front hall. He experienced a flicker of surprise at how easy this was, despite the servant's impressive physique, before saying, "Fetch Henley." It was no good asking a stranger for his mother.

"Mr. Henley is not available," answered the footman, looking ready to wrestle him out the door again.

"Nonsense. He will be sitting in his pantry at this hour, probably reading some tedious volume of military history. If you don't summon him at once, you will be very sorry."

The footman took a step back, clearly impressed by the way Richard spoke as well as his knowledge of the household.

"I've known Henley since I was a boy," Richard added. "Get him."

The servant retreated another step from the look in his eyes, and then obviously decided that this was a matter for the butler to judge himself. He disappeared through the rear door with a flutter of coattails.

The place looked exactly the same, Richard thought, gazing at the gilt sconces and curving staircase, the furnishings of the parlor on the left. Which was odd. His mother had a penchant for redecorating, particularly in those rooms most seen by guests.

He heard no sound of conversation or music from above. He could just run up the stairs to the drawing room. But he hung back, postponing the moment a little longer. Henley would know everything that was going on in the house and how his mother was likely to receive his return. He envisioned the coming scene with a grimace.

The door at the back of the hall opened, and the tall spare figure of Henley strode through. "How may I assist . . . ?" he began in freezing accents, then stopped. He peered at Richard, came closer. "My lord?"

"Hello, Henley. I'm back."

The old butler seemed stunned.

"I survived the shipwreck," said Richard, to give

him time to recover. "But I was flung ashore in the middle of a jungle. It's taken me all this time to make my way home."

"Is it really you?" Uncharacteristically, Henley approached and took hold of Richard's forearm, as if to verify that it was indeed living flesh.

"Alive and well."

The butler released him, then glanced up the stairs apprehensively.

"My mother's all right, isn't she?"

"Her ladyship is at this moment holding a séance to contact your spirit, my lord," was the emotionless reply.

"What?"

"She began them three months after you were declared lost."

Richard started up the stairs.

"My lord, if you appear in the middle of . . ." But his lordship obviously wasn't listening. It really *was* young Richard, Henley assured himself. He did recognize him, although it had taken a moment to see that pampered exquisite in the powerful man who had taken his place.

THE DRAWING ROOM was so dim that Richard couldn't see anything at first. An odd humming sound emanated from the center of the chamber, where he gradually made out a group of people sitting at a round table illuminated by one wavering candle. They were holding hands, he realized disgustedly. And the rather disturbing sound was coming from someone who faced the other direction. All he could see was a bulky silhouette with an outsized head that must be some sort of turban.

"We call across the great gulf of dissolution to the other realm," chanted a high, nasal voice. "We reach through the mists and darkness that obscure it. We seek this woman's son, Richard, tragically lost at sea in the flower of his youth."

Richard snorted softly.

"Bring him hither my messengers," commanded the voice. "Azráel. Phileto. Bring him!"

Richard was about to interrupt when he was startled by a whoosh like a great rush of wind. How the devil did they manage that?

"He is coming!" claimed the voice. "He is near. Spirit, give us a sign. Show us your presence."

Richard could take no more. He strode forward. "Mother, what the devil are you doing?"

An ear-splitting shriek rent the air, followed by a confusion of other shouts and exclamations. People started up in the dimness, overturning chairs, stumbling into each other, and crying out again. Someone started sobbing. Realizing that he had not chosen the ideal moment to address his mother, Richard moved to secure the candle, which was in danger of being knocked over. Taking it up, he began lighting others in the sconces around the room.

"There he is!" cried a male voice. "Good god!"

Richard continued lighting candles. The drawing room grew brighter, and he was able to see that it held eight people besides his mother. He didn't know any of them, though the orchestrator of the supposed séance was obvious—a burly, square-shouldered man wearing a massive jeweled turban with a feather. Ignoring them, he went to the chair where his mother sat and knelt beside it. "I beg your pardon for bursting in on you at such a moment," he said.

"You did it, Herr Schelling. You brought him back!" was the dazed reply.

To Richard's disgust, the large turbaned man put a hand on his breast and bowed in acknowledgment.

"Mother, I was not dead." He felt ridiculous saying it. "I was cast ashore in South America, and I had to make my way back on foot. I'm sorry I could not get word to you."

His mother simply stared at him as if he were indeed a ghost.

She was a bit thinner, but her gown was still in the height of fashion and her hair and ornaments exquisite. She looked like the mother he had left—a dedicated member of the *haut ton*. He took her hand, both to comfort her and to show her that he was solid flesh. "The ship I took began to go down in a storm," he added, hoping that details would make his return real to her. "The sailors put me in a longboat. Before they could join me it was swept away. I came ashore in a jungle."

His mother put her free hand on his cheek. Her hazel eyes, very like his own, brightened with a haze of tears.

How could he have considered not coming back? Richard wondered. It would have been cruel, unforgivable.

"I thought you were gone," she whispered, too low for anyone else to hear. "My god." She gripped his hand so hard her knuckles whitened.

"I'm back," he assured her, "and perfectly well."

"You won't go away again!"

He wouldn't be able to, Richard saw. Not for a while anyway. He shook his head.

"Brought him back from the dead," someone in the room murmured with a hush of awe. Richard was annoyed to see the turbaned man preen a little in response. He had to get rid of these people. "Mother . . ."

A tear spilled and ran down her cheek.

Richard stood, meeting the fascinated gazes of an ill-assorted group of strangers. "Perhaps you would all go now. I would like to talk with my mother."

Several left immediately. Others lingered a few minutes to make formal farewells. Finally, only the large turbaned man was left.

"Richard, this is Herr Schelling," said his mother in a shaky voice.

Schelling gave another of his deep bows. "I have been privileged to study with the Adepts of the East," he said, with a slight but noticeable German accent.

"Have you?" said Richard.

"We have much to learn from the Masters of the Hidden World."

"Indeed? But not tonight, perhaps. If you would excuse us?" The man was a pompous charlatan, but Richard had no desire to argue with him.

"I would not dream of intruding on this tender reunion," Schelling answered, without making any move to go. "My dear Lady Fielding, you are serene? Your humors are balanced?"

"No," said Richard's mother. "I am feeling quite agitated."

"Very natural," Schelling practically crooned. "Hardly to be avoided in the circumstances. You must visualize the Great Light, allow your unbalance to flow into it and be floated away."

Richard was appalled to see his mother actually close her eyes and take a deep breath. His disappearance had affected her far more than he had imagined it would.

Schelling, too, had closed his eyes. His hands rose and waved like seaweed in an ocean current. "Yes, I feel the balance being restored, the serenity returning." He opened his eyes. "Perhaps you would like to join us, Richard?"

He couldn't believe the fellow's effrontery. He gave him a look designed to wither him where he stood and said, "No, thank you. The balance of my humors is perfectly satisfactory."

Schelling looked pitying. He shook his head.

He was going to see that this faker never crossed his mother's threshold again. In fact, it would be a pleasure to send him back to Germany, if that was where he really came from. "I'll see you out," he said to Herr Schelling, and took the man's elbow in a grip that made him gasp.

He was not daunted, however. Over his shoulder, he said, "I will see you on Wednesday then, my dear Lady Fielding."

"Oh," replied Richard's mother. "Yes, I suppose . . . why not?"

For any number of reasons, thought Richard as he hustled the man out and handed him over to Henley. When he returned to the drawing room, his mother was still sitting amid the overturned chairs. "You look so different," she said.

He could only nod. It didn't seem the right time to deal with such a large question.

"It doesn't matter. You're home." She gazed at him as if trying to see the old Richard in the man who stood before her. "Thank God, you're home."

"Yes, Mother." He took her hand once again. She clutched it like a lifeline.

THREE

EMILY SAT BESIDE her aunt and watched dancers turn like flowers across the parquet floor. The musicians at this, her first ball, had struck up a waltz, and she was not allowed to waltz, because she had not yet been approved by one of the powerful patronesses of Almack's. The rule echoed in her head, along with the many others her aunt had set out for her. There was an intricate code of behavior involved in a London season, she had found. She hadn't known there were so many rules in the world. It was the chief difference between her former life and the new existence that had so unexpectedly opened up before her. Emily felt as if she had traveled to a foreign country, where the culture was totally unfamiliar. Yet there was something alluring about it, too. This new country was full of clear expectations, of calm routines that were extremely soothing after all her years of turmoil.

Her aunt Julia was her native guide, Emily thought with a slight smile. She was also a duchess, of course, and just a little bit frightening. It was odd, because her aunt looked so much like her mother—the same red-gold hair and large blue eyes. Her chin was a bit squarer, and her nose a trifle more arched. But anyone would guess that this woman and her mother were sisters. Which made it all the more disconcerting that they appeared to have nothing at all in common. Aunt Julia lived in a magnificent townhouse in Grosvenor Square. The vast scale of it all had taken her breath away—the tall footmen and butler who had ushered her through the wide door, the richness of the furnishings, and the formality of every small detail. And her aunt's manner, her bearing, couldn't have been more different from Emily's easygoing mother's. She was serene, cool, affable without sacrificing an iota of dignity. Emily couldn't imagine her ever shouting or throwing a piece of crockery. No guest at her table would stand on a chair or topple out of one in a drunken stupor. It was quite relaxing.

And Aunt Julia had thrown herself into Emily's introduction into society with an endearing enthusiasm, declaring that it had always been a great disappointment to her that she had no daughters. She had been efficient, decisive, always utterly clear—like a general planning a campaign, assembling her stores and ammunition, preparing to launch an offensive.

Emily had been impressed, and appreciative, though it was a little uncomfortable being the object of so much concentrated attention after her unregarded youth.

Her aunt's efforts seemed designed to refashion her from head to heels. And wasn't that all to the good? She had wanted a different sort of life. It was logical that she should change to meet it.

Above all else, her aunt was plotting to introduce her to legions of the "right sort of young man." This was the goal of all their activity, all the admonition and advice. Emily wondered what these young men would be like. As far as she knew, she had never encountered such a creature. The right sort of young man, she repeated silently, watching the dancers. She tried to picture one in her mind. Tall, with an athletic figure, an expression that promised intelligence, strength, generosity. He wouldn't have to be incredibly handsome, but there would be something appealing about him that . . . She was picturing Richard Sheldon, Emily realized with a shock.

Something had seemed very right about him, she acknowledged. When they had walked together across the field, she had felt so . . . alive. She had felt his heartbeat under her hand.

Emily shook her head. What was the matter with her? She was never going to see him again. Why had she thought of him at all?

"Sit like a queen," said her aunt Julia. "How you carry yourself is very important."

Guiltily, Emily straightened. She was so used to leaning back in her chair and daydreaming. It was the one thing she was worried about—her errant imagination and the remarks that came out of her mouth as a result of it. There were things one was supposed to talk about, and many more things one was never to mention. Most particularly, the thousands of questions that buzzed in Emily's head were not acceptable conversation. Indeed, she had already shocked her seemingly imperturbable aunt more than once with the things she knew—and those she didn't.

Holding her head high, she gave her aunt a side-long glance. Her mother had assured her that Aunt Julia knew everything there was to know about society and that she could have no better advisor in negotiating its intricacies. Emily felt deeply grateful to have such a guide.

In her aunt's house everything ran so smoothly that her needs were fulfilled almost before she recognized them. It was completely unlike home, as if she had been transported into one of those fairy tales where magical servitors anticipate every wish. And then the poor heroine makes a mistake and is plunged into disaster, Emily couldn't help thinking.

Realizing that she was leaning back again, she sat straighter. A London season couldn't be any more difficult than the vicissitudes of her life so far. In fact, she was thoroughly trained in dealing with the unexpected. Why, her father had once invited a pick-pocket to dinner to meet the dean of the local cathedral. Could she encounter a more awkward situation among the *haut ton*? Not likely.

"That is Elsmere," murmured her aunt, discreetly indicating a young man dancing by. "Very eligible."

Emily turned back to the dance floor. The waltz was graceful. To be held so close to a man one hardly knew must be rather interesting. The dancers shifted and Emily gave an involuntary gasp.

"What is it?" said her aunt.

"That gentleman there—dancing with the woman in yellow."

The duchess searched the crowd.

"Isn't that . . . Mr. Sheldon?"

Her aunt examined him for a moment. "He looks a bit . . . different. But yes, his name is Sheldon. Not mister, however. He is Baron Warrington." She frowned. "Someone told me he had been lost at sea."

"Baron," echoed Emily. He had said nothing about that.

"You know him?"

"He . . . he had an accident on the road and stopped at our house."

"Really?"

Her aunt's tone made Emily uneasy. "Just for a few minutes."

"Don't tell me you developed a *tendre* for him?"

Intimidated by the ferocity of Aunt Julia's expression, Emily shook her head. "We scarcely exchanged five words." Which was true. No need to mention the walk across the field.

"Quite unsuitable, you know. He hasn't a sou. That family's been all to pieces since my father's day."

Mr. Sheldon—Baron Warrington—waltzed quite expertly Emily noticed. "So he is not the 'right sort?' " she wondered a little wistfully.

"Emily! You must *not* say such things!" Aunt Julia looked around, making certain no one had overheard.

A young lady showed no interest in the question of matrimony, Emily remembered. All that sort of thing was handled by her elders. Which was a splendid thought, really, particularly after years of having to deal with everything herself. "I beg your pardon," she murmured.

Satisfied, her aunt turned back to the crowd. "No, he isn't," she conceded very quietly. "Not only is he penniless, his manners aren't exactly . . . engaging."

This surprised Emily. "He was perfectly polite to Papa, even when he wished to paint him as Samson."

"Emily!"

She flushed. "I'm sorry. I forgot."

Aunt Julia had informed her that her parents' ramshackle establishment and their scandalous past was a social liability. The gossips would like nothing better than to revive the story about their elopement, which would be very embarrassing.

"He met Alasdair?" The duchess looked distressed.

When Emily nodded, her aunt looked despairing. "He will wreck everything."

"How?"

"He is a famous wit," replied the duchess bitterly. "He will make a fine story of Alasdair. Oh lud, Olivia, too. If I had known . . ."

"He didn't seem like the sort of person who would . . ."

"He ruined the Stanley chit. Caused her to retire to some godforsaken place in Scotland and breed terriers. Only because her nose was a trifle . . . large. What he will say about Alasdair . . ." She struggled for control. "It was long ago, of course. Perhaps he never heard the story."

"He called Mama 'the Marquess of Shelbury's lost daughter,'" Emily felt obliged to tell her.

The duchess moaned.

"Mama wasn't the least bit embarrassed."

"She never comes to London," was the acerbic reply. "It is easy to care nothing for society's opinion when you don't get within a hundred miles of it."

Emily acknowledged the truth of that. But she still couldn't reconcile the Richard Sheldon she had met with the man her aunt was describing. "B-baron Warrington was quite civil to all of us."

The duchess turned and focused her gaze on Emily. "Why?"

"What?"

"Did he need help from you?"

"He . . . he wanted to borrow a horse."

"Hah." Aunt Julia looked triumphant. "You see."

"But aunt . . ."

The duchess's attention had shifted. "He has been away for an age," she murmured. "Where, I wonder? If there was anything disreputable about it . . ."

"Aunt!"

"Warrington has no scruples. So we can't afford any."

The waltz ended. The baron escorted his partner off the floor. He was dressed in the height of fashion now, Emily noted, and he looked irritated.

"The best defense is a frontal assault," muttered Aunt Julia. She appeared to be running calculations in her head. "Come. You will have to renew your acquaintance. I have met his mother," she announced in more normal tones.

"Perhaps later," Emily ventured, her feelings wildly mixed. "He is probably already . . ."

"Nonsense. Come."

She had no choice but to follow her aunt across the floor. Richard Sheldon had gone to stand beside an older woman who somewhat resembled him. He looked very handsome, but there were a number of very handsome men in the crowded ballroom. He stood out like a hawk among roosters. What was it that made him so different? It was something in his stance, Emily decided, in the way his hands hung at his sides and his body moved inside his clothes.

"Lady Fielding," said her aunt, very much the duchess. "How do you do?"

The woman standing next to Richard looked surprised, and then very pleased, to be addressed. "Very well, thank you, duchess. You know my son, Richard?"

"Warrington, isn't it?" replied Emily's aunt. "I believe you are acquainted with my boy Philip." There was no trace of concern in her aunt's expression or tone, Emily noted.

Richard nodded. He hadn't taken his eyes off her, Emily thought. He was staring as if he were a hawk indeed. Her aunt had assured her she looked lovely. Her ball gown was finer than any garment she had ever owned, of pale blue satin overlaid with white gauze and trimmed with blue ribbons. A matching ribbon threaded through her hair, which had been sculpted into an intricate mass of curls. It had taken almost an hour to achieve the style, and the wisps and ringlets that the fashionable haircutter had teased out around her forehead and cheeks tickled and made her want to brush them back, which she had been strictly forbidden to do.

"May I introduce my niece, Emily Crane," said Aunt Julia grandly. "I am presenting her this season."

"Indeed?" Lady Fielding gave Emily a polite smile. "I hope you are enjoying yourself."

Before Emily could speak, her aunt said, "This is her first ball. She knows very few people in London as yet."

Lady Fielding looked at her son. So did the duchess.

Richard gave a small bow. "Would you care to dance?" he said.

Emily's eyes flew to her aunt, expecting some excuse for a refusal. After what she had said about Mr. Sheldon, she couldn't send Emily off alone with him.

But the duchess merely smiled benignly.

What was she up to? What did she expect her to do? They were all looking at her. She stammered out an acceptance. Richard took possession of her hand as if he owned it and swept her out to join the country dance just forming.

The transformation was amazing, Richard thought as they began the first figure. The pretty young woman he had met in the country had been polished into a fashionable beauty in an amazingly short space of time.

They moved down the line of dancers and turned at the end, holding up their arms for the next couple to pass under.

Emily outshone most of the other women in the room—which wasn't really surprising if the duchess of Welford had taken her in hand.

"I didn't realize you were coming up to London," he said as they turned.

"It was decided later."

Perhaps it wouldn't be so bad being stuck here in town after all. Up to now, beset by his mother's anxiety whenever he was out of her sight, he had despaired. The simple act of replenishing his wardrobe—a task that had once occupied all his faculties—had rubbed him raw. The fact that all his old things were too tight in the chest and arms, which he once would have seen as a marvelous opportunity to rig himself out in the very latest mode, now was merely an annoyance. Emily Crane promised a refreshing break from the irritations of society.

He looked down at her, remembering the feel of her slender body against his, her calm acceptance of the oddest events. That memory was more vivid than anything that had ever happened to him in rooms like this. Her eyes were downcast. He ought to speak Richard realized. "Your mother remained in contact with her sister?"

She threw him a quick glance, looking almost frightened, then nodded.

"I wouldn't have thought they would get on. It's hard to imagine people more different."

This earned him another glance, but no reply.

"One of the leading hostesses of the *ton* and a woman who doesn't care a whit for society," he elaborated, thinking that he might not have been clear. "It's amazing to think that they grew up in the same household."

He expected that Emily would expand on this

interesting conundrum, but she only nodded, her expression stiff.

"I wouldn't have thought your father would send you to stay with a duchess," he added, smiling to show he meant it as a small joke.

Emily made a choking sound.

What was wrong with her? She hadn't seemed at all shy when he met her before, certainly not tongue-tied or missish. "What do you think of London?" he asked, confident that she would have an original perspective.

"It is very interesting. My aunt took me to see the pictures at the Royal Academy."

"Indeed? An odd choice of amusements."

She gazed up at him, her blue eyes wary.

"Paintings are hardly a novelty in your life, growing up, as you did, with artists. Your aunt might have chosen something less familiar." She was acting as if he spoke a language that she scarcely comprehended; and as if she weren't very happy to be dancing with him.

"What did you think of them?" he inquired, a bit curtly.

"Of . . . ?"

"The paintings at the Royal Academy. I assume your father's work is more . . . animated than what the Academy hangs?"

Emily bit her lower lip.

What had happened to her? Or perhaps he had been mistaken in his first impression. He had been rather groggy. Tonight, she was as boring as any deb—more so. "Which pictures, precisely, did you like?" He heard the sarcasm in his voice.

"The portrait of the duke of Wellington was very fine."

"So *everyone* says."

"Yes, well, they say the likeness is—"

"Striking. So I have been told. *Repeatedly.*"

The snub made her flush.

Richard felt a twinge of regret, immediately submerged by impatience. He had a strong desire to walk away. It took a considerable effort of self-control to keep dancing.

"You . . . you haven't been to see the show?"

"No. I've been rather busy." Richard's mind wandered back to his own concerns. Busy trying to reassure his mother and separate her from Herr Schelling, busy fending off his friends' assumptions that he would be resuming his old life as if he had never been away. They were all fools, he thought, looking around the ballroom. What would they do if their luxurious life were suddenly snatched away?

He realized that Emily had said something. "What?"

She flinched slightly. "I wondered if you are in town for the whole season?"

"I hope not."

She looked surprised at his vehemence.

"You are, I suppose?"

Emily nodded.

"My felicitations."

Her chin came up at this, but it was a pale shadow of the spirit he thought he had seen in the country.

"My aunt has been very generous," she declared.

"Has she?"

Emily blinked at him.

"What else has she to do? Gossip?"

This elicited a look so timorous that he lost all desire to converse with her. Clearly, he had mistaken her character.

They completed a figure of the dance in silence.

"I trust you are fully recovered?" said Emily then.

"Recovered?" he echoed.

"From the . . . the incident on the road."

"Ah." Couldn't she dare the word *attack?* "Of course."

"And you have not had any further . . . ?"

Richard waited, but she didn't finish the sentence. "What?" he asked finally.

"Nothing."

Nothing was the word for it, Richard concluded. She had nothing more in her head than any of the other wide-eyed young debs. He had never had much interest in such creatures, and he had absolutely none now. The music ended; and with relief, Richard returned Emily to the duchess and left her there.

EMILY WATCHED HIM walk away, feeling rather low. Baron Warrington was quite a different creature from the man she had met at home. He was cold and sarcastic. He spoke as if he were setting traps. She had tried to behave as her aunt had instructed, to show him that she could be at ease in society, where he seemed so perfectly at home. But she had been thrown off by the fear that he meant to gossip about her parents to all his London acquaintances. Would he turn the details of her home into anecdotes for the sniggers of the *ton?* She had experienced that kind of snide mockery often enough in her life, and she didn't like it in the least.

"Did you enjoy the dance?" asked the duchess sharply.

"Not particularly."

"Emily."

A young lady does not have strong opinions, Emily remembered, especially negative ones. "I . . . I mean, yes, aunt, it was very pleasant."

Her aunt nodded like a governess acknowledging a correct answer. "Was he rude to you?"

"No. Not exactly."

"What do you mean?"

"He was just . . . rather sarcastic."

"He is well known for that."

She had totally mistaken his character in their brief earlier meeting. Her aunt did seem to know best about these unfamiliar creatures—the denizens of society.

"We will call on Lady Fielding tomorrow," declared the duchess.

Emily gaped at her.

"We must lose no time in cultivating the acquaintance."

"But aunt, I don't really want . . ." She could do without further setdowns from Richard Sheldon.

Aunt Julia waved this aside. "If Warrington is seen to spend time with you, escort you here and there, it will be far more difficult for him to spread scandalous stories about your family."

"I don't think he will wish to escort me any-where."

"His wishes are irrelevant."

"But . . ."

Her aunt silenced her with a gesture. "You needn't be concerned about this. That is why a girl has a sponsor in society—to manage such things."

Her cousin George, Aunt Julia's second son, joined them. He had been drafted as Emily's official escort this evening. Large, blond, and good-natured, he closely resembled his father the duke, who had greeted Emily's arrival in his house with absent courtesy. She had a strong suspicion that the duke, and all three sons of the household, viewed her chiefly as an amusement for Aunt Julia, as if she had suddenly taken up horticulture or knitting.

"That Anne is queer as Dick's hatband," said George. He had been dancing with the daughter of the house, whose presentation ball this was.

"Slang, George," admonished her aunt.

"I beg your pardon, ma'am. But she is a bit much."

The countess of Holburn's daughter Anne was tall and sturdy with dark hair and somewhat prominent green eyes. She had an almost insolent air, and when they were introduced, she had concentrated all her attention on George, scarcely glancing at Emily or her aunt.

"You will clearly outshine *her*," said the duchess, scanning the room critically. "I haven't seen Maundseley's girl since she was ten. Have you, George? You know her brother."

"Bad skin," replied her son.

"Ah," said the duchess with obvious satisfaction.

"And the Wetherby chit seems frightened of her own shadow. No threat there."

"You make the Season sound like some sort of contest, Aunt," Emily ventured.

"Not at all," was the airy response. The duchess didn't shift her gaze from the crowd.

George caught the eye of a servant and provided them all with champagne. Remembering her instructions, Emily merely sipped.

A few minutes later, when her aunt was diverted by an acquaintance, Emily looked up at George. He seemed very much at home in this setting. "Do you know Lord Warrington?" she asked him.

"Eh?" He started as if one of the gilt chairs had spoken to him. "Warrington? Of course." He seemed miffed at the suggestion that he might not know someone.

"What sort of man is he?"

George goggled at her.

It probably was the sort of question she wasn't supposed to ask, but she didn't care. Fixing her cousin with a steady gaze, she waited.

"Er . . . he's . . ." George frowned in unaccustomed concentration. "Got a deuced sharp tongue. Modish; up to every rig and row in town." His gaze sharpened suddenly. "You ain't setting your cap in that direction, are you, because . . ."

"No." She gave him a look that made his mouth snap shut. "Is Lord Warrington a great gossip?"

"Fellows don't gossip," George protested. At her raised eyebrows, he added, "Know all the *on dits*, of course. Warrington tells a dashed good story. A wit, you know. I remember one time he was . . ." He flushed and stopped abruptly.

"At others' expense?"

George didn't seem to understand what she meant, but his account agreed with his mother's. Emily felt a lowering of her spirits.

"Ah, here is Beatrice with a partner for you," declared the duchess. "Young Hanford, I believe. Very good."

The countess stopped in front of them, facing her aunt. Emily had a sudden image of two duelists extending their pistols, preparing to fire. The air seemed to quiver as the two women smiled at each other.

Emily took the hand of the smiling young man, and moved into the dance. And into the small hours of the morning, this process went on. Either the countess or Aunt Julia would approach with a gentleman in tow, present him, and then send them out onto the floor. Their appearance varied, but all of them were the honorable this or lord that, and they all seemed to say the same things to her. And to expect the same responses. The one time she ventured to stray from the accepted subject, her partner looked down with such a startled expression that Emily subsided, afraid she had made a terrible gaff.

How had Cinderella really felt at the ball? she wondered on the way home. How would she have liked hours of fittings for her new finery, instead of having it conjured up in a moment by her fairy godmother? And what had she found to talk about with Prince Charming?

Four

YOU HAVE A FITTING for your new riding habit at eleven," said the duchess the following morning at the breakfast table. "Henry's chosen you a horse." She ticked off two items on a long list that lay beside her plate. "Tonight is the Wetherbys' rout party. We'll call on Lady Fielding in the afternoon."

"Perhaps another day would be better," ventured Emily.

Her aunt shook her head. "On the contrary. It is vital that we move quickly, before he has time to . . ." She waved her hand, indicating disaster.

"I don't think . . . that is, couldn't we wait . . . ?"

Her aunt looked at Emily with raised eyebrows. "I thought you had decided to be presented?"

Puzzled, Emily nodded.

"You yourself decided?"

What did she mean by that?

"Making one's entrance into society is a delicate process. Particularly when you have certain . . . disadvantages."

Emily frowned at her.

"That is not a criticism, merely a statement of fact. I know the system intimately and am expert in working it. I thought you had accepted my guidance."

"Yes, but . . ."

"Good. I do have your best interests at heart, you know."

She did, Emily thought. She had opened her home; she had spent a great deal of money on Emily with apparent pleasure. She was totally engrossed in advancing her niece's interests. And this was familiar territory for her, alien as it seemed to Emily. She reminded herself that she *did* want a more settled life. Aunt Julia was trying to get it for her.

THIS REASONING DID NOTHING to calm Emily's nerves as they drove the short distance to Lady Fielding's house. Richard probably wouldn't even be there. Of course he wouldn't be there. Undoubtedly he had his own chambers elsewhere. Reassured, she relaxed in the seat.

When they pulled up, however, they found another carriage waiting. They had barely stepped down when Richard emerged from the front door with his mother on his arm.

"We appear to have called at an inopportune time," commented the duchess.

"No, no. We were just going to the park," said Lady Fielding. "Take the carriage back to the stables, Ben. Please come in, duchess."

Richard looked annoyed, Emily thought.

"Why don't we all go to the park?" said her aunt. "We can take my barouche."

With a small flurry of conversation, it was settled. Richard handed the three ladies into the carriage and climbed in after them. The driver slapped the reins, and they were off.

"A delightful day for a drive," suggested the duchess blandly. Lady Fielding agreed, and the two older women initiated a flow of commonplaces to fill the silence. Emily risked a glance at Richard, sitting beside her on the forward seat. He looked intensely bored. Her aunt was staring at her, Emily realized. Guiltily, she straightened in her seat and smiled. Her aunt nodded very slightly and looked away.

The park was busy, as it was, in fact, a very fine spring day. The duchess and Lady Fielding acknowledged acquaintances as they passed. Emily had just concluded that this outing would not be so difficult after all when the duchess said, "Perhaps you would like to walk a little, Emily?"

She had to repress a start at being called back from her own thoughts. "Oh . . . yes."

The carriage was stopped and the footman jumped down to open the door. Emily stepped to the gravel drive and hesitated. Was her aunt coming? But both the older women were looking at Richard, who responded by joining her and offering his arm. Not joyously, Emily noted.

"Would you care to see the Grecian temple?" asked Richard in a colorless voice.

Emily glanced up at him. He looked like a man going through the motions. There was no trace of the person she had helped across the fields, the one who had spoken to her forthrightly and without affectation. That was because she had imagined him, Emily told herself sharply. "Yes, thank you."

He led her along a landscaped path toward a small building ornamented with columns and carvings. Flowers had been planted all around it, and in urns along the pediment. "It's pretty," Emily ventured.

"If you like fakery."

This silenced her. They strolled toward the temple, properly in full view of the duchess and Lady Fielding, who sat chatting in the carriage.

His arm was hard and unyielding under her hand. His face was equally stiff. No one was going to believe that he was enjoying her company. Her aunt's scheme was doomed. She looked around the park, desperate for some suitable, interesting topic. A spot of color caught her eye. "Look."

Richard turned and the boredom vanished from his expression. "It's a balloon."

"What?" Emily watched the gaily striped sphere drift upward. It was high above the rooftops already.

"A balloon. A silk bag filled with gas that is lighter than air. That's why it rises."

"Lighter than air? How could anything be lighter?"

"The various gases it contains have different properties. If one separates out the less dense element, it will lift even quite heavy objects." His gaze was fixed on the still rising balloon. "It gives us flight."

"Us?" echoed Emily.

"Mankind. There are aeronauts in the basket hanging below the bag. You can just see it."

She squinted. There was indeed something dangling from the bright sphere.

"An ancient dream finally coming true," Richard murmured.

"Wishing for wings, you mean?"

He stared down at her with such intensity that Emily was abashed. "How will they get down?" she asked to divert him.

He continued to gaze at her for another moment. "They let out gas to descend, drop weights to rise higher."

"You know a great deal about it," said Emily, impressed.

Abruptly, he looked self-conscious. Turning away from the balloon, he led her along the front of the Grecian temple. "I have read about such things," he answered, his voice once more emotionless. "Shall we return to the carriage?"

Emily started to ask another question. But something moved in the corner of her eye, and she turned, startled. An urn on the roof of the temple was toppling slowly over the edge of the pediment. In the next instant, Emily was snatched off her feet and tumbled to the ground in Richard Sheldon's arms. The urn crashed into the pavement where they had been standing and shattered in a rain of soil and stems.

Emily felt the flying shards of pottery strike Richard's back. His body had wrapped around hers, shielding her almost completely from the projectiles and taking most of the impact of their fall. She rested in his embrace, breathless and a little dazed. He had moved so fast, and so decisively. There had been no time to think. He had somehow just known. It had been the same when he lunged at Jonathan in the field behind her house, Emily remembered; this very large man suddenly became a blur of lethal motion.

A man shouted behind them. Shrieks sounded from the direction of their carriage.

Richard's body was all muscle, like sprung steel. It felt as if he could hold her forever, effortlessly. Emily began to feel odd, tingling with energy and languorous all at once.

"Are you all right?" he asked.

His lips were inches from her ear, which made the question seem intimate and intensely personal. A flush of heat washed over Emily. She made a soft affirmative sound that surprised her.

Richard untangled himself and rose, pulling her up after him. Emily swayed a little on her feet.

In the next instant, Lady Fielding hurled herself at Richard, keening at the top of her lungs. He caught her and held her against his chest. "It's all right, Mother. No harm done."

"You were nearly killed!"

"Not at all. We had stepped out of the way. Mother, calm yourself."

Stepped out of the way? That hardly described it. But watching Lady Fielding wail and wring her hands, Emily could see why he would make light of the incident. She took a deep breath. There had been something just before the urn fell, some small movement barely glimpsed. She took another breath, regaining her equilibrium. Emily started around the temple to look for some sign of what it might be.

"Are you all right?" asked her aunt.

"Yes, I am just going to . . ."

"What a very distressing accident."

"I'm not sure . . ."

"I believe we had better get Lady Fielding home. She is quite . . . distraught." The duchess's expression showed her low opinion of such displays of emotion. It also seemed to contain a glint of satisfaction.

"I want to look behind the temple."

"Behind it? Whatever for?"

Emily didn't feel her aunt would respond well to her suspicions. "We should tell someone about this . . . accident," she ventured instead.

"You may be sure I shall. Disgraceful carelessness."

Lady Fielding had descended into hysterics, Emily saw. She could not keep her from home. With great reluctance, looking back over her shoulder more than once, she returned to the carriage. On the drive back, she bent all her faculties to recalling that moment when she had seen—what? A movement? The urn itself, or someone pushing it?

The duchess was soothing Lady Fielding with her

vinaigrette. The latter had subsided into weeping now.

At the house, the duchess took over, sending a messenger for Lady Fielding's physician and summoning her dresser and a covey of maids. All of them supported Richard's mother up the stairs, leaving Richard and Emily standing in the front hall gazing after them.

"She is easily upset since my . . . absence," said Richard, as if to himself.

Emily had, of course, heard the story of his shipwreck. It was a choice bit of gossip among the *ton*. "I'm sure she'll be all right."

He nodded, eyes still on the stairs, then turned to her. "You should sit down. Would you care for anything? No doubt you are quite shaken by the—"

"I think someone pushed that urn. I may have seen . . . well, I'm not sure."

Richard looked skeptical.

"There was something," she insisted. "A movement. Why should the urn fall otherwise?"

"A crack in the base," he suggested. "A flaw in the wall under it."

"But after the way those men attacked you on the road . . ."

"Footpads."

"They did not act like footpads. Don't you think it suspicious that they—?"

"My dear Miss Crane, you read too many sensational novels."

"I don't read any."

"You will *not* mention this foolishness to my mother."

Emily drew herself up. "I would never do such a thing."

"Or to anyone else either." He shook his head. "What an *on dit* that would make. Warrington thinks himself persecuted. I suppose I was deliberately marooned in the wilderness as well?"

Emily hadn't thought of this. "Could it have been arranged?"

Richard gave a harsh laugh. "Indeed. By someone in direct communication with the Almighty. Or perhaps a sorcerer who summons storms? I beg you to curb these idiotic flights of fancy, Miss Crane."

"You have to admit—"

"Stop it!" His voice was like a whip. "I have no patience with this lunacy. You will drop it at once."

Before Emily could reply, her aunt appeared at the head of the stairs and began to descend.

"How is she?" asked Richard.

"Better. She is asking for you."

Richard started up, then hesitated. "Do you need . . . ?"

The duchess waved him on. "No need to see us out."

With a nod of thanks, he strode up the stairs. Emily turned to walk out with her aunt. She didn't see Richard pause on the upper landing and stare intently after her.

"A volatile woman," commented the duchess as they returned to their carriage. "She has endured a difficult time, of course. But a bit more fortitude . . ." She shook her head as they started off.

What was behind the attacks? Emily wondered. If she was right, a determined killer was after Lord Warrington. She bit her lower lip. Was she right? Was she imagining things? She frowned. The men at the pond had been solid and very real. But today . . . she couldn't be sure. Perhaps the movement had been the balloon? There was no way to know. And it was no business of hers, in any case. Lord Warrington clearly did not want her opinion. She should put the matter from her mind. But she couldn't.

STEPPING DOWN FROM the carriage in Grosvenor Square, Emily noticed that a caller was departing from one of the neighbors, escorted by all four daughters of the house. That was odd. Only the eldest was out. The younger sisters would not be receiving callers. As her aunt entered the house with a sweep of draperies, she hesitated. The caller made his final farewells and sauntered down the pavement toward her. "Daniel Fitzgibbon," she blurted out.

The man stopped, stared at her, and then came forward slowly. He didn't look gratified by her notice. And no wonder—the last time Emily had seen him, he had been head of a company of motley traveling players just one step ahead of a magistrate.

Coming up to her, he bowed most elegantly. "Miss Crane."

"How . . . how are you?"

"Very well, thank you. And you?" He glanced up at the imposing mansion behind them.

"I'm staying with my aunt."

"Ah."

"What are you . . . ?" Emily hesitated once

again. Her father had befriended this man, and she rather liked him herself. But he did have some dubious habits; things had been known to go missing from the towns where his company of actors performed. If he was playing these tricks on her aunt's neighbors . . . Emily glanced uneasily at the house. Aunt Julia would *not* approve of the connection.

Fitzgibbon smiled as if he could follow her thought processes. "I am an exceedingly fashionable dancing master to the young ladies of the *haut ton,*" he told her.

Emily couldn't help but stare.

The man raised his eyebrows, waiting.

"Dancing master?"

He gave her a slight bow. "I am a very fine dancer."

Emily remembered the complicated dances in some of his performances. "Yes, but . . . how did you come to be teaching?"

The footman holding the front door coughed discreetly. Emily heard her aunt's questioning voice from inside.

"A complicated story," said Fitzgibbon. He made a gesture indicating that he did not wish to tell it in a public street. "Will you bubble me?" he added with some urgency.

"No. That is . . . I don't . . ."

"Emily?" said her aunt, appearing in the doorway.

Bowing once again, Fitzgibbon handed her a card, tipped his hat, and walked quickly away.

"Who is that you were talking to?"

Emily slipped the card into her reticule. "The

Talbots have engaged him as dancing master for the girls." She hurried up the steps and into the house.

"Dancing? Is that the fellow everyone's talking of? Maria Talbot was telling me he's even got Margaret moving with a bit of grace." She frowned. "But I do not understand why you were speaking with him."

"I . . . I was thinking I could use some lessons," Emily said in a rush. "I have had so little practice dancing."

"Hmm. Perhaps." Her aunt turned and started up the stairs. "I am glad to see you taking an interest in your social skills," she added with more warmth.

Emily kept her head down as she followed Aunt Julia upstairs. She hadn't exactly lied to her. No, she had simply neglected to tell the truth jeered another inner voice.

In her own room, she took out Fitzgibbon's card, only to discover that the name engraved on it was Edwin Gerrity. What if she had mentioned his name? She sat down abruptly in the armchair under the window. How many of her father's collection of eccentrics were now in London? she wondered suddenly. They included a great many disreputable figures, and a few out-and-out scoundrels. If Daniel Fitzgibbon, thieving actor, could so easily become Edwin Gerrity and enter the houses of the *haut ton*, what else might happen? The possibilities daunted her. Aunt Julia would be furious.

Emily went to the small writing desk in the corner and put the card safely inside. She had to keep her two lives firmly separated. There was no room in this household for characters like Fitzgibbon/Gerrity. Imagining him here was as difficult as picturing her

Aunt Julia among Papa's paints. She swallowed. Completely separate, she thought. It was the only answer. Everything would be fine as long as she held to that resolve.

RICHARD FOLDED HIS ARMS across his chest as his mother's carriage started off along the cobblestones. He glowered at the tufted blue velvet lining the interior. He had tried to forbid this expedition. But his mother had resorted to tears and laments about the incident in the park, and he had had to yield. He had also had to accompany her, wasting his time and spoiling his temper. But he wasn't about to send her alone into the clutches of Herr Schelling.

She sat happily beside him, gazing out the window. When would she recover her spirits? When would she be able to contemplate his leaving London without falling into a despond? This fearful, clinging woman was so unlike the mother he remembered.

A wave of compassion overtook him. He had changed. No doubt she felt the same bewilderment over the son who had returned to her. And she had mourned his death for a long time. She could be allowed more than a week or two to recover. "Are you warm enough, Mother?"

She turned and smiled at him. "Yes, thank you, dear."

Her expression touched him. He had given her a good deal of pain over the last year. And in the years before that. The old persona was all too easy to resume, but he wasn't going to do that.

"It is so good to have you home again," she added. "Nothing was the same with you . . . gone."

A year ago, he would have dismissed this as maudlin sentiment, Richard thought. But he could see the emotion in her eyes.

"Even the Season seemed a lot of silly posturing." She looked self-conscious and gave a brief laugh. "How people would stare to hear me say that. Of course, it is all right now that you are back."

Richard watched her visibly gather the elements of her social self around her. Family connections went deeper than the roles individuals played in the world, he saw. But one didn't always understand that until a crisis struck.

"I'm afraid Herr Schelling lives quite out of the world. In Kensington," said his mother in another tone entirely. "But he says the vibrations there are good for his work."

"Indeed?"

She nodded. "There is a rift in the etheric envelope that allows him to reach through to the other realm."

"A what?"

Lady Fielding gestured airily. "A rift. I don't understand it precisely, of course."

"Of course." Because it was gibberish, Richard added silently.

"But it does help Herr Schelling do the most amazing things."

"Such as?"

His exceedingly dry tone earned him a doubtful glance.

"Besides communicating with my supposedly deceased spirit," he added.

"That was a mistake," she acknowledged. "But Herr Schelling was wondering . . . you do not think, Richard, that you received any sort of etheric communications when you were trapped in that awful jungle?"

"No, Mother, I do not."

"You might not have noticed them, you see, because they are very subtle. . . ."

"Vanishingly so."

"Richard."

He subsided. He had promised to keep his sentiments to himself on this expedition. It was going to be even more difficult than he had imagined.

Herr Schelling lived in a respectable looking house on a quiet street in this unfashionable suburb. The maid who admitted them looked quite ordinary, as did the furnishings Richard glimpsed, though they were rather luxurious for a man in his position. Apparently, Herr Schelling paid some heed to the physical plane as well as the etheric.

The upstairs room to which they were taken was different. Its only furniture was a large round table in the center, set on a circular carpet decorated with stars and surrounded by straight chairs. All the walls were muffled with heavy dark draperies. The only light came from a branch of candles set on the table.

A few people stood about the room, talking softly. Herr Schelling surged forward from among them and held out both his hands. "My dear Lady Fielding. How splendid to see you in my humble abode once more."

Richard almost snorted. What sort of man could actually utter the words "humble abode"?

"Lord Warrington," said their host. "You also are most welcome."

Restraining himself, Richard merely nodded.

"I believe we are ready." Schelling turned and gestured. Richard followed his mother to a pair of chairs and sat beside her. When they were settled, a large weeping woman was led in and seated. Herr Schelling materialized next to her, wearing his bulging turban now. When had he put it on? Where had he gotten it? Richard looked around the room, noting how hard it was to see anything in the shrouded corners. The man was slippery as a barrel of eels.

Schelling snuffed all but one of the candles, then sat in the last empty chair. Those seated next to him took his extended hands and the entire group began to link hands as well. Richard allowed his mother to grasp his hand, but he nearly balked when the other was taken in a limp clammy grasp. Turning to protest, he found a thin, timorous woman who evaded his gaze as if it were a blow. The limp fingers trembled in his. Grimacing, Richard turned away again. He should have forced his mother to stay home. He should have argued much more vehemently.

Their host moaned, and the circle stirred with anticipation. The candle flame fluttered in an errant breeze.

"We call across the great gulf of dissolution to the other realm," Schelling chanted in a high, nasal voice. "We reach through the mists and darkness that obscure it. We seek Wendel, newly passed over in the prime of his life."

Some relative of the weeping woman, Richard concluded. His distaste for this farce nearly overwhelmed him.

"Bring him hither, my messengers," continued Schelling. "Azrael. Phileto. Bring him!"

The draperies stirred. The candle dipped and smoked. There was a creaking sound.

"He is coming!" intoned their host. "He is near."

A dog began barking somewhere. Richard almost laughed aloud at the intrusion of this prosaic noise. Did Herr Schelling keep a pug?

"Wendel?" cried a tremulous voice. "Is that you, Wendel?"

The barking grew more rapid.

"Wendel!"

A strangled choke escaped Richard, the product of outrage and laughter colliding and being stifled by consideration for his mother's feelings. All this rigmarole for a dead dog? This put him in his place—the group apparently ranked deceased sons and pets about equal.

"He cannot speak," said Herr Schelling, to Richard's disappointment. "But I sense he is well."

"Does . . . does he have enough to eat?" quavered the large woman.

This was unconscionable, Richard thought—playing on the grief of this woman, as on his mother's. He was going to see that Schelling was thrown out of England.

There was not much more. Schelling made a few more moaning sounds and then "came back to himself." The candles were relit. Clasped hands were released. The maid appeared to invite the group downstairs for refreshment, Schelling pretending to be too drained to act the host. Richard hung back a bit to let the others go ahead, then took his mother's arm firmly. "We're going," he said.

"But the evening isn't . . ."

"Now," he insisted. He led her down to the entry and out into the street. "How can you tolerate that man?" he asked his mother.

"He has abilities."

"To contact a dead dog?"

Lady Fielding looked doubtful. "It was a little odd, wasn't it? We never had a dog before."

"I think you should give up seeing him."

"He was such a help to me."

"He is a charlatan. Do you imagine that nonsense tonight was real?"

His mother looked thoughtful. "It does seem strange that there are dogs in the spirit realm."

Richard rubbed his eyes with one hand.

"It might have been a hoax," she added.

He blinked in surprise and pleasure. "Of course it was a . . ."

"Myra has given him a number of gifts, you know. Perhaps he wished to make some return for her generosity."

"Gifts?"

Lady Fielding nodded. "He doesn't ask for anything, naturally."

"Doesn't he?"

"Oh, no. Too proud. But his assistant lets one know how difficult it is for him to sustain his work."

"Indeed. What is her name?" That would be a place to start, he thought.

"Umm. Sarah, I believe." She nodded to herself. "I have been thinking of asking him to contact Walter."

Richard sat bolt upright on the cushions.

"I do miss him, you know."

He nodded. He could acknowledge now that his stepfather had been a kind and generous man. How much more his mother must feel.

She frowned. "Perhaps you think I should look for your father instead."

Richard scarcely remembered his father. Even had he believed in Schelling's powers, he wouldn't have thought to seek him.

"But it has been so long . . ."

"You cannot reach either of them, Mother. Schelling's claims are utterly false."

"It would be wonderful to hear Walter's voice once more," she replied, as if she hadn't heard a word. "He always knew just the thing to say. He was so . . . comforting."

"He was a good man. But—I'm sorry, Mother—he is gone."

"Well, I know that."

Her change of tone gave Richard hopes for a moment.

"I would just like to talk to him, you know," she went on, deflating them. "I'll send a note round to Herr Schelling tomorrow. He'll know just what to do."

Staring grimly out into the night, Richard made no reply.

FIVE

THE DUCHESS CAME into Emily's bedchamber and ran an expert eye over her. Emily shifted a little under that critical gaze, telling herself that her gown of sea green muslin was impeccable and her hair was styled in a most becoming cloud of curls. "Very nice," her aunt said.

This was high praise from Aunt Julia. Emily gathered her dark green wrap and followed her out to the stairs.

"I think you will like Vauxhall Gardens," the duchess declared as they walked. "The fireworks are very pretty." Emily murmured her agreement.

"We have received a prodigious number of invitations. I do believe you are making a hit. And we certainly needn't worry about Warrington any longer after his disgraceful behavior in the park."

"Disgraceful?"

"Throwing you down in that odious way and positively rolling about on the ground. Everyone is talking of it." She raised a hand. "No one blames you, of course. It was all Warrington. He was . . . ferocious." Her expression showed how shocking she had found the incident.

"He saved me from being crushed by that urn," objected Emily.

"A gentleman would have done so in quite another manner."

"How?"

The duchess gave her an admonitory glance. "I don't know, my dear, but he certainly would not have grabbed you so . . . aggressively and thrown you into the dirt." She shook her head. "Warrington's unfortunate experience at sea must have upset the balance of his mind."

"He acted boldly to save us both from being hurt. I don't know what you expected him to—"

"You sound almost admiring. Emily, you must not—*must not*—get some romantic notion in your head that—"

"It is nothing of the kind."

The duchess frowned at her, looking every inch the outraged duenna.

It took Emily a moment to realize the extent of her transgression. "I'm sorry I interrupted you, Aunt."

"You must watch your tongue, Emily. We have

spoken about this. A young girl does not have opinions, let alone such very . . . insistent ones."

Emily nodded. It was rather hard, to have been encouraged for her first twenty years to have strong opinions and now to be told that this was not what was wanted at all.

In the front hall, two of her cousins, George and Philip, were waiting to escort them. Tall and blond, they looked elegant and imperturbable in their evening dress. Did they mind being commandeered to take her about London? She never could tell how the men of this household felt about anything. Her father, the only male she knew well, was such a different creature. *His* feelings were never in doubt.

All such concerns fled when they reached the river and embarked for Vauxhall. The gardens glittered on the other side of the water, and music drifted in the soft spring air when they stepped to shore again. There were colored lanterns hanging in the trees, Emily saw with delight. Paths wandered through the vegetation. She could see a glowing fountain at the far end of one and a small pillared structure down another. "It's beautiful," she said.

Philip looked down at her. "Mater thought you'd like it."

Fashionably dressed groups strolled here and there, chattering like exotic denizens of a fairy story. Her aunt was truly making an effort to see that she enjoyed her London season, and she was very grateful.

They walked down the broadest avenue, George and the duchess in front. Emily tried to see everything at once. All the paths looked intriguing. The colored lights through the new green leaves were lovely. The music was growing louder. It was an enchanted landscape. "Can we go there?" she asked her cousin, indicating a particularly enticing walk.

Philip shook his head. "Mater likes to sit in the Pavilion. Nothing down there but trees. George'll order the ham and some rack punch," her cousin promised her kindly.

"Can't we walk a little first?"

Philip started to refuse. Emily looked for her aunt, who had drawn a good way ahead. A large raucous group surged out of a path on the left and engulfed them in a tipsy, jostling mass. "Here now," said Philip indignantly, but no one paid any attention. The group went careening around them laughing and gesturing, heading for the gates. They looked like law clerks or shop assistants, Emily thought, and they looked like they were having a very good time.

One of the young men stumbled hard into Philip and clutched his lapels to stay upright. Philip roared with outrage and cursed him. Some of the others began to jeer, laughing more than ever when Philip raised his walking stick and threatened to thrash his assailant.

Emily backed up a step, then another. Philip was red in the face and shouting, but it didn't seem to her that he was in any real danger. She had seen mobs bent on violence, and this wasn't one of them.

She took another step back. The temptation was irresistible. She would just go a little way down the path that had so drawn her and then find Philip when his dispute was settled.

The walk was as enchanting as she'd expected,

winding through the lantern-hung trees like a secret path through a magic forest. Emily was lured farther, first by a gazebo that was a fantasy of wrought iron and glass, and then by a series of sculptures that seemed to be Greek gods and goddesses. By the time she remembered that she must get back to her aunt, she had lost track of the turns she had taken and the direction she had come.

Aunt Julia would be livid. She had never meant to stay away so long. Her cousins were probably searching for her, and none too happy about the task.

Quickly, she started to walk. Coming to a place where two paths crossed, she tried to remember which one had brought her here. But she had been engrossed in the sights of the place, letting her feet take care of themselves. She had no memory of this turn.

Taking a breath, she chose a path, telling herself it looked quite familiar.

Ten minutes later, Emily had to concede that most of the paths looked alike. She had not come upon the gazebo or the statues again. She was lost and there was no one to be seen. She had obviously wandered into a deserted area of the gardens, and she didn't need to be told that this was not a wise idea. If she could just find a busy avenue, someone would direct her to the Pavilion. She stood on tiptoe, trying to see over the bushes for the direction that offered the most light. It was impossible to say. She would just have to walk.

She moved down the paths rapidly, her expression set.

But she couldn't seem to find a populated place.

Emily was beginning to feel the first tremors of panic when she passed under an arch of branches and into an open space where two men sat at the edge of a dry fountain looking down into it. "Lord Warrington?" she said, astonished.

He stood, as did the other man. "What the deuce are you doing here?"

Emily hurried forward, too relieved to notice his scowl. "I'm lost. Could you tell me how to find the Pavilion, please? My aunt will be so worried."

A wordless exclamation from the unknown man drew her attention. He looked like a superior sort of workman. His hands were covered with something green and slimy looking.

"Why the devil are you wandering around Vauxhall alone?" asked Richard.

"I . . . I was just looking at a path, and then I made a turn . . ."

"Easy to lose your way here," said the other man.

Richard threw him a look that Emily couldn't interpret. "I will escort you to the Pavilion," he said stiffly.

"If you just tell me the way . . ."

"Naturally I will not send you off alone," he put in, as if she had arranged this whole incident just to inconvenience him. He stepped forward and offered his arm. Since she really didn't want to go alone, Emily swallowed her protest and took it.

They started off along a path that seemed quite the wrong direction to her. Which was no doubt the problem, she thought wryly. It was enormously comforting to hold Richard's arm and watch him choose the way with complete confidence. "What were you doing with that man?" she asked, her curiosity returning.

"Nothing that concerns you."

There was a fleck of the green stuff on his coat, she noticed. It looked like the scum one found growing in ponds. "Was he working on the fountain?"

Richard nodded.

"But why were you—"

"It is none of your affair," he interrupted almost savagely.

Emily's chin came up. "I *beg* your pardon."

A stiff silence descended. He really was an insufferable man.

"I am interested in the waterworks they have here," said Richard suddenly. "They are very complicated and intricate."

"Oh."

"Not a fit pursuit for a man of fashion," he added with a sneer. "Your new friends among the *ton* will find it vastly amusing."

She looked up at him. His mouth was tight, his face half turned away. He seemed both angry and humiliated. "Why would they find it amusing?"

He didn't appear to understand the question.

"Why shouldn't you be interested in how things work?"

Richard stopped walking. He stood there looking down at her. "It isn't . . . done. A nobleman doesn't care about machinery, or new inventions." His lips turned down. "Or the future."

"You are a nobleman, and you do."

"*I* am . . . " He stopped and looked perplexed. "I have never let it be seen. Not even by . . ."

Emily waited for him to go on. When he didn't, she said, "It was very interesting about the balloon. Far more interesting than hunting and horse races and silly wagers in the clubs."

He gave a short laugh. "You have been talking to the bright young sprigs."

"It is all they talk about. What is so intricate about the waterworks here?"

Richard hesitated.

"My aunt said they have a great many fountains."

Enthusiasm struggled with doubt in Richard's expression. "A huge number. They pump water from the river and run it through pipes under the entire garden. There is a marvelous system of valves to move the water from place to place. Finch oversees it all."

"The man you were with just now?"

He nodded. "He knows a vast amount about machinery."

"How did you meet him?" It seemed reasonable to her that Richard should be interested in the subject, but she couldn't imagine how he had become acquainted with someone like Mr. Finch.

"I sought him out," was the defiant reply. "Since I have been back in London . . ." He stopped, his jaw set. Deeply interested, Emily waited for him to say more. But he didn't.

"That was clever of you," she offered finally.

"Clever?" He looked baffled. Richard's gaze bore into hers. He seemed to be searching for something in her face. Emily couldn't look away. She realized that she wanted him to find whatever it was he sought.

The lanterns and leaves and strains of music

seemed to recede. She was conscious of nothing but Richard and the wary amazement that had crossed his face. Emily was suddenly very aware of his height, of the strength of his arm under her fingers. She could hear her heart beating.

He continued to gaze at her as if she were some fantastic creature that he couldn't quite believe in. Emily found herself longing for that belief. Lost in the timeless moment, she leaned closer.

Richard's head bent. His lips touched hers, and something glorious flamed into life, astounding her. The touch sent a tremor through every nerve in her body. It ignited her, made her want to melt into his strength.

The kiss deepened. Richard's arms slid around her and drew her tight against him. His hands moved, exciting and dangerous, along her back. The hard angles of his body enticed her toward total surrender.

Emily had never imagined anything like this. She hadn't known that she could catch fire, go up in a conflagration of sensation that promised worlds. She gave herself up to it, letting his touch guide her in this fabulous, unfamiliar universe.

Richard pulled away, and Emily nearly cried out with disappointment. He let his hands drop to his sides. He was breathing hard, and his eyes looked wild. "I beg your pardon," he said thickly. "I . . ." One of his fists clenched on the word. He fell silent.

Emily suddenly remembered all her aunt's strictures. What was Richard thinking of her? Did he imagine she habitually kissed men she scarcely knew? She drew away from him, trying to show that was the furthest thing from the truth.

He responded by taking a step backward.

She wanted to say something to ease the tension that vibrated between them, but she couldn't find the right words.

Richard turned away. Her hand reached out without conscious volition, then dropped again.

"This way," he said, starting off. He didn't offer his arm again. Emily followed, and in a few minutes, they emerged from the trees onto a broad, brightly lit avenue full of fashionable strollers. Richard's expression became more even distant. "The Pavilion is down here."

They walked side by side along the crowded pathway. Emily wondered if she looked as self-conscious as he did. She fumbled for something to say. Her aunt was wrong about Richard. He was not the supercilious, malicious man she described. He was . . . she couldn't say precisely, but she knew she wanted an opportunity to find out.

The Pavilion loomed ahead. When would she see him again? Her aunt was unlikely to arrange another outing with Lord Warrington. Something she had heard at a party popped into her mind. "Have you seen the steam locomotive on Hampstead Heath?" she blurted out.

Richard looked startled. "Not yet."

"I should so like to. It is quite amazing, I believe."

He gazed down at her. She couldn't decide if he was apprehensive or bemused.

"Perhaps you would escort me?" added Emily breathlessly.

"I . . . if you like."

"Thank you. Thursday?"

He nodded just as Emily heard a sharp exclamation up ahead. In the next instant, she was swept up by her aunt and being questioned and scolded for her heedlessness. Somehow, Richard was dismissed in the midst of the explanations. And from the remarks made in the carriage going home, Emily was very glad she had made her own arrangements.

EMILY WALKED along the busy London street, conscious of her fashionable clothes, the smart maid who walked beside her, the tall footman who escorted them both. It was so very different from anything in her life before the last few weeks, and yet she was on her way to visit one of her father's disreputable old friends.

Her Aunt Julia had made inquiries about Gerrity, the dancing master, and had agreed that Emily could benefit from some expert instruction. The only thing was, there was no dancing class this afternoon. She was going to see Daniel Fitzgibbon—Gerrity, she reminded herself—for quite a different purpose.

Emily was received with careful ceremony. The servants were safely disposed belowstairs, and she was ushered up to the drawing room by a solemn butler. Only when the door was closed and latched did her host grin at her and say, "Mary's here too, y'see."

Emily smiled at Mrs. Fitzgibbon, a small plump woman of unshakable placidity. She smiled and picked up a teapot. "Lemon or cream, dear?"

A tightness that she hadn't even recognized relaxed as Emily sat down opposite her and accepted a cup. She needn't worry about saying or doing the wrong thing here, or about letting slip some forbidden bit of information about her family.

"Your parents are well?" asked Fitzgibbon.

"Yes. I had a letter just yesterday. Papa has acquired a ferret."

Mary Fitzgibbon laughed quietly. "For ratting?" inquired her husband.

Emily shook her head. "He thought it would pose for a painting he's working on. It stole one of the apples from the still life and ran up a curtain to eat it. He shouted at it until Mama came and suggested another subject."

"What became of the poor animal?" wondered Mary.

"It's living on top of the hall clock, stealing food from the kitchen."

The three of them shared a smiling moment, appreciating the Honorable Alasdair Crane's well-known eccentricities.

"How do you come to be in London?" asked Emily then.

"Mary wanted a more settled life. She was tired of traveling. And Sarah wanted to see the city."

"She's here?" The Fitzgibbons' daughter, Sarah, was Emily's own age, and they had played together as children. She got only a nod in return. Sensing some awkwardness, she added, "It is so good to see old friends. My aunt's house is . . . very formal."

"She's known as a high stickler," said Daniel.

"But she is kind to you?" asked Mary.

"Oh, yes. Are there others from home in London?"

"Jack Townsend's here," Daniel replied. "Fleecing young sprigs at the gaming hells." He cocked his head. "Not that he cheats, mind. Well, he don't need to. He's deuced clever with the cards."

Emily nodded, remembering this dapper adventurer from her parents' dinner table. "Gentleman Jack" had saved her father from being horsewhipped by an irate neighbor whose foxhounds had had an altercation with David and Jonathan.

"Flora got herself on stage in Covent Garden," her host continued. "Seems to have hooked a great swell, too. He's set her up in style in . . ."

"Daniel," admonished his wife.

"Eh? Oh." He eyed Emily uneasily. "Mrs. Taylor has a boarding house in Kensington. Rooms for displaced gentlewomen."

"And work for them?"

He shrugged.

Emily took it as agreement. Mrs. Taylor was an unusual breed of crusader. She deplored the way society treated certain classes of women, exploiting them as governesses, companions, or poor relations and then often abandoning them with a pittance when they were older. She gave them refuge and taught them a variety of dubious skills, from genteel thievery to confidence tricks.

"There's others about as well. Here and there."

"It's odd to know they are nearby, and I probably shan't see them."

"There's more than one London," responded Daniel. "You could live all your life and never venture from one to the other." He nodded sagely. "Hardly anyone does."

"Do you think Papa's . . . friends would help me with something?" Emily asked.

"Of course they would, dear," said Mary Fitzgibbon. When it appeared her husband would object, she gave him a look. "Her father has put himself out for most of them."

"I know, but I can't speak for Jack, or Eddie. Besides, what could they do for her?" He turned to Emily. "Begging your pardon, but you're staying with a duchess and moving in circles quite above their touch."

"I just want them to watch out for someone. An . . . acquaintance of mine. Papa knows him, too."

"What did he do?"

"Nothing. That is . . . I don't think he did. But someone is trying to kill him."

Both of the Fitzgibbons looked startled.

Emily knew it sounded outlandish. But she had been doing a great deal of thinking in the last few days, and she had come to some clear conclusions. Lord Warrington was in danger, which he refused to see. Someone had to do something.

And it was so much more interesting than simply going to balls and evening parties. The Season was amusing and interesting, but a trifle limiting, Emily admitted. Watching out for Lord Warrington would add a fascination to events that didn't seem to require all her abilities. She was used to watching out for her parents. Could it be she actually missed this? Of course not. She was happy to be free of the endless alarms and debates, living in ease and luxury.

But she couldn't allow a fellow human being to be harmed, she added righteously. Her conscience would rebel. She was obliged to help. She could do a good deed, and occupy her mental faculties at the same time. Splendid. Praiseworthy, even. There was nothing more to it than that.

"They tried to drown him back home, and then to crush him with an urn here in London. He was in a shipwreck, too, but I'm not sure . . . He thinks it is all accidents. I could not convince him otherwise. So he is not being careful, you see. And I cannot watch over him all the time, because I am not free to come and go as I like."

"Why should you watch over him?" asked Mary, her eyes glinting with curiosity.

"I don't wish to see him murdered," Emily answered a bit quickly. "And they tried first right outside our house. I feel . . . responsible."

"That's nonsense." Daniel looked perplexed. "Why should you?"

"Well, I . . . I was there, you see. I untied him. And when the urn fell in the park. And he isn't paying the least heed to it. It is . . . it is like watching a runaway team about to trample someone. You must try to pull them away."

Her host seemed about to dispute this, but Mary spoke first. "Who is he?"

"His name is Sheldon. Lord Warrington, that is."

"A lord?" snorted Daniel. "We've nothing to do with lords."

"You're visiting among the *ton*," said Emily.

"Jack is in the gaming houses, and Flora at the theater. And I'm sure all of you hear things." She spoke the last words firmly, knowing quite well that they gathered information along with other valuable commodities.

"We can pass the word," agreed Mary. She ignored her husband's surprised look. "What does this lord look like?"

"Oh." Emily blinked, unaware of Mary's close scrutiny. "He's tall," she began, "and, and very . . . well muscled. His skin is bronzed; he has been in the Indies. Brown hair and hazel eyes that are extremely . . . penetrating."

"Engaging manners, I suppose?"

Daniel gaped at his wife. Emily bit her lower lip as she struggled to form a reply. Richard was abrupt and sarcastic. But his rare smile was certainly engaging. He acted decisively in a crisis. She had felt so safe in his arms. Hurriedly, she banished this thought. "His manners are . . . indescribable."

Mary nodded as if she had gained important information. "We'll see what can be done." Her husband shrugged, then nodded.

"Thank you."

"Your dad shielded us from the magistrates," was the placid reply.

Emily smiled at them, then rose to go. "You will let me know if you hear anything?"

The Fitzgibbons said they would and stood to see her out.

"May I call again to see Sarah? I so love talking to her."

The earlier awkwardness returned. Daniel shifted from one foot to another.

"She is all right?"

There was another pause, then Mary replied. "She's not ill or anything. But we're a bit on the outs."

"Why?"

"She's gone to work for some German feller who reads fortunes," Daniel blurted out.

"Not fortunes," corrected Mary. "He contacts their dead relatives."

Daniel made a derisive noise.

"Dead?" said Emily.

"He holds—what d'you call them—séances. Pierces the veil and gets messages from those who've passed on."

Daniel snorted again. "He's supposed to have brought some swell back from the dead."

"People, mostly women, give him gifts," explained Mary. "He pays Sarah well, treats her well, too."

Her husband growled. "So she says."

"So I know," was the confident reply.

"You don't wish her to work there?" ventured Emily.

"It's not that I object to taking money from marks," stated Daniel, as if he had made this argument many times before. "But I draw the line at making light of death and the hereafter. It ain't a game, you know? There's some things not to be meddled with."

"I'll tell Sarah you were asking after her," said Mary.

Smiling her thanks, Emily turned to the door.

"No good'll come of it," Daniel muttered. "She ought to stick to honest thievery."

A bit bemused by his unexpected philosophy, Emily went on her way.

SIX

⚜

"THERE IS NO MORE income to be squeezed from your Somerset properties," declared Elijah Taft.

Richard looked at the craggy old man who sat opposite him in his mother's library. He had known Taft all his life, a dour West Country man with a daunting knowledge of estate management. Taft's belligerence was completely justified by their history. In the past, Richard had condescended to see Taft only when he wanted money and had berated him soundly when there wasn't any. Yet Richard still found that the man's attitude galled. "They're in poor shape, aren't they?"

Taft bristled. "When you put nothing into your

land, my lord, when you pull our every spare penny and let buildings fall to ruin and fields . . ."

Richard held up a hand. It was true; he had never made the least effort to manage his patrimony, or indeed to learn much about it. The decaying house depressed him. But even if he had tried, there was no money to mend anything or salvage acres that had been neglected for more than a generation. "Cottages and barns need to be repaired, I suppose. And other things."

"A thousand other things, my lord. And there's no more income to be gotten out of . . ."

"I know," Richard said sharply. The man might be right, but it made the situation no easier to face. "The problem is, there is no money. That's always been the problem, hasn't it?"

"There was a reasonable income—once."

"But my father was not a reasonable man."

Taft said nothing. He didn't need to. His face showed his agreement.

"And my grandfather not much more so, I understand."

"He did his best," was the gruff reply.

Taft and his grandfather had grown up together, Richard knew. They had been fast friends from early boyhood, and Taft had taken on the management of that Lord Warrington's affairs as a mission as well as a job. He had made the property his lifework. No one knew it better or cared more for every inch of the land. "I don't have the thousands of pounds that are no doubt needed to set things right," he pointed out.

"If every cent was put back in," Taft began.

"You wish me to live on nothing at all?" He would be more dependent on his mother than ever.

Taft's glower was familiar from days gone by.

Richard was assailed by an unfamiliar bitterness. It was all well and good to decide to change. But circumstances didn't always allow one to do so. "The house is falling to pieces, full of mice and damp. Perhaps we should just pull it down and have done with it."

The flare of rage in Taft's eyes was almost daunting.

He didn't really mean to tear the place down, Richard thought. He was only dispirited by the damage that generations of neglect had left behind. The task of saving the estate seemed overwhelming, and rather lonely as well. He started to withdraw the words.

"You worthless excuse for a man," Taft blurted out, obviously laboring under intense emotion. "You don't deserve the place—"

"You forget yourself!" snapped Richard.

As Taft struggled for control, Richard grappled with a fury that he acknowledged as unfair. But that didn't make it any less fiery. It was one thing to criticize oneself; it was quite another to have accusations thrown in one's face by an employee. "If you find my character so distasteful, perhaps you would like to end our association."

He couldn't help feeling a twinge of satisfaction at Taft's stricken look. "I . . . I beg your pardon, my lord. I have devoted my life to keeping . . ."

Guilt made Richard brusque. "Yes, yes. Very

well." The clock on the mantel chimed. "I have an engagement."

Taft rose. He had recovered somewhat, the lines of his face once more hard and craggy. He bowed his head in curt acknowledgment and went out.

He would have to find a way to begin repairs, Richard thought. Perhaps he would allow Taft to make use of all the income for a time. If nothing else, he would leave the land in a better state than he found it. But this sounded long and difficult even to the new Lord Warrington. He couldn't imagine being like Taft, spending his whole life in a hopeless cause.

Putting these thoughts from his mind, Richard called for his curricle to be brought round. The steam locomotive he was to see this afternoon intrigued him far more than estate management. He would always be more interested in new mechanisms and inventions than in land and crops. It was another of the things that made him so different from his peers.

Different. And open to ridicule and blank incomprehension if he showed it—except to one person in London. Taking his hat and gloves from a footman, Richard allowed his thoughts to linger on Emily Crane. He could still feel that kiss on his lips, feel the effect in every fiber of his flesh. She was damnably alluring.

London was turning out to be more enjoyable than he had expected, Richard mused. Perhaps he would stay in town for the whole of the Season.

RICHARD DROPPED HIS HANDS and let the team increase its pace on this straight stretch of road. It had been an odd afternoon. The locomotive had been fascinating, but Emily Crane had been . . . he didn't know what to call it. Impertinent? Her conversation had veered from his relatives to his position in society to the dangers of holding a grudge. She had gone on for quite some time about the possibility of making enemies among the *haut ton*. She seemed to see it as some kind of battleground, rife with verbal rapier work and relentless vendettas. What had she been up to in her short time in town? She was a decidedly unusual girl.

To top it off, the groom perched behind them in the curricle appeared to have overindulged during their luncheon at the inn. He was continually nodding off and then jerking awake again to gaze around blearily. Richard was beginning to fear that he would lose his grip and fall.

Emily cleared her throat nervously. Richard braced himself for another odd remark. "Lord Warrington?"

"Yes?"

"I . . . there was something I wished to speak to you about." Emily took a deep breath and then spoke in a rush. "My aunt tells me that gossip about my parents could be quite harmful to me. So I wanted to ask you please not to mention that you . . . that is, that they . . . your visit to them."

The request surprised Richard, and annoyed him. "Do you imagine that I spend my time gossiping?"

"I . . . I didn't mean . . ."

"Do you imagine I tell malicious tales for the pleasure of it?"

She bit her lower lip.

Richard was assailed by a rush of wholly unprecedented embarrassment. Had Emily Crane heard all about the old Lord Warrington? Embarrassment became humiliation. No doubt she had, and had probably despised the man described.

The emotion he felt then stunned him. In all of his twenty-nine years, he had never worried about what a woman might think of his character. He hadn't cared. The old Warrington had had only one purpose for a woman.

"I don't spread rumors or indulge in tittle-tattle," he added stiffly, wondering if she would believe him. "I have more important things to do with my time."

"You talked to me of nothing but my parents at the ball," Emily snapped. "How was I to know that you would not . . ."

"I didn't know you were trying to conceal their identity. That scheme is unlikely to fly, you know."

"I am not trying . . ."

"What *are* you trying to do?"

Emily hesitated. "My aunt is very knowledgeable about society."

"Undoubtedly."

"I am not."

Richard felt a spark of interest.

"I must be guided by her advice."

"Must you?"

Emily looked up at him. She was an enigma, he thought. He couldn't predict her as he could so many people he met. "You wish to succeed in society?"

"Why shouldn't I?" She looked him straight in the eye as if daring him to answer.

Richard was startled by a strong pulse of desire. His hands had found her body delightfully rounded in all the right places, he remembered. Her red-gold hair, brushing his chin, had been like threads of flame. Sternly, he called himself to order. This was out of the question—he certainly didn't need any more complications in his life.

The sound of hooves pounded up behind them. Richard pulled a little to the side to let the other vehicle pass. It came abreast of them—a light carriage and four going flat out. The driver had a hood pulled up over his head, obscuring his features. How the devil did he see the road with that thing on? If this were some young blood racing for a wager, he would most likely be foxed as well. And deadly dangerous.

Richard started to slow the curricle, but at that moment, the other carriage veered slightly and slammed into it, rocking the lighter vehicle. Both teams shied, one of the leaders squealing. Richard fought the reins, every muscle in his body taut.

The other carriage hit them again. The driver must be sodden drunk, Richard concluded. He pulled hard on the ribbons, trying to halt his thoroughly spooked horses. The leader threw back his head in a challenge and tried to bite his opposite number.

Richard hauled harder as the other carriage careened into them again. In the midst of the chaos, he noticed a small gloved hand clutching the seat beside him. Emily wasn't making a sound, he noted with approval. Then all his attention was claimed by the plunging team. There was something wrong.

They were moving away from the curricle to the left. Risking a glance downward, Richard saw that the traces had parted. The only links between the curricle and the horses were the reins in his hands.

The team turned farther, eager to get away from the melee now that it was free. Richard gripped the leathers, but it was no good. They weren't pulling the curricle any longer, and if he held on he was likely to be dragged from the seat. With a supreme act of will, he let go. The horses raced off, dragging the broken traces behind them. He heard a muted cry from Emily just as the rogue carriage hit them again and sent the curricle plunging down a hill toward a grove of trees. He had a bumping, reeling vision of sky, branches, a huge spray of water, then blackness.

RICHARD WOKE TO DARKNESS and rain pounding on his face and chest. When he tried to sit up his whole body protested in one great ache. Where was his spear? His sling? Groping for them, he searched the area for predators.

He found mud. He was half-submerged in it. Then his hand brushed his coat tail, came up to his shirtfront. He sniffed the air. He wasn't in the jungle. He had come home, he remembered. He was home. No great spotted cats or bone crushing snakes were likely to drop on him.

Bringing his hand to his face, he rubbed his pounding head. There had been a carriage . . . a fall. Struggling up, pulling his boots from the sucking mud, he squinted into the darkness. There was a full moon behind the rain clouds. He could make out the hulk of the curricle, sagging in the middle of a small pond. There seemed to be trees beyond—probably the trees they had crashed through, he decided, as memory sharpened. He had been thrown clear.

He scanned his surroundings. The rain was letting up a bit. He could hear something else, a rhythmic sound. Squelching his way toward it, he discovered his groom, flat on his back on the sodden soil, snoring. Richard shook him. When he got no response, he hauled the man up by his lapels and shook hard. The groom snorted and gurgled, but he didn't wake. How could the idiot sleep in these conditions? He must have emptied a barrel of ale. Richard dropped him, resisting the strong urge to give him a kick. He had to find Emily, yet he was almost afraid to. With her more fragile frame, was she lying broken somewhere nearby?

A movement caught his eye. A pale figure staggered upright, wavered. Striding over to it, he was just in time to catch Emily in his arms.

She clung to him. A hint of warmth penetrated his soaked shirt from her body. She was shuddering with cold and probably shock. "Are you hurt?" he said.

"B-bruised and battered," she responded, her teeth chattering.

She said it remarkably calmly, all in all.

The rain intensified again, pouring over them, the drops beating on his head. The spring night wasn't frigid, but with the wet and the wind, it was enough to do them harm. He had to find some shelter. Holding Emily close to his side, he led her over to the somnolent groom. "Wait here. I'll find someplace out of the rain."

She nodded, then sank down next to the groom. "Is he sl-sleeping?"

"Apparently. I'll be as quick as I can."

Richard left them there and took his bearings. The road was beyond the trees and up a bank if he remembered correctly. He could scramble up there and hope to flag down a passing carriage, but travelers would be few or none on a night such as this. He needed a house. Peering through the rain, he looked for a light. There was nothing. He walked up the low bank of the pond. Rain pounded on his face and shoulders and dripped from his fingertips. He would have preferred the jungle, he thought ironically. There, at least, he could have built a shelter. But this landscape offered no convenient plants with great broad leaves.

He walked a little farther, straining to penetrate the curtains of rain. There seemed to be something . . . a dark mass against the slightly lighter clouds up ahead. Moving faster, he came to it. Not a house, not even a barn; it was a small three-sided shed for storing fodder. But the overhanging roof kept out most of the rain. There were mounds of dry straw inside. It would do.

Returning to the others, he told Emily about the shelter as he helped her up. "I can walk," she said when he would have supported her. "Help your poor groom."

"Poor!"

"There must be something wrong with him to sleep like that."

"He's drunk," retorted Richard. But he grasped the man's shoulders and began to drag him across the muddy field.

Slowly, they made their way to the shed. "Oh," said Emily when she stepped inside. "It is so good to be out of that rain."

Richard grunted his agreement as he deposited the groom on a pile of hay. Emily had wrapped her arms around herself, still visibly shivering. "I have no means to make a fire. There may be a house nearby, but to find it in this . . ."

"You mustn't go out there again," she objected.

"I don't intend to. We will have to cover ourselves with the hay."

She turned to it immediately, surprising Richard at the lack of argument. Burrowing into one of the piles, she started to create a nest for herself. After a moment, he bent to help her pile the hay on top. He could not see her face, but his hand encountered hers and paused. "You're freezing," he said. Her fingers were like ice.

"I am cold. The hay will help." She nestled down into it.

Richard turned to throw some of it over the groom, then made his own place in the cramped shed. When he was done, there were scarcely six inches between him and Emily, and little more separating him from the servant.

He lay there in the darkness waiting for the chill to fade. The rain beat on the slanted roof. The groom snored. He could hear Emily's teeth chattering, the rustling in the hay caused by her shivers. She made no complaint. She didn't cry or moan or accuse. She was simply lying there, quietly freezing, not asking for anyone's help.

An unfamiliar pressure arose in Richard's chest. He had never experienced anything like it. Did it have something to do with the new Richard Sheldon? Was it something he'd acquired during his ordeal?

It was almost painful. It pushed him, without words, to act.

Reaching out, he pulled Emily into the crook of his arm. She fit neatly under his open driving coat against his side.

She made a small sound of protest.

"You must get warm," he said.

She didn't reply, but neither did she draw away. She was shivering violently now. But as heat began to spread between them, the shudders lessened, and finally faded. She relaxed slightly in his embrace, though he could tell that she still wasn't completely at ease.

How could she be? It was not a situation that encouraged nonchalance. He could feel the soft curve of her breast against his ribs, the pressure of her thigh on his own. Her breath ruffled against his cheek, and the beat of her heart made a counterpoint to his accelerating pulse.

He remembered the kiss in Vauxhall Gardens, and the way she had responded to his touch, with an innocent eagerness that had driven him wild. The feel of her lingered in his fingertips, on his lips. He could recall every nuance of those moments—the delicate, yielding texture of her mouth, the slender suppleness that nestled against him now. Making love to Emily would be glorious. She was such a beguiling mixture of inexperience and wisdom.

Her contours softened into his, and Richard almost groaned aloud. His body was demanding the pleasures his mind had visualized so clearly. It was all he could do to keep his hands still, to discipline the drive of desire.

Emily's breathing grew more regular. She had fallen asleep.

Richard clenched his jaw. She trusted him. She had little reason to do so, but she did. She snuggled closer, and this time Richard caught his breath. He was unbearably aroused. He wanted her as he couldn't remember ever wanting any woman. And he wasn't going to do anything about it.

The thought made him smile slightly. How the old Richard Sheldon would jeer at this restraint. Nothing had been allowed to interfere with his desires. He would have found Emily's trusting openness laughable.

Of course, no one had trusted him, Richard acknowledged. It was different, seemingly, when one had to deal with such complications. Because there was more going on than simple physical arousal, compelling as that was. He felt odd. When he considered Emily, he felt—pity, or no—that wasn't it.

Her reaction to their plight had impressed him, he reasoned. She had been brave, astonishingly uncomplaining. He admired that.

She turned slightly in his arms, and Richard let out a quick breath. Her hands were curled on her breast. They would only have to move a little to caress . . .

He stopped himself. This was not acceptable. He was losing his grip on himself. And that was a thing he no longer allowed. If he had learned one thing in his fight for survival, it was control.

He'd taken a sharp pummeling in the accident, he told himself. That was it. Perhaps he was slightly delirious. He would take more care.

He looked around their crude shelter, then down at Emily, curled so confidingly against him. He had a sense of consequences rippling out from this night, already far beyond his control. He ought to have gone on searching for a house or . . . something.

The sound of the rain contradicted him. He had done what he could. And now he would simply have to endure. He would hold her, keep her safe and warm, until he could get her home again. And he would resist the urge to touch her, to see if he could rouse the desperate need he was feeling in the exquisite body pressed against his. It couldn't be any harder than slogging through a steaming swamp for days on end. It had to be easier than facing a jungle cat with little more than his teeth and nails to defend him.

But it wasn't. The heat they'd generated burned through him, and the soft caress of her breath drove him mad. It was hours before the rhythm of the rain and the rush of wind finally lulled him into a restless sleep.

Around dawn, the groom stirred. He sat up, holding his head as if it might split in two, then staggered out into the long grass. He squinted at the daylight, spat, and reeled off in the direction of the pond like a desert wanderer spotting succor.

EMILY WOKE TO THE SOUND of voices. Her aunt was calling her, she thought groggily. Perhaps she had overslept. Aunt Julia equated early rising with virtue and steadiness of character. Why hadn't the maid brought her tea? She moved, and was rewarded by a whole medley of aches and strains, a prickle of hay in her face, and a sudden stunning awareness of another body pressed close to hers. She blinked to clear her vision and found herself gazing at Richard Sheldon's face from a distance of inches. She was folded in his coat. His arm was draped over her. So was one of his legs. Even as her face flamed, Emily realized that the position was not precisely unpleasant. It was unprecedented in her life, of course, and very unsettling. But the pounding of her heart and the shortness of her breath were . . . stimulating.

An earsplitting shriek cut through these ruminations. It also caused Richard to jerk awake just as Emily was struggling up out of their cocoon. When she managed to sit, she found herself facing her Aunt Julia, her cousin George, and two of the duchess's footmen. All of them looked profoundly shocked.

"Emily," cried the duchess. "What . . . ?" Her mouth opened and closed, but she appeared unable to find words.

Emily struggled to escape the hay. It was clinging to her clothes and no doubt her hair as well. She must look like . . . well, she didn't want to think about it.

A strong hand helped her rise. Richard came to his feet beside her. Emily tried to gather her wits.

"What are you doing?" her aunt managed finally.

"The curricle overturned," said Richard.

The duchess gazed at him with horror.

"I . . . we were all thrown. It was some time before we recovered, and then . . . with the rain and . . . we were forced to shelter here. My groom was . . . ah . . . injured."

"What groom?" asked George belligerently. He was tapping his stick against his thigh.

Richard looked around the empty shed.

"This is dreadful," moaned the duchess. "This is disastrous. Olivia will . . ." She turned even paler. "Alasdair! He will have an apoplexy. He'll kill someone." She looked at Richard as if in no doubt of the victim.

"But Aunt, we only . . ."

"Don't tell me what you did!" She started to wring her hands. "Lady Jersey will make such a story of this."

"Not if Lord Warrington is a man of honor," said George. He looked thunderous.

Richard looked worse, thought Emily. He looked murderous. Muscles shifted in his jaw as he stood rigid. His hazel eyes burned. She worried suddenly that he would go for George's throat.

"I will call on the duke as soon as I am able," he said, spitting out the words.

George gave a curt nod. His mother wrung her hands a final time, then clasped them tight together.

"Miss Crane should be taken home," Richard added.

The duchess surged forward to gather Emily. George ushered them both out of the shed. "I will tell my father to expect you," he said over his shoulder.

"Count on it," was the clipped reply.

Emily stumbled a bit as she was helped over the rough ground. She still felt disoriented. She couldn't seem to think. It seemed an endless way to her aunt's carriage.

"But will it do?" said the duchess to her son.

"I've left Ned to find that groom. We should be able to hush it up."

"Nothing . . . improper occurred," stammered Emily.

Her aunt looked scandalized. "Nothing? Do you call lying in a man's . . . ? I can't even speak of it. What would your parents say to me if they heard?"

Her father wouldn't say anything, Emily thought. Aunt Julia had been right before. He would kill someone. She wasn't sure about her mother. "No one will know."

The duchess shook her head. "We will do our best. But such things get out. The servants will gossip. If Warrington doesn't . . ."

"He would never tell anyone," interrupted Emily.

Her aunt and cousin stared at her as if she had lost her wits.

She remembered their opinion of Richard's sharp tongue and tendency toward malice. But it wasn't true. He wasn't like that at all. Was he?

"He won't if I have anything to do with it," answered George grimly.

She didn't believe it, Emily decided. He had

never maligned her parents, after all. Despite what nearly everyone said, she found she trusted him.

Exhausted by her ordeal, Emily climbed into the carriage and sank back on the cushions. Things would be clearer when she was rested.

EMILY WAS SITTING in the morning room the next day when her aunt entered with Richard in tow.

"Lord Warrington has something to say to you." The duchess looked strained but resolute. "Your uncle and I have given him our consent."

"Consent?"

Her aunt merely slipped back out of the room.

Richard came closer. His gaze was cold and his expression grim. "I've come, of course, to ask you to be my wife," he said without preliminaries.

Emily had been half-expecting this, half-rejecting the idea as ridiculous. "Of course?"

Richard waited in icy silence. His expression was forbidding. He might have been carved from stone.

She wasn't going to go along with this. Her aunt had arranged the scene, but no one could make her follow the prescribed steps. "That carriage attacked us."

He blinked, startled.

"It was absolutely blatant."

Surprise made Richard look a little less intimidating.

"And I have been wondering if your groom was given some drug. The way he was sleeping," she pointed out. "It was unnatural."

One corner of his mouth twitched.

"And the traces were cut, weren't they? I could see that."

"Could you?"

She nodded, pleased to have elicited a reaction. "They had to befuddle the groom to do that."

"They?"

"Whoever did it," she added impatiently.

"Ah."

At least he was looking a little more human, Emily thought, not so frightening. "You must admit now that someone is trying to harm you."

"I am not required to admit anything." He grimaced. "Except stupidity that goes beyond all bounds."

She chose to ignore this. "Whoever was driving that carriage deliberately ran you off the road."

"If they did, it is no business of yours."

"You do admit it!"

He brushed off the statement with a gesture.

"The urn, the footpads, it is all . . ."

"An odd series of . . . occurrences."

"Occurrences? They were plain murderous attacks!"

"Whatever they are, they are my affair. I will deal with them."

"But you must—"

"I will judge what I *must* do," he interrupted angrily. "Indeed, I already have."

Like come here today and offer for her when it appeared to be the last thing in the world he wanted to do. A tremor of unhappiness shook her, and she closed her fists against it. He wasn't going to listen to sensible advice. He wasn't going to take steps to protect himself. Would he even try to discover what was behind the attacks?

"You have not answered my first question."

He was going to let himself be killed through sheer stubbornness.

"I don't imagine you've forgotten it."

He needed help. But he would never admit it. On the contrary, he would act like a fool to prove he didn't.

Richard raised his eyebrows. His gaze was stony.

It would be much easier to watch over him if they were engaged, Emily realized. Later, of course, she would break it off. She would never entrap a man into marriage.

"Well?"

She took a shaky breath. It was all for his own good. She cared . . . she cared only that a fellow human being was in jeopardy. She swallowed. Her heart was beating very fast. "Yes," she said.

Richard winced. "Yes?"

"I . . . I accept your proposal."

He looked like a man who has received dire news and is just apprehending the full extent of the disaster.

Stricken, Emily swallowed again. It would only be for a little while, and then she could explain to him that she had never meant to go through with it. He would be safe by then, and she would be . . . she would have figured out the puzzle. She struggled to pull in some air.

"I see." He stood straighter. "That is clear then."

The coldness of his tone and the anger in his face

were too much. Emily opened her mouth to retract everything.

The door opened and the duchess peeked around the panels. "Have you settled things between you?"

"It appears we are engaged," replied Richard.

The duchess came into the room and gazed at Emily with a kind of despair. Then she visibly pulled herself together. "I'll send the notice off to the *Morning Post* at once."

"I'm sure you will," replied Richard contemptuously.

At that, Aunt Julia was every inch the duchess. She raked him with a look so haughty that Emily quailed.

This was supposed to be one of the happiest moments of her life, she thought. An accepted proposal should mean excitement about the future, tender emotions, and a flurry of felicitations. Instead she felt a sinking sensation and, when she looked at Richard, a tremor of tears. Should she take back her acceptance?

"You have subjected my niece to mortal danger," said the duchess through her teeth. "You have very nearly destroyed her position in society. I don't believe you have anything to complain of."

Richard looked as if he might explode. Emily braced herself for she didn't know what. But when he finally spoke, he said only, "As things appear to be settled, I will take my leave."

Her aunt began a protest, but he didn't wait for it. He was striding out the door before she managed two words. "Well," she said. "Well."

Emily reminded herself that the engagement

would only be temporary. She would find the assailant and end the attacks, and then she could show
Richard that she was above all this sort of thing.

"It is not the match I hoped for," said her aunt.
She paused to grapple with this prodigious understatement. "But under the circumstances . . ." She
swallowed as if something was caught in her throat.
"Oh, lud," she murmured.

She was going to have to move fast, Emily
thought. She had to find the solution before all this
flew right out of control.

SEVEN

RICHARD SAT in the library of his mother's house, his legs extended, a glass of brandy held loosely in one hand. It was past midnight. The household was asleep, and the streets outside had grown quiet. How he had dreamed, six months ago in the jungle, of sitting just so, of being home again. Now, he was, and he almost wished himself back in the wilderness.

Trapped into marriage. It was the last thing he would ever have expected. In fact, he couldn't quite believe it even now. Since he had first entered society, he had had the address—some had called it ruthlessness—to discourage any scheming females. A woman who approached him when he didn't wish it was soon sorry. Not that many pursued a man without fortune. It wasn't a record to be proud of, he acknowledged, but it had kept the question of marriage at bay.

Yet here he was. The notices would appear in the papers tomorrow. It was out of his control. He was as helpless as he had been when the storm swept over the ship and he'd been marooned two thousand miles from home.

He hated it.

Richard sipped his brandy and wondered if Emily Crane had somehow engineered the whole, from the moment of their meeting at her house. But after a moment, he shook his head. It was impossible. All that Emily had done was acquiesce. His mouth hardened; not that he forgave her for that. He would never forgive her.

He tossed off the rest of the brandy and refilled the glass. A toast to his coming nuptials, he thought bitterly. He had meant to marry, of course, someday. He owed it to his name. An heiress was clearly called for to repair his fortunes. But this had always figured as a distant event in his mind. He had never imagined such a humiliating position. Grimacing, Richard addressed himself to the brandy once more. It didn't matter what he wanted. He'd gotten Emily Crane.

He'd gotten the thing he had always hoped to avoid—one of those society marriages where husband and wife shared little more than a residence. They were common enough; and in the past, he had even found their vicissitudes amusing. But he had vainly imagined he could evade that fate, even with the illusory heiress.

Richard snorted in self-mockery. It seemed the old Warrington had had some mawkish romantic notions, despite his careless treatment of women. Perhaps this forced marriage was no more than he deserved.

He turned from this depressing subject to the other matter. He saw again the hooded driver, heard his carriage slam against the side of the curricle. Whatever he might say to Emily Crane, to himself he had to admit that the crash had been no accident. The man had meant to overturn them.

And someone had definitely tampered with the traces. When he examined them, they'd been cleanly cut through. The groom denied imbibing more than a mug of ale. He might be lying, of course; but his record was spotless, and the butler vouched for him. It seemed that someone had actually slipped him a drug and cut the reins.

Richard shifted in the chair, conscious of the aches and bruises throughout his body. He might easily have broken his neck in that spill. Had that really been the idea?

If so, then the other incidents that seemed to obsess Miss Crane might deserve his attention after all. He had dismissed her suspicions, seeing them as fanciful embroideries, female hysteria. Even though Emily had never shown a single sign of excessive sensibility, an inner voice pointed out.

Richard rubbed his forehead, as if that could ease the tension in his brain. He had not seen those other incidents. She might have been mistaken about the footpads, the urn. And they had seemed so trivial after all he'd been through. But taken together . . .

He sipped brandy. Why should anyone want him dead? He had no enemies on that scale. He had no money to tempt his heir. The idea that his cousin Donald, a wealthy man in his own right, would kill to assume a mere barony—it was ludicrous. There was absolutely no reason for him to be the victim of a murderous plot, and yet he was very near to conceding that he was.

The door latch clicked. Richard's muscles tightened reflexively. But when the panels swung open they revealed only his mother in a long white nightgown and mobcap, a paisley shawl swathing her shoulders. "Richard?"

He rose and went to her. "Yes, Mother. Why aren't you asleep?"

"I was just wondering if you were all right."

A complex question. "Of course I am."

"That awful accident." She gestured vaguely. "So worrisome."

"But I came out of it perfectly well. You should go back to bed. You look tired." She did indeed, he thought. Tired, and older than her fifty years.

His mother sighed, looking around the room. "I hardly ever come here since Walter died. He always sat here."

His stepfather had loved books, Richard remembered. He had indeed spent countless evenings in this room with a favorite volume and a glass of brandy. How strange that he had chosen the same retreat, when he had scarcely entered it during his stepfather's life. A pang of regret startled Richard, as unfamiliar as most of the feelings that plagued him lately.

His mother had wandered over to the bookshelves, scanning the spines as if they held some message for her.

"Would you like a little brandy?" Richard asked. "Perhaps it would help you sleep."

"And this engagement," she said, still gazing at the books, not appearing to have heard him. "It is so sudden."

"Come and sit down, Mother." He guided her to an armchair and poured out another glass of brandy before sitting opposite. They had been through all this earlier, but clearly it had not sufficed. He could hardly blame her.

"I didn't even know you liked the young lady. You've known her such a short time."

"These things happen quickly sometimes," he offered.

"And you say she has no fortune at all?"

He shook his head.

"I don't wish to interfere, but do you think that is really wise, Richard?"

It was the antithesis of wise. It was a disaster from start to finish.

His mother sampled her brandy. Gazing at the amber liquid with approval, she repeated the dose. "One can't live on love, you know. I thought your father was the most glorious young man on earth. But once we were married, it was . . . difficult." She drank again.

"Mother, I—"

"My family opposed the match, but I wouldn't listen." She looked straight at Richard, not the least bit befuddled.

He was amazed, and wholly at a loss. It seemed

grossly unfair that he had to defend an engagement he had never wanted in the first place. "Miss Crane is . . ." He grimaced slightly, not knowing how to finish.

She waited. The silence stretched out uncomfortably. Finally, his mother sighed and sipped from her glass again. "It is a good family. The duchess has been very kind."

Richard refrained from comment. He was picturing his mother's introduction to Alasdair Crane.

"If you need some help with setting up your own household—"

"I won't take your money," interrupted Richard harshly.

She looked surprised. As well she might. He had never refused her money before.

"But how will you . . . ?"

"I don't know! But I will manage it on my own." Perhaps he would take Emily to live on his Somerset estates, he thought savagely. A few weeks of leaking roofs and rotting floorboards—not to mention the odd rat—would show her what sort of bargain she'd made. She'd demonstrated a remarkable fortitude, a treacherous inner voice commented. He stifled it by draining his glass and reaching for the decanter.

His mother looked a bit daunted. She seemed to cast about for a new subject. "Did I tell you Lydia is coming for a visit? I haven't seen her for an age. She's Walter's niece, you know."

Lydia Farrell was one of the members of his stepfather's family who had received a legacy from him, Richard remembered. He had resented them fiercely at the time.

"Such a lovely girl."

Lydia must be well into her thirties, Richard calculated. He thought she was married and had a couple of children. He hadn't seen her since he was a stripling. In his hazy recollection she was a skinny, silent creature with little to recommend her. "She lives in Wales?"

"I'm sure she must be heartily sick of the country. We'll show her a bit of town life."

The idea appeared to please her, which was enough for Richard. His mother badly needed a diversion.

"I wonder if I can get her vouchers for Almack's." She looked down into her glass, found it was empty, and held it out to him.

"You are going to be thoroughly foxed, Mother."

She gave a trill of laughter. "Don't be silly. Just a sip more."

She didn't laugh nearly as much as she used to, Richard thought as he poured it. He sent a silent thanks to his almost cousin Lydia. Though she didn't know it, her timing was impeccable.

EMILY SAT VERY STRAIGHT as one of the footmen placed a filet of sole on her plate, then moved along to her uncle, who sat at the head of the long table. She never quite got used to the formality of dinner in a ducal household. A liveried servant was posted behind every chair. And there were always two full courses and a remove. Her aunt and uncle, and tonight her cousin George as well, seemed to take it for granted. They only remarked on the ceremony if something went amiss, or if a dish was particularly good.

"What did you do today, Emily?" inquired the duke.

She smiled at him. He tried to be kind, she knew, but he spoke to her as if she were twelve years old instead of almost twenty. "I rode in the park."

He nodded as he sampled the sole. "Your horse is satisfactory?"

"Yes, thank you. You couldn't have found a better one for me."

He acknowledged this benignly.

"She's a spanking rider," said George.

"Slang, George," said the duchess automatically.

Under other circumstance, Emily would have told them that her father had taught her to ride, and that he was ridiculously proud of her fine seat. But she wasn't to mention her parents. Under other circumstances, they might have been chatting about bride clothes and wedding arrangements, but that topic was equally awkward. In fact, she couldn't think of a single thing to say, even though she found the scrape of cutlery in the silence oppressive.

Thankfully, the gentlemen fell into a discussion of the duke's racing stables, which obviously interested them far more than anything Emily might have said. She finished her fish and sipped her wine. She had wished for more stability and convention, she remembered. She hadn't realized her wish would be granted with a vengeance.

The sound of raised voices drifted back from the front of the house, followed by a thud. A door slammed. Emily's aunt frowned and cocked her head at the noise.

An argument had broken out in the entry hall. There was another thud. "What on earth?" said the duchess. "John, go and see."

One of the footmen bowed and went out. The apparent altercation continued.

"What is that?" asked Uncle Henry, apparently just noticing the disturbance.

His wife shrugged. "I have no idea. I've sent . . ."

"I damned well will interrupt them," declared a masculine voice. "Get out of my way, idiot."

"What in blazes?" George started to rise, but Emily was well ahead of him. "Papa!" she cried to the rakish figure who came striding into the room just then, and threw herself onto his chest.

Alasdair Crane embraced her with one arm while gazing around the room with a mixture of contempt and amusement. "Hullo, Julia," he said. "Duke."

"Alasdair," responded the former in a faint voice. "Where is . . . ?"

"Right here," said Olivia Crane, walking gracefully into the dining room. "I beg your pardon for descending on you unannounced."

Emily transferred her hug to her mother, who returned it full measure.

"Alasdair was in a hurry," she added, looking amused.

"Hurry?" bellowed the said Alasdair. "Damned right I was in a hurry. What the devil have you been up to, Julia?"

The duchess raised her eyebrows and gave him a

look that would have withered any member of society on the spot.

It had no effect whatsoever on her brother-in-law. "We send Emily to you, against my better judgment, mind." He glowered at Olivia, who smiled serenely back. "And before she's been in London a month, we hear she's engaged."

As she watched her aunt struggle with her temper, Emily was overwhelmed with relief and affection. She was incredibly glad to see her parents. Though it had been only a few weeks, she had missed them far more than she realized.

"Engaged!" roared Alasdair. "Without so much as a by-your-leave. To some fellow I've never heard of. It's insupportable." He had stepped close to Aunt Julia and was looming over her in a way that she clearly disliked. "Nothing to say for yourself?"

"I see that your manners haven't improved, Alasdair," was the cold reply.

"Not likely to, since I haven't any."

"Indeed," murmured the duchess.

"Are you Philip or George?" Emily's mother said.

Her cousin made a strangled noise in his throat. "Er, George."

"I am your aunt. Your other aunt."

"I know."

His stunned expression seemed to amuse Olivia a good deal. "Hello, Henry," she said to the duke.

The latter nodded. Of all his family, only he seemed unperturbed by the interruption.

"I *am* sorry for the sudden arrival, Julia," she added. "But once we got the news, we had to come up, of course."

"How did you get the news?" wondered her sister faintly.

A good question, Emily thought. She hadn't had time to write herself, and she was certain her aunt had not done so.

"Not from you," exploded Alasdair. "Is there something havey cavey about this business? Because I'll have you know I won't stand for any . . ."

The duchess went pale. George choked again. Emily's mother seemed to be enjoying herself. "I still have a few friends in London," she said. "Cynthia sent me the notice."

Her sister's lips turned down. "She always was a little sneak." Her expression showed that she regretted the remark as soon as it was made.

"What's there to be sneaking about?" demanded Alasdair. "I'll have the whole story, by God. And if there's anything smoky about it, someone will pay." He glared around the room pugnaciously. George gulped.

"It was rather . . . soon for an engagement," said Olivia.

Alasdair growled.

"Emily is lovely," countered the duchess. "Can you be surprised that she captivated a young man. . . ."

Another rumble from Alasdair made her falter briefly.

"And there was a prior acquaintance," she added. "So it is not really . . ."

"What?" Alasdair glowered. "Emily wasn't acquainted with any young sprigs of fashion."

"It was the gentleman who had trouble on the road," Olivia told him, clearly not for the first time.

"Eh?"

"The one you wanted to paint as Samson," explained Emily, then wished she'd held her tongue as her father's irate gaze swung in her direction.

"That vagabond?" He looked incredulous, then enraged. He turned on the duchess again. "You've engaged *my* daughter to some wandering scoundrel who can't even keep a horse under him?"

This seemed unfair even to Emily. "He is Lord Warrington, Papa."

As usual, he ignored any point that might weaken his argument. "This will all have to be gone into in detail. I have not given my consent, and I think it highly unlikely that I will do so."

"We will certainly talk with the young man," said Olivia soothingly. She smiled. "And as long as we are in town, we can renew some old acquaintances. You can put us up for a few days, Julia?"

Her sister looked horrified.

"I . . . that is . . . are you sure you would not be more comfortable . . . Papa . . ."

"Well, Papa did say that I was never to darken his door again," Olivia pointed out. "And he and Alasdair have never really gotten on."

From the way her aunt's eyes widened, Emily took this to be a considerable understatement.

"And with Emily here . . ." Olivia let her voice trail off and fixed her sister with a steady gaze.

The duchess looked wildly around the room. Her son evaded her gaze. Her husband shrugged, disavowing responsibility. Emily kept her eyes on the floor.

While she felt some sympathy for her aunt, her long-ing for her parents' company was far greater. "Of course you are . . . welcome," she murmured at last.

Her sister gave her a genuine smile. "Thank you, Julia. Really, we won't trouble you in the least."

If the duchess believed that, Emily thought. . . . But clearly, she didn't.

Later that evening, a more expected arrival was taking place as Lady Fielding greeted her late hus-band's niece. Richard returned from dinner at his club in the midst of these effusions and in time to admire Lydia Farrell's dashing traveling costume and the favorable changes time had wrought in his rela-tive by marriage.

She was no longer skinny and diffident. Quite the contrary. The years had generously rounded her fig-ure. Her face was slightly fuller as well, which became her, her complexion was ruddy rather than pale, and her dark brown hair gleamed with vitality. All the country air, he decided. "How do you do, Lord War-rington?"

"Oh, you must call him Richard," exclaimed his mother. "We are all family here."

"I don't think I could do that," was the cool re-ply.

The look that went with it told Richard that he had been even ruder than he remembered when they had met years ago. "Please do," he said.

She seemed surprised, and examined his expres-sion before saying, "Then you must call me Lydia."

"Good," said Lady Fielding as she led the way to the drawing room. "I'm so glad you've come. It has been so long."

"More than ten years." Lydia threw him another sidelong glance. "I believe Richard was still at school the last time we met."

"A scrubby schoolboy, in fact. And you were barely out of the schoolroom."

She smiled ruefully. "It has been a long time. But I don't think I ever called you scrubby."

"Even though I richly deserved it."

He had startled her again.

"You were extremely polite," he added.

"I expect I was a mass of nerves. My upbringing was very retired, you know. I had no idea how to go on in society."

"You grew up in Wales?"

She nodded, turning away. "What a lovely room." She sank gracefully down on a sofa. "And how wonderful not to be bouncing in a carriage any longer."

Lady Fielding prepared to pour tea; and Richard leaned back in a chair, taking a cup when he was offered it. Lydia raised one brow. Clearly, she had expected him to excuse himself.

"How is your family?" asked his mother.

"Very well, thank you. Jeremy and Thomas—my sons—are at school now. William is deep in the spring planting, as he is every year. I tried to convince him to come with me, but he hates society. He said he would rather be shut in a cellar for a month than trapped in a ballroom for one night."

Richard smiled at his mother's incredulous expression.

"But you must . . . surely even in Wales there is some society?" she said.

"Oh yes. We dine with friends, and there is even an assembly hall not too far away." She gestured as if dismissing this topic. "Tell me about London. I have only been here once before, when I was presented years ago."

As his mother began to relay all the latest gossip, Lydia appeared amused and interested. His mother was more animated than he had seen her for a long time. This visit was really a fortunate accident. Perhaps it would solve one of the host of problems that beset him.

EMILY SIGNALED A HACK near the duchess's townhouse, and quickly climbed in. The household was in disarray this morning as her parents settled in and her aunt brooded about the consequences of their visit. No one had seen her slip out alone, and no one was likely to miss her for an hour or two.

The cab let her out at the Fitzgibbons' house.

"Have you heard anything?" she asked when they were seated in the drawing room.

Daniel looked solemn. "There's a whisper—no more than that, mind—that some bullyboys have been after your Lord Warrington."

"He is not my . . ."

"We saw the announcement in the paper," put in Mrs. Fitzgibbon. She smiled at Emily over her knitting.

"Oh." It was public knowledge now. Emily's heart quailed when she remembered the evening party they were to attend tonight and all the attention the news would draw. Her parents would probably want to go along. A small shudder shook her.

"We wish you very happy," added Mary Fitzgibbon.

"Oh. Er, thank you." Mary was eyeing her dubiously. She would have to learn to do better than that. She would be pelted with congratulations—sincere or not—tonight. "Bullyboys?" she managed.

Daniel shrugged. "The sort you can hire to cosh a bloke or slip him into the river."

"Killers, you mean?" Her voice squeaked a little on the words.

Her host nodded. "Nobody we would know, you understand. Or our friends, either. I don't hold with violence, so I don't hear, you might say, directly. Can't vouch for the truth of it."

"He has been attacked, though."

"Well, there you are then."

Emily sat still for a moment, trying to take it in. It was one thing to have suspicions, and quite another to have them confirmed. Confronted with actual flesh and blood killers, she felt daunted.

"So that's that," added Daniel. "Happy to have been . . ."

"Can you find out anything more about these men? Particularly who hired them?"

Daniel shook his head. "I don't care to get mixed up with . . ."

"We could ask the Bruiser," suggested Mary.

He glared at her and made a gesture as if cutting off further talk.

Mary absorbed it placidly. "It's her promised husband. We can't just let it go."

"The Bruiser'd be no help," was the response. "And dealing with the likes of him ain't what I like at all."

"I don't want to get you in trouble," began Emily.

"You're exaggerating, Daniel," declared Mrs. Fitzgibbon. "And the boy was a great help when Jack had his . . . little problem."

"Boy!"

"You know quite well he is little more."

Daniel looked extremely unhappy. "They'll be a price."

"I would be happy to pay whatever . . ."

"If money's all he asks," growled Daniel.

"You worry far too much," said his wife. She smiled at Emily. "It's what's kept us one step ahead of . . . difficulties. But this is quite all right."

"If you're sure." Emily frowned at Daniel's woebegone expression.

His wife gave him a look.

"I reckon it'll be all right," he conceded.

She let out her breath. "Thank you. I don't know what I would do without your help."

"Happy to do it, my dear," answered Mrs. Fitzgibbon. Her husband merely grimaced.

In the hack on the way home, Emily thought over what she had heard. The worst sort of ruffians were apparently after Richard. She must tell him this right away. She would have to get him alone, make him listen.

Then she remembered; they were engaged. They would be expected, and allowed, to talk privately together. She relaxed a little in the seat. She had been right to go along with the betrothal. The matter was even more urgent than she'd known. But now she would be able to really help Richard resolve it. And then, of course, she would break off the engagement. It wasn't going to do anyone any harm. It was all going to work. There would be difficulties, but she would overcome them.

She was feeling quite sanguine as she slipped back into the duchess's house and made her way upstairs. It wasn't until she heard her father's bellow from an upper room that she remembered the difficulties might be greater than she knew.

EIGHT

❦

"**O**H DEAR," said Emily when she walked into the party and discovered the hostess's scheme of entertainment. She was calling the event "Homage to the Arts," and she had various examples stationed around the edges of the reception rooms. Emily could see a burly man in the far corner applying a chisel to a block of stone and a group of actors playing a scene on the other side. There was music in the air. Undoubtedly a painter sat in some other part of the house plying his craft. Nothing could be more calculated to enrage her father, who was already out of sorts at the mere thought of attending a *ton* party.

She moved quickly into the crowd, putting some

distance between herself and the inevitable explosion and callously abandoning her aunt, whose worst fears were about to be realized. Several acquaintances offered their felicitations as she moved through the rooms. Emily accepted them without pausing, searching for a refuge from complications.

Richard was standing in the far salon, watching a pair of dancers stationed in the corner, in an area set off by velvet ropes twined with flowers. In this constricted space, they were taking poses from a ballet, unable to really execute the steps. Richard looked torn between amusement and disgust at the sight.

Emily went to stand beside him just as a young sprig of fashion offered the dancers a bottle of champagne, which they eagerly accepted. "That should make it a bit easier for them," she said.

Richard turned and discovered her.

"Perhaps we should do the same for all the 'arts,' " she added.

"You don't approve of our hostess's scheme?"

"It's insulting."

He raised his eyebrows.

"She's exhibiting artists as if they were animals in a zoo. And all these people"—she indicated the crowd around them—"are treating them just that way."

"You are an unaccountable creature."

Emily was taken aback.

"Your conversation is a muddle of inanities and impertinence. But then you come out with an interesting observation—like that one. I cannot make you out."

"Inanities?" she glared at him.

He was nodding when the festivities were interrupted by a roar and clatter from another room.

"What was that?" Richard moved in the direction of the sounds.

Emily sighed. "I expect it was my father."

"He is here?"

"He and Mama came up to town yesterday."

"Ah." His expression hardened. "Come to see the new son-in-law, have they?" His tone was cutting.

"To thrash him more likely," Emily couldn't help answering. At his startled look, she added, "My father is . . . he is not like other people, you know."

"I did observe that. His arrival must be very awkward for you."

"Oh, I'm used to him." She had to smile. "My aunt is in quite a taking. When he said he was coming here tonight, I thought she would faint."

"I thought you wished to conceal your parentage."

"What?" She drew herself up straighter.

"You asked me not to speak of them—not to gossip, if I recollect correctly." His voice implied that he certainly did.

All of her aunt's fears would be realized now, Emily realized. If Aunt Julia were right, her own debut in society might be wrecked by the gossip. She looked around the room at the glittering crowd. It would be too bad; but the truth was, she had much more important matters on her mind. "My aunt was worried. And she convinced me that I must be, too."

"But you have changed your mind?"

Emily nodded impatiently. "I must speak to you about something important."

"Now that you have snared a husband," he added.

"What?"

"You needn't care about society's opinion, since you have gotten what you came for?"

Emily struggled briefly to contain her outrage. He didn't understand anything, she told herself. Taking a calming breath, she bent a little toward him and lowered her voice. "I have some information that you must hear."

"Information?"

"Yes. There are—"

"You are a mass of contradictions."

"You must listen to me."

"Either you are the most devious, heartless little schemer I have ever encountered . . ."

Emily glared at him.

"Or you are demented. I suppose, given your upbringing, I should be charitable and choose the latter. But it is difficult for a man who has been entrapped into marriage to be charitable."

She stood very still, telling herself again that he had a right to be angry. But his words and contemptuous expression still cut her to the quick. "I did not mean . . ." she began, and found she couldn't continue.

"You do understand that I have no fortune?"

Emily fought to hide her agitation from the people around them. Eventually, Richard would understand. She took another calming breath and rushed on before he could stop her again. "Some . . . friends of mine have heard rumors about the attacks on you. Ruffians may have been hired to harm you."

Richard stared down at her.

"They are trying to find out who this may be," Emily added hurriedly. "If we could find them, then we could discover who is behind . . ."

"We?"

His gaze made Emily falter. "Well, that is . . ."

"I have told you it is none of your affair," he continued, but he said it as if he were mystified, rather than offended, by her persistence.

"You admit that someone is after you, then?"

His frown didn't seem directed wholly at her. "I have been forced to acknowledge that something odd is going on."

"Thank God," replied Emily, feeling immense relief.

"Why should you care?"

He really had the most piercing gaze, she thought. It took her a moment to gather her faculties. "I care about anyone who is in trouble,"

He obviously found this unsatisfactory.

"And I was there at the beginning, you know. When those two men were trying to drown you. I have some . . . some responsibility, since I chased them off."

"You?"

"The dogs and I."

He looked bemused.

"And it's interesting," she finished.

"What?"

Instantly, she regretted that final phrase. "It's an . . . an obligation."

He examined her as if he had never seen such a

creature before. "Having, as you see it, saved my life, you now feel obligated to safeguard it?"

"That's it." Relieved, Emily smiled at him.

"Ridiculous," he pronounced. "The obligation—if one did exist—would be on my side."

"But if you save something, you cannot just abandon it afterward."

He looked offended. "We're not talking of a half-dead kitten, or an injured fox." There seemed to be amusement in his voice as well, though she couldn't be sure.

"So I should just let you be killed?"

"I assure you I am exceedingly difficult to kill."

"But a systematic attack . . ."

"Where did you hear of such a thing?"

"I told you. Friends of mine . . ."

"What sort of friends would be privy to that kind of information?" He looked around the crowded room, his lip curling a little. "Certainly not those you have made in London?"

"Old friends."

"Miss Crane, you are being deliberately unhelpful."

"I cannot tell you who they are. They would not wish to be known to you." The Fitzgibbons would be exceedingly unhappy if she betrayed their true identity, or their connection with some of the town's more unsavory elements.

"Indeed. But I am to take the word of these mysterious individuals . . ."

"Well, what other clues do you have?"

He raised an eyebrow.

"How else will you find out who is after you?"

"I have certain resources of my own."

"Are you going to refuse help just because it comes from me?" Emily was horrified to hear her voice break slightly as she spoke.

He seemed to be trying to formulate an answer when a low musical voice interrupted with, "I beg your pardon."

Emily turned, and almost collided with a tall attractive woman bearing down on them. Emily stepped out of her way.

"Richard, you must rescue me," said the newcomer. "I believe your mother has introduced me to everyone here, and I have forgotten all their names."

Emily watched Richard smile down at her. The woman was dark haired and quite beautiful, and she had an enviable ease and confidence.

"And some mad earl smashed the painter's easel," she continued. "He threatened to slather the hostess in red paint for 'mocking creative life blood.' I had no idea that *ton* parties were so . . . active."

A small sound escaped Emily. That had to be her father, though he was only the son of an earl.

The woman was looking inquiringly at her, as if wondering why she didn't take herself off.

"This is Emily Crane, Lydia," said Richard. "Miss Crane my, er, cousin Lydia Farrell."

"Ah. Miss Crane, I'm sorry I didn't recognize you. I've just come up to London. May I offer my felicitations." Her gaze was speculative and appraising.

"Thank you," answered Emily faintly.

Lydia looked from her to Richard. "Am I interrupting? I don't mean to intrude on your *tête à tête*."

Emily had a strong desire to say yes, but she held

her tongue as Richard assured his cousin that she was quite welcome. He certainly seemed to find her so. The conversation had been a fiasco from start to finish. It was hard to see how it could have been worse.

"Sheldon," bellowed a deep voice behind her.

Emily closed her eyes in despair. Things can always get worse, she reminded herself.

"Or Warrington, whatever you call yourself," continued her father, descending on their little group like the wrath of God. "I want a word with you."

Richard merely waited. He didn't look the least intimidated.

"I have not given my consent to this engagement!"

Was that a spark of hope in Richard's eyes? It certainly looked like one. People were starting to turn and listen. A few were drawing closer as if part of the entertainment was beginning.

"And I don't like it above half," her father went on. "Puffing it off in the papers without consulting me." Alasdair Crane huffed like a goaded bull. "Not quite the thing, eh?" He waited for an answer, but no one gave him one.

Emily watched a series of expressions pass across Richard's face. To her, they looked like temptation, compunction, and regret. She wondered what the crowd made of them. "Have you, er, spoken with the duchess?" asked Richard finally.

"Julia has nothing to do with the matter. We're talking about *my* daughter." He glared at the other guests, who now surrounded them in a clump. "All of you hear me?" he demanded. "Did I speak loud enough for you jackals?"

Emily was shaken by a crazed desire to laugh. Since she also felt utterly humiliated and unaccountably afraid, what came out was more like a bleat.

"And you, my girl. You ought to have known better than to accept him without consulting your parents."

The laugh was in her throat, side by side with a moan. She gulped and nodded.

Her mother came gliding up and put a hand on Alasdair's arm. She whispered something to him.

"I've said what I meant to," he answered aloud. "You come round and see me," he commanded Richard. "I have some questions for you."

Richard was actually smiling, Emily saw with incredulity. He bowed his head in acknowledgment.

"Come along," added her father peremptorily to Emily. As she followed her parents through the murmuring crowd, Emily saw Richard's cousin thread her arm through his and smile warmly up at him.

WHEN RICHARD PRESENTED himself at the duchess of Welford's splendid townhouse the next day, he found he was looking forward to the visit with a surprising amount of anticipation. He had been summoned by Alasdair Crane, after all, and he could only foresee the unexpected.

The butler ushered him into a small parlor near the back of the house. It was well away from the main rooms, he realized with a smile. The duchess must have given orders to keep her unpredictable brother-in-law as far from her as possible.

The door opened, and Alasdair Crane came in. But the bluster and outrage of their last encounter was gone. The man looked almost forlorn, Richard thought.

"I have no studio here," he said, as if this would naturally be Richard's first concern. "I cannot paint. And Olivia is making me buy new clothes." He fingered the lapels of his coat—which did indeed look new—as if the mere sight of it pained him.

"That . . . that is too bad." Richard had to hide a smile.

"It's intolerable. She knows that."

Was he supposed to offer some sort of solution? "Perhaps you could use a room on the upper floors for a studio?" The place must have thirty rooms.

Crane shook his head. "Julia claims the smell of paint makes her ill." He grimaced. "I've always doubted that she and Olivia were really sisters. Old Shelbury's such a dry stick. I shouldn't wonder if their mother played him false." This idea seemed to cheer him. "Olivia's father must have been a different sort altogether—an artist even."

Richard couldn't contain a short laugh.

It attracted Crane's full attention. "What are you doing here, anyway?"

"You summoned me, sir."

"I did? Oh yes." He shook his head again. "Can't think clearly when I'm not painting. It's this engagement, isn't it?"

"I believe so," answered Richard, making an effort to keep his voice steady.

"Yes, that's it." Emily's father walked over to a

sofa near the fireplace, his steps heavy. "May as well sit down."

He did so, and Richard followed suit. Silence fell.

"Look at that light," said Crane suddenly.

Turning to follow his gaze, Richard saw a shaft of sunshine streaming through one of the windows and pooling on the yellow carpet.

"Like butter. Butter spangled as an opera dancer's tights."

A bit surprised, Richard nodded. The motes of dust floating in the light did make it look rather like that.

"It'll be gone in half an hour and I won't have touched a brush to canvas."

"I'm sorry." He actually was, Richard realized. The man's deprivation was so real, his face so forlorn. Moved by a sudden impulse, Richard said, "When did you know you wanted to paint?"

Alasdair didn't look the least bit surprised by the question. "I was four years old. I was playing with some building blocks in the nursery when my sister's governess began a lesson in watercolors." His dark eyes bored into Richard's. "Her brush swept across the paper like a bluebird's wing, and suddenly I couldn't see anything else. She let me try, and . . ." He made a gesture signifying that everything had flowed from there.

"So it was a gift, a talent. You didn't have to struggle and wonder what your purpose might be."

Alasdair Crane shook his head, his attention fully on Richard for perhaps the first time in their short acquaintance. "You don't want to paint?"

Richard smiled slightly. The man's obsession was

almost endearing. "No, I've never wanted that. But I do want . . . something like that," Richard blurted out. Part of him couldn't believe he was confiding in a stranger, but another pushed him to get any guidance he could. "A task or a pursuit that compels me."

Alasdair nodded as if this were the most reasonable statement in the world.

Richard felt a curious relief, along with satisfaction. He had known Alasdair Crane would understand this desire.

"What do you love?"

Richard frowned, at a loss.

"Think about it. Find what you love, and follow it, and that will be enough for you."

"But . . ." This seemed both too simple, and immensely complicated. "How will that tell me what to do?"

"The doing's not the problem." Crane waved a hand. "Or, it is. But not the main one. When you have the passion, wrestling with the details of the work is a splendid fight."

Richard puzzled over his words. They sounded good, but he was no further along in finding a next step.

Giving the shaft of sunlight a longing look, Crane said. "So you want to marry Emily?"

Richard gathered his wits. There was no suitable reply to the question. It would not be honest to agree, and to disagree would create considerable havoc. He could understand the duchess's decision not to tell the Cranes the circumstances behind the engagement. Emily's father would probably try to call him out. Or just shoot him.

"Olivia reminded me what it was like to have one's wishes opposed." Crane sat a bit straighter on the sofa. "I would have killed anyone who tried to keep her from me. I still would." He gave a sharp nod.

"You are to be envied, sir."

"I know it." He grimaced. "It was damned unsettling, finding myself in Shelbury's shoes, acting just like him."

"I'm sure you could never be like the marquess."

"You would have thought so, but now that it's a daughter of my own . . ." He scowled. "Hostages to fortune, that's what the bard called them. And with only the one child . . ." He sighed. "The important thing is to see her happy. That's what Olivia says, and I agree. So if it's you she wants . . ." He examined Richard and seemed to find him wanting. "You're mighty cool about this."

Richard groped for words.

"In your place, I'd've made it clear by this time that I didn't give a rap what her parents thought—or anyone else." He peered at Richard. "I'd've consigned them all to perdition."

"Perhaps we are of different temperaments." Oddly, Crane's accusations stung.

"You're not afraid of me. I can see that."

"No."

"You don't much care what I think." He frowned.

"I hope for your good opinion, of course."

Alasdair snorted. "Fustian."

"Not at all. You have shaped your life to your own design. I admire that."

"Trying to turn me up sweet?"

Richard shrugged, letting him take or leave his remarks. He had meant them, though.

"I don't understand you." Crane leaned forward as if decreasing the distance between them would help. "You've said nothing about Emily in all this."

They were back to the sticky part. To tell the truth would be to go back on his word. It occurred to Richard that this was the first time in his life that he had seriously inconvenienced himself for another person. He had a sudden sense of vertigo.

Crane sat back, resting his hands on his knees. "Well?"

"Not everyone can . . . express himself as fully as you do."

This brought no break in the hard scrutiny.

"I'm not an artist. It is not so easy to say how I feel." That was certainly true.

The older man continued to watch him, though his gaze seemed slightly less hostile.

"You will be wondering about my prospects," said Richard, attempting a diversion. "I have to admit they are not good. My estates in Somerset are heavily encumbered, and one in Wales left me by my stepfather is mainly rock. My income is . . . limited."

Crane shook his head as if bewildered.

"The cottage at Morne is Elizabethan. There are some beautiful vistas. Very paintable." Paintable? he thought incredulously. This eccentric man was reducing him to idiocy.

"I don't know how to do this," replied Crane. He sounded pathetically bewildered. "I'm not some sort of old Roman paterfamilias." He blinked at Richard, then rose. "I need Olivia. Where is Olivia?" He made his way to the door, leaving Richard alone in the small parlor.

It was a relief. He felt as if he'd been interrogated, though he hadn't really. It would have been enormously satisfying to declare a great love, to fling his passion in the face of all opposition, to dare anyone to thwart him. He longed to have such feelings, such certainty . . .

There was very little sound here at the back of the house. The silence enveloped Richard. He wondered if Crane meant to return, or if he should go? Sitting back on the sofa, he waited.

IN HER BEDCHAMBER UPSTAIRS, Emily had been enduring a similar trial. Her mother had come to her about the time Richard arrived and settled in for a cozy chat. "It seems so long since we had a chance to talk," she began.

They didn't talk very often at home, Emily thought, and braced herself for difficulties.

"I didn't expect that you would become engaged so soon. I thought you would have a season at least." She made a deprecating gesture. "Of course one cannot control these things. When you fall desperately in love . . ."

She paused, giving Emily the opportunity to profess her passion. Emily swallowed. Should she tell her the truth?

Looking a little concerned, her mother went on. "I remember the first time I spoke to your father. It was a rout party. His mother had made him go, and he was so magnificently angry." She smiled. "He tried to be quite savage with me, reviling my dress and the petty emptiness of society." Her blue eyes twinkled. "And I told him it was all a kind of art. I had heard about him, you see, and made it my business to meet him. It wasn't two weeks before we . . ." She broke off with a self-conscious laugh. "Well, never mind that ancient history. We were talking of you."

Emily had to tell her something. When I met Richard Sheldon, two men were trying to kill him, she thought wildly.

"I suppose you found Mr. Sheldon—Lord Warrington, that is—ah, interesting when he was at our house?" Olivia prompted finally.

"Yes."

"And then you met again in London."

"At a ball. We danced." That had been quite unpleasant, she remembered. "And walked in the park, and . . ." In a sudden panic, she wondered whether her aunt had confided the whole story to her mother. She hadn't told Papa, of course. No one would do such a silly thing as that.

"And you fell in love," said her mother. "He is a handsome man."

The concerned look that accompanied this spurred Emily to action. She nodded vigorously. "He . . . he was shipwrecked in the jungle and had to fight his way out. It took months and months. There were huge snakes and, er, panthers."

"Really?" Her mother was looking a bit puzzled.

"I think that is admirable," Emily blundered on. "It shows true courage and, er, initiative, don't you think?"

"Umm."

"He is quite at home in society, too. He knows everyone."

"Does he?"

And someone is plotting to kill him, and I want to find out who, so I agreed to an engagement when my aunt found me sleeping in his arms. No, it didn't sound good. Emily stole a look at her mother. She wasn't afraid she would be scandalized. Quite the opposite, actually. She would undoubtedly feel that nothing warranted a forced marriage, and the whole thing should be called off as soon as possible. Despite everything, Emily didn't want that.

"But, my dear . . ."

"So he is just everything I want in a man."

"You make it sound like a recipe," objected her mother.

"I'm not like you. I don't get swept away by great gusts of feeling." It was true, Emily thought, with a brush of melancholy.

Her mother frowned. "You have always been such a practical, self-possessed girl," was the worried response.

Emily almost smiled. "Some parents would find that reassuring."

"We love you very much, Emily. And we want to see you happy—as happy as we have been."

"Perhaps that isn't possible," she muttered.

"What?"

"I'm sure I'll be very happy," she declared.

"But the way you speak of . . ." They were interrupted by her father's voice, bellowing Olivia's name. "Oh, dear."

Her expression alarmed Emily. "What has Papa been doing?"

"Talking to Lord Warrington. At least, I hope that is all he has been doing."

Emily rose in consternation. But before she could make another move, her father burst into the room looking plaintive. "I can't make him out," he complained. "He don't seem to give a farthing for . . ."

"What did you do to him?"

The intensity in her voice seemed to gratify both of Emily's parents. They exchanged a glance.

"I didn't do anything. You should see him, Olivia. You're much better at ferreting out . . ."

"*I* will see him." Emily started for the door. "You stay here."

In a flurry of skirts, she was gone.

"Well, *that's* more like it," said Alasdair.

EMILY PEERED into four empty rooms before she found Richard in the small back parlor. He was standing by a window looking undecided when she burst in and came to a sudden halt just inside the door. "Oh, there you are." Having achieved her object, Emily could think of nothing else to say.

"Here I am," he agreed.

He always looked so at ease. It was admirable, and rather irritating. "I hope my father did not . . ." Did not what? Of course he had ranted and accused and done all the other things that had made any young man she encountered think they were all mad.

"He is a very interesting man," replied Richard. "I envy him his passion for his work."

"You do?"

He nodded. "It is a gift—to know so clearly what you wish to do, and to concentrate every faculty upon it."

This sort of reaction was unprecedented in Emily's experience. She couldn't quite believe it. "He didn't shout at you?"

Richard shrugged. "Oh, yes, a bit. More last night, you know."

She certainly did. "And you . . . didn't you mind?"

"It seems to be just part of what he is," was the astonishing response.

Her mouth was a little open, Emily realized. She closed it.

"Perhaps it comes of being an artist."

Maybe being in London, in her aunt's house, had muted her father's usual outrageous behavior. Then she remembered the smashed easel. That wasn't it.

"I'm glad you came down. I wanted to speak to you," Richard added.

For some reason, Emily's pulse accelerated.

"About what you said last night—these rumors you mentioned. I suppose I shall have to look into them." He grimaced. "Ridiculous as the idea still seems."

"You were attacked—"

"I've conceded the point. If you will just tell me where to find these friends of yours." She started to speak, and he waved her to silence. "And don't tell me again that you cannot say."

"I can't." Daniel would be furious. "I'll find out if they've learned anything else and tell you at once."

"Unacceptable."

"I won't betray them to you."

"Betray? What am I, the Inquisition?" He frowned at her. "Just who are these people? They are beginning to sound rather unsavory."

Emily gave a small shrug.

"What would your father say if he knew you were associating with dubious characters?"

She couldn't restrain a laugh.

Richard raised one dark brow. "Ah. I suppose they are friends of his." He surveyed her. "Perhaps I should ask him about them, then?"

Her hand went out in an involuntary gesture. "No!"

"Ah?"

"You mustn't tell him about . . . any of this."

"Because he would prevent you from seeing these 'friends?' " He watched her. "No, I can see that isn't it."

"If he knows about the attacks, he might find out about other things as well."

"What other . . . ?" Richard appeared to understand suddenly. "About the true nature of our engagement, perhaps?"

She avoided his eyes. Silence lengthened. Finally, when she could stand it no longer, she looked up. He was gazing at her as if she fascinated him.

"I am beginning to have serious doubts about you."

"What?"

"You do understand that I have no fortune whatsoever. In fact, I can scarcely support a household of my own. It will be a very poor one."

"I don't care . . ." began Emily, then was stopped by the expression on his face.

"I am not known as a pleasant or a generous man." His scrutiny intensified.

She tried to keep her expression blank.

"Yes, I can see that you've heard that."

He was watching her as the hawk does a rabbit. She needed to say something sensible, Emily thought, to divert him. But nothing occurred to her.

"So, we have a man of uncertain temper and no resources. And we have a beautiful young woman who is likely to attract many admirers."

She glanced at him, and quickly away. The look in his eyes was making her breathless.

"Miss Crane, precisely why did you become engaged to me?"

She looked down. "The . . . the scandal. My aunt said . . ."

"Yes. She alarmed us both with her hysteria over the scandal, didn't she?"

Emily risked another look. He seemed exhilarated, like a man on the trail of a promising quarry.

"Or did she?" He was staring as if he wanted to see right through her. "When you first came to London, you took instruction from the duchess."

"She knows all about society," Emily protested, understanding just how the fox feels.

Richard was nodding. "She does indeed. And so you followed her advice." He looked triumphant. "And it was a dead bore, wasn't it?"

"I don't know what you mean."

"No?" He shook his head. "I couldn't fathom the difference in you—from the decisive young woman I met in the country to a simpering ninnyhammer."

"I was not!"

"Oh, you were." He smiled mockingly at her. "I assure you, you were."

"Young ladies of fashion . . ."

"Are simpering ninnyhammers. I will certainly grant you that. And the duchess would be just the person to mold one." Richard looked as if he were having a wonderful time. "So you found it a dead bore. And you fixed on these . . . incidents."

"Attacks," corrected Emily.

He made a dismissive gesture. "And you began to think about them, because they were vastly more interesting than a London season."

"I enjoy going into society. Having new gowns and meeting new people."

"You did for a while." He smiled at her. "A short while."

Emily tossed her head. "You know nothing about it."

"Don't I?" His smile was more like a grin now. "So you asked these mysterious friends for help, and busied yourself in other ways. And then there was the carriage accident."

"Attack," she corrected again. She was beginning to be angry at his teasing.

He nodded. "And the night in the fields."

He looked a little self-conscious then. Emily felt her cheeks warm at the memory.

Richard cleared his throat. "The duchess reacted

predictably. And you accepted my suit." His gaze sharpened. "Why?"

"She told me I would be ruined if . . ."

"Yes, yes." He brushed this aside. "I cannot believe that Alasdair Crane's daughter would give a snap of her fingers for that."

"Let him find out about it, and see how wrong you are!"

He digested this. "Well, yes. But it was extremely unlikely that he would find out. Your aunt would never tell him, and he sees no one in society."

"Someone would have told my mother," she protested. But she knew it sounded weak.

"Possibly. But from what I have seen of your mother, she would be inclined to listen to your side of the story. And she appears eminently capable of handling your father."

There was no denying this.

"You wanted to stay on the trail of the attacks," he mused. "And it would have been almost impossible to do so unless . . ." He watched her with deepening fascination. "Do you have the slightest wish to marry me?"

"No!" declared Emily, goaded beyond endurance. "And I have no intention of doing so."

For the first time in the conversation, he appeared at a loss. "Yet, you did accept me."

"I intended to break it off as soon as . . ."

"You had solved the mystery. I knew it!"

"You don't know anything!"

"Indeed? Are you claiming that I'm wrong?"

She would have liked nothing better. The fact

that she couldn't made Emily even angrier. He was so despicably smug.

"So you weren't trying to get your hooks into me. It all begins to make sense."

"My . . . ?" Rage choked her for a moment. "I hope they do kill you!"

"Now, now, when you have made such efforts on my behalf?"

"You don't deserve them." She smoldered at his amused expression. "I should have let those men throw you in the pond."

"And miss everything that has happened since? You can't mean it."

He was laughing at her. Emily folded her arms and gritted her teeth. "I am declaring the engagement at an end as of this instant."

This penetrated his mockery. "Just like that?"

"Precisely like that."

He considered.

In a moment, he would show his relief at being rid of her. Despite her anger the idea stung.

"There's no need to be hasty," he said.

"What?"

"You had a certain plan in mind," he went on slowly. He seemed to be working something out in his head. When he met her gaze she felt an odd sort of tremor. "You won't introduce me to these useful friends of yours?"

"I can't."

He ruminated further. "Why shouldn't we work together?"

"Together?"

"You appear to have some valuable . . . acquaintances. I am more able to act on their information."

She felt a thrill of excitement. She did want to see the thing through to the end—even if he was the most infuriating man on the face of the earth.

"The engagement is in name only," he added.

Emily nodded. "Absolutely."

"We will find a way to end it when the game is up."

"I will certainly do so."

He gave a nod, and after a moment, held out his hand. "We are agreed then?"

She hesitated. "We will pursue the attackers together?"

"In our individual spheres."

She wasn't sure she liked this.

"You appear to have the only information on how to begin," he added.

Slowly, she took his hand. It was very large, and warm.

He eyed her with something like admiration. "You are very like your father after all."

"Don't be ridiculous. I am nothing like my father."

Richard's answering smile was as irritating as ever.

NINE

THE FOLLOWING MORNING, Emily set off right after breakfast to visit the Fitzgibbons. She found only Mary at home. Daniel was holding a dancing class at the mansion of one of his noble patrons.

"Did Daniel speak to the . . . Bruiser?" Emily asked her.

Her hostess nodded placidly. As usual, her hands were busy with knitting needles. "The poor boy's wits are a bit addled by this time, but he said he would see what he could discover among his friends."

"Addled?" This didn't sound promising.

"It happens to the best of them, which I'm afraid

the Bruiser never was. No one can take that sort of punishment forever."

"Punishment?"

Mary nodded, then noticed Emily's confusion. "He is a fighter, my dear. Fisticuffs."

"Oh." Emily had heard of the bare-knuckle matches that were so popular with the sporting set.

"Not a very successful one. That's why he may be useful."

"I don't understand."

"It's men like the Bruiser who would be engaged to do someone harm. They have no other profession, you see, and if they do not win their matches . . . they are discarded by the Fancy and must turn to other shifts."

"It sounds dreadful. Perhaps I shouldn't have asked you to speak to him."

"Oh, we've known the Bruiser since he was a lad. He'll be all right. Some of his friends now"—she made a disapproving sound—"we steer clear of them."

Emily nodded. "But if his wits are addled . . ."

"He has enough left to ask a few simple questions. He was a right sharp little boy." She sighed. "We tried to keep him out of the ring, but he was mad for boxing as soon as he saw it."

Suppressing her doubts, Emily thanked her for their efforts. "You will tell me as soon as he finds out anything?"

"Of course, dear."

Emily sat with her a few minutes longer, chatting about Daniel's success in London and some old friends. She was just rising to go when there were sounds of an arrival below. They heard voices outside the room, and then a slight brown-haired girl walked in, grinning when she saw the two of them.

"Sarah," exclaimed Emily and Mary at the same moment.

"I didn't expect you this morning," added the latter.

"Herr doktor isn't feeling the thing. He's laid up in bed."

"Is it serious?" asked her mother.

Sarah shook her head. "A feverish cold, though you'd think it was the cholera from the way he carries on. Hullo, Emily."

"How are you? I've been hoping to see you."

Sarah grinned again. "Could have come to one of our 'evenings.' My gentleman could call up a spirit for you. Maybe Rex, eh?"

"He was a dog." With a nasty temper and yellow fangs. She had no desire to see him again.

Sarah made an offhand gesture. "Schelling does dogs, cats, people, whatever you like. We had a pony once, come to think of it. This weepy cove loved it when he was a little lad."

"Language, Sarah," admonished her mother.

"This 'melancholy gentleman' had loved it," she amended.

"You are working for this . . . ?"

"Student of the Adepts of the East," Sarah supplied. "That I am. I nursemaid the visitors. Talk up his powers and tell them stories of what he's done for other poor souls. The usual line of patter. And I keep them out of the way of . . . things they don't need to see."

"Do you like it?" wondered Emily. She remembered Sarah as an enthusiastic child actress and an endlessly inventive playmate.

"I've learned some new dodges. Dad doesn't like it, I know. Says we're taking advantage of the bereaved. But some of them find it real comforting."

"What sort of people come?"

"All sorts." Sarah gave her a sidelong look. "That fiancé of yours has been to see Herr Schelling."

"What?" Emily was dumbfounded.

"Warrington, isn't it? That's what the paper said."

"Yes, but . . ."

"He was escorting his mother. And he seemed right put out about it."

"Lady Fielding came to Schelling's?"

"Oh, she's one of our regulars. Herr doktor uses her case as a draw."

"Her . . . ?"

"Her son was lost at sea. Well, you must know all about that. Lady Fielding was broken up about it. Schelling gave her a good show, and then his lordship up and walks in on one of the sessions! Scared the living daylights out of everyone there and made Schelling's reputation, I can tell you."

Richard must have hated that, Emily thought.

"So you're actually getting married?"

For a moment, Emily thought she had somehow divined the reality behind her engagement. Then she realized that it was just the amazement of a childhood friend.

"I don't intend to get leg-shackled for a good long while."

"Sarah," exclaimed her mother, who had been calmly knitting through this conversation.

"Contract a suitable alliance," corrected Sarah with fond mockery. "The other says it a lot better, Ma."

"I don't want you to use . . ."

"Vulgar cant phrases. You didn't send me to school so I could talk like a navvy." Sarah grinned at Emily, who couldn't help grinning back.

"Well, we didn't."

"Your lord's a big handsome fella," said Sarah teasingly.

Emily nodded uncomfortably. She didn't like deceiving her friends.

"When's the wedding?"

"Oh . . . not for a while." Struck by inspiration, she added, "Mama and Papa have come up to town to meet him."

"They're here in London?" cried Mrs. Fitzgibbon.

She nodded. "Papa's already created a small scandal at a *ton* party."

Mary laughed. "Mr. Crane has his own ways. But he's always been very kind to us."

"I'll tell him you're here. I'm sure he will want to see you." It would be a relief for her father to spend time with old friends like these. Then a reservation surfaced. "I'd rather you didn't tell him about the inquiries we are making. He might not . . . that is . . ."

They gave her identical shrewd stares, which showed Emily that Sarah had been brought fully up to date on her previous visit.

"Men are much happier if they don't know *everything*," replied Mrs. Fitzgibbon.

"Their brains are limited," agreed Sarah. "It doesn't do to tax them."

Relieved, Emily nodded.

"He and Daniel will be too busy reminiscing to worry their heads about anything else."

"Do you recall that time Dad and your father were lifting a pint at the pub?" Sarah paused. "Don't recall what town it was. We were always on the move."

"And so were we," said Emily. The Fitzgibbons' acting troop had always found them in whatever house they had shifted to from year to year.

"It was Kent, I think. Anyway, the local vicar came in, and it seemed he was very low church."

Emily nodded in recognition. "He started haranguing them about the evils of playacting and wanton actresses parading their 'nakedness' on the stage."

"We certainly never had anything like *that*," huffed Mrs. Fitzgibbon.

"And so Dad told him," supplied Sarah.

"But he didn't listen. That sort of person never does." Emily was smiling broadly by this time.

"They can't hear for talking," put in Sarah's mother.

"And so your father stood up and gave him one of his 'earl' looks," continued Sarah. "Told him he wasn't wanted and to take himself off."

"Which didn't set well with the vicar at all."

"He called your father a maker of graven images."

"And Papa upended a pint of bitter over him. Someone else's pint."

"It's fortunate the townspeople didn't like that vicar above half," commented Mrs. Fitzgibbon. "Otherwise both of them would have ended up in gaol." She was smiling, though, at the girls' laughter. "Aye, we did have some good times."

"I'll send Papa over soon," said Emily, rising to go. They would be starting to wonder where she was.

Saying her good-byes, she left the house with a smile. She was still in a mellow mood when she reached the duchess's house and heard that a "family party" had been arranged for that evening. Richard would be bringing his mother to see them. The possibilities in such a gathering were enough to sober her most thoroughly.

RICHARD BARELY LISTENED to his mother chatting with Lydia Farrell. As their carriage made its way through the streets to the duchess of Welford's house, he was thinking about Emily and the odd succession of events that had brought them to this moment. He had never known a woman like her. Most probably, considering her eccentric upbringing, there was no other woman like her. He could imagine her, he realized, at his side in South America, hacking her way through the jungle vegetation, eating whatever they managed to capture with their own hands.

The mental picture surprised him considerably. Why should he be thinking such a thing? That was the past, and Emily Crane had nothing to do with it. She had nothing to do with anything. She might be of some small use in this matter of the supposed attacks on him. He ought to be thinking about those.

"You're very pensive," commented Lydia.

Richard looked up to find her watching him.

"I suppose this first family party is enough excuse," she added.

"First . . . ? Oh, yes."

"You have met Miss Crane's parents before?"

He nodded.

"I have heard they are exceedingly odd," complained his mother. "And of course there was that scandal, years ago. This really wasn't a very wise choice, Richard."

He repressed a grimace.

"They are staying with the duchess, and she is the best of good *ton*. But after his behavior at Geraldine's artistic evening, I declare I am afraid of Mr. Crane."

"It was only an easel he broke," Richard reminded her.

"Yes," agreed Lydia in an ironic drawl. "He only threatened to cover the hostess with paint and box her ears."

Richard's mother groaned.

"Don't worry, Aunt. Richard will protect us."

She seemed to enjoy mocking him, Richard thought. Apparently he hadn't convinced her that the old reprehensible Warrington was a thing of the past. "I'm sure that won't be necessary."

"You must stay by me, Richard," demanded his mother. "Don't leave me alone with him."

"I confess I am looking forward to this evening with the liveliest anticipation," commented Lydia.

"It will be a perfectly conventional visit," Richard assured her. "I daresay you will be rather bored."

"Surely not. I've never met anyone who eloped to Gretna Green, let alone the daughter of a marquess."

Richard's mother groaned again.

THEY WERE CONDUCTED upstairs to a large reception room in the duchess's house—not the main drawing room, Richard noticed. Nor was there any sign of the Welford family. Emily came forward to greet them and made the introductions with a certain constraint. Everyone sat down. There was a short silence.

"So, you are an artist, Mr. Crane?" said Lydia.

He scowled. "When I am allowed to be."

"Allowed?"

Richard could hear the amusement in his cousin's voice. He hoped she could restrain herself from doing mischief.

"I cannot paint here," Crane declared belligerently.

"The landscape of London does not inspire . . . ?"

"Inspire?" He made the word a curse. "I am always inspired. Olivia's damn sister won't have the smell of paint in her house."

Richard heard his mother gasp.

"She can't be any kin of yours," Alasdair complained to his wife. "I mean to say—the smell?"

"But Mrs. Crane and the duchess resemble each other so closely," said Lydia.

Richard tried to signal her to silence.

"Are *you* enjoying London, Mrs. Farrell?" said Emily.

"Prodigiously." Her lazy smile implied that the current scene was a rich source of this enjoyment.

"It is my first time in London." Emily's tone and expression showed a determination to avoid explosions.

"Yes, I know."

"Lady Fielding," said Emily's mother, "I understand you have attended a number of spirit calling sessions."

Richard gave her a sharp look. Where had she heard that in her short time in town? He noticed that Emily was gazing at her mother with exasperation. His mother was nodding with more enthusiasm than she had shown so far.

"Have you found them convincing?" Olivia added.

"I beg your pardon?"

"I believe these people employ all sorts of tricks."

His mother drew herself up. "Herr Schelling is a gifted man. He has no need of tricks."

"Nonsense," answered Mr. Crane. "It is impossible to communicate with the dead. They're . . . dead."

"Just so," murmured Lydia with a laugh in her voice.

"Herr Schelling can reach beyond the veil," insisted Richard's mother. "He brought Richard back."

Everyone turned to look at Richard. Even Emily, he noticed with annoyance. "I wasn't dead," he said curtly, feeling ridiculous.

"You were the next thing to it," argued his mother. "In that dreadful jungle."

"Jungle?" said Alasdair. "I have always wanted to see a jungle. Astonishing variety of color, I hear." He gazed at Richard.

"Very colorful," he muttered.

The door opened. At precisely the same instant, Richard and Emily both said, "Ah, here is the tea tray," and rose, bumping into each other as they moved toward the footman carrying the tray.

Lydia stifled a laugh. Olivia Crane looked at her with raised brows.

Refreshments were offered and poured, occupying a few minutes. But all too soon, everyone was settled again. Richard was searching his mind for a safe topic when his mother addressed Emily's. "How do you occupy yourself in the country while your husband is painting, Mrs. Crane?"

"I paint as well."

"You paint . . . ?"

"Pictures," was the dry response. "A woman is fully as capable, artistically, as a man."

From Emily's expression, Richard judged that this was a common topic, and not one she was pleased to have broached here and now. He felt a rush of sympathy for her.

"Though, of course, it is made much more difficult for a woman."

"Is it?" Lady Fielding murmured.

"Hampered by ridiculous conventions, refused admission to the studios." Olivia Crane shook her head in righteous indignation. "As if the sight of a naked body could corrupt anyone."

Lydia and Lady Fielding choked on their tea.

"But a girl must be protected . . ." ventured Richard's mother after a moment.

"Protected from learning? From expressing herself in any way? What rot!"

Richard covered a bark of laughter with a cough. He had never heard a lady of Olivia Crane's standing use such an expression, and he was sure his mother never had either. She looked as if she had been turned to stone. His cousin, however, appeared fascinated.

"But you must admit, there are those who would take advantage of a young girl's . . . enthusiasms," Lydia said.

"Oh, yes. Girls should be given pistols, and taught to shoot them, as soon as they reach twelve years of age. If I had not found Alasdair . . ."

The Cranes exchanged a scaring look. Richard was at the same time shocked and envious. Emily appeared to have dropped into despair, he noticed. His cousin was avid. His mother was eyeing Emily with suspicion, as if wondering whether she had fire-arms concealed in the folds of her skirts. Should he overturn his teacup? Simulate a fit?

"Can't we just have a normal conversation?" cried Emily.

Everyone turned to look at her. She quailed slightly, but didn't retreat.

"What is a normal conversation?" asked her mother.

"Seems quite normal to me," grumbled her father at the same time.

"You must have had them when you were

young?" Emily answered desperately. "When you went about in society."

"You mean the sort of thing Julia talks about?" Her mother seemed genuinely perplexed, and interested in what she meant.

"Gossip and sport?" barked Alasdair.

"How would I know? I have never seen it. You never talk about anything . . ."

"Normal?" wondered Lydia.

Richard gave her a look, asking that she be quiet. She pressed her lips together obediently, though her eyes continued to dance.

"Never mind," said Emily. She looked at Richard's mother. "Please forgive my outburst."

Her father looked outraged at this apology. He would have spoken, but his wife put a hand on his arm. "Have you been to the opera this season, Lady Fielding?" she asked.

The following half hour was filled with irreproachable, and deadly dull, exchanges about the events of the season, the theater, and possible family connections that—after some truly tortuous examination—turned out not to exist. It was, Richard supposed, a normal conversation for members of the *ton* on such an occasion. And he was finding it deuced difficult to stay awake.

"We should be going," said his mother. "So pleasant," she added, fooling nobody.

Their farewells weren't prolonged. Emily looked relieved, Richard noticed, but also miserable. The occasion hadn't gone well, true. But did it really matter? He lingered a moment in the hall, letting his mother and cousin walk on. "Was that the sort of normal conversation you wanted?" he heard Olivia Crane ask.

"How should I know?" Emily replied. "I've only Aunt Julia to go by, and . . ."

"I haven't been so bored in twenty-five years," complained her father. "And don't tell me you weren't, my girl, because I could see your eyelids drooping."

"No, Papa," conceded Emily in a tired voice.

"YOU CANNOT MARRY that girl," said Richard's mother when he joined them in the carriage. "It's impossible, out of the question."

"Why do you say that, Aunt?"

It was easy for Lydia to enjoy all this, Richard thought. None of it involved her.

"She is utterly unsuitable. That unladylike comment about 'normal' conversation! What if she were to repeat it in a more public place? And her parents . . ."

"They are unusual," began Richard.

"They are outrageous. Was she joking? About the pistols? I suppose it must have been a joke—though she didn't *look* as if it was—but it was in the poorest possible taste."

"I think she meant it," offered Lydia.

"Pistols!" repeated Richard's mother. "Can you imagine? Young girls running around brandishing pistols?" She looked from one to the other of her companions. "How can you smile?"

"Well, it is quite a picture," answered Lydia.

Lady Fielding blew out an exasperated breath. "I forbid you to marry her, Richard."

This was an odd twist. He had no intention of marrying her, yet he couldn't tell his mother that without revealing things she wasn't to know. He found he didn't much want to, in any case.

"Do you hear me?"

"I am twenty-nine years old, Mother."

"And acting like a moonstruck stripling. How could you have engaged yourself to such a . . . a hoyden?"

"You are not being fair."

"Fair?"

"Her behavior is perfectly . . ." What? Richard wondered. Understandable? Acceptable? Agreeable?

"Dreadful," declared his mother. "You must break it off, at once."

"Even if I wished to, it would not be the act of a gentleman." And he didn't wish to, he realized. He was having far too much fun. How long had it been since he had had fun?

"We must contrive something. Some excuse. It shouldn't be difficult, with *that* girl."

"You aren't to interfere, Mother." He would enjoy the situation to the full, and then, of course, they would end it. That was clearly agreed.

"You expect me to simply let you ruin your life—"

"I am not doing any such thing. And I am perfectly capable of managing my own life, thank you."

"Oh, really?" His mother leaned toward him. "You have engaged yourself to a chit who hasn't a penny to her name. How do you expect to live? I will not help you, not with such a girl as that."

"I have already said I don't want your help," replied Richard through his teeth.

Lydia threw him an unreadable look.

"And *her* parents obviously haven't two shillings to . . ."

"I will be speaking to Taft about what may be done to . . ."

"I do not understand you at all any more. This is just a disaster. Tell him, Lydia."

"I don't think, Aunt . . ."

"Enough." Richard faced their startled looks directly. "This is my affair. You will leave it to me."

He had been a bit too forceful, he saw. His mother, in particular, looked frightened. He had to be more careful. But it was damned difficult when he seemed to be besieged from all sides.

TEN

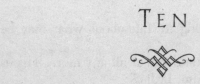

EMILY WAS ALONE the next morning when Richard was announced. Her father had finally snapped at breakfast and insisted that they find their own lodgings if they were to stay in town. Her mother had seen the wisdom of this without much urging, and so they had gone off to look for a suitable place.

It was just as well. Richard could tell her, in that roundabout way people used, that his mother had been horrified by the freewheeling Cranes and that he really could have nothing further to do with her. She had heard the same thing, spoken with more or less finesse, a score of times. Her parents' absence would make it quick and easy. No one said such things to Alasdair Crane's face, of course.

But when Richard was ushered into the small parlor they had been using, Emily felt a pang. She didn't want to hear him trying to spare her feelings as he explained that the visit yesterday had been . . . really . . . rather . . . unusual and—and all the rest of it. "Just say it straight out," she said when he greeted her.

"I beg your pardon?"

"What you have come to say. There's no need to spare my feelings."

He looked puzzled.

"I've heard it all before. Repeatedly."

Richard frowned. "I came to say I thought we should make a clear plan."

She couldn't take it in at once.

"Decide what we are going to do," he added, "how we will proceed."

"Proceed?"

"What did you think I was going to say?"

Emily was too surprised to evade. "That your mother was scandalized by us, and you could not keep up the connection."

Richard looked startled, then self-conscious.

She was right. His mother had reacted just like all the neighbors and acquaintances who had found the Cranes "unsteady" and "unsound."

"You believe I would say something so rude?"

"Plenty of others have done so." At his expression, she added, "Oh, not in so many words. But I soon learned what they really meant when they told me the children I had been playing with could not come out or the girl who had joined in my walks was taken ill or the young man who had called was busy with estate matters."

"They objected to . . . ?"

"Everything. They way we lived, my father's temper, my mother's ideas."

"I see."

Emily berated herself silently. If he really had not come to say those things, she had herself given him the notion.

"That must have been very difficult."

"I love my parents. And I admire the way they have done what they liked." Pity was even worse than avoidance; she knew from bitter experience.

"Yes. But having chosen for themselves, they might have paid some heed to the consequences for you."

"They gave me what they prized most." She could never bear to hear them criticized.

"What?"

"Freedom to find my own way."

"That is a gift indeed."

Emily gazed at him. People of their own station in life never saw it that way. Others—Sarah Fitzgibbon, for example—understood, but never the so-called gentry.

"And a bit of a burden perhaps?"

She blinked.

"Obeying the rules is easy, after all. There is no need to think or choose among alternatives. Still less to chart a new course."

He seemed to be talking to himself rather than to

her, but Emily understood exactly what he meant. "Where to begin?" she murmured.

He turned to her with an arrested expression, and started to speak. But then he appeared to change his mind, or not to know it fully. There was a silence that eventually grew awkward.

Emily was about to break it when he said, "Have you found it?"

"What?"

"Your own way."

He wasn't like anyone she'd ever known. And he wasn't at all like the person her aunt and others had made him out to be. It was very confusing, and it made it difficult to answer. Something in his eyes, though, pushed her toward honesty. "Not yet."

Richard nodded once as if he too were searching for a place, a way to function in the world. Emily dismissed the idea as ridiculous. He was firmly established in society.

"Perhaps we should sit down?"

She started. "I beg your pardon. Of course."

They sat opposite each other in front of the hearth.

"Have you any more news from your mysterious friends?"

"They have found someone who may be able to discover the identity of the attackers."

"Someone?"

Emily nodded.

"You do not intend to tell me anything about this person?"

"I can't."

"Because your friends have forbidden you to do so?"

"They would be angry if I . . ."

"Have you asked them?" he wondered.

"I don't need to ask. I know how they feel."

Richard considered this. He looked annoyed. "You know, it will be impossible to pursue this matter if we do not trust one another."

"It is not that I—"

"And can we? We are barely acquainted. You cannot be sure I will not betray your friends somehow. And I do not know how far I may confide in you."

Protest rose to her lips, and no further.

"Perhaps our collaboration is doomed before it starts."

"I don't . . ."

He held up a hand for silence. She pressed her lips together. "Unless we are both willing to take a chance."

For some reason, this simple sentence took Emily's breath away. He meant only that they would tell each other everything they discovered. There was no reason in the world for her pulse to pound—no reason for her to feel that he was suggesting a revolution in her life. He was gazing steadily at her, expectant. The risk of speaking seemed overwhelming, as if the wrong words might wreak havoc beyond her comprehension. "I will ask the . . . my friends if I may tell you," she managed.

He nodded, satisfied. "Good."

Emily's relief was equally out of proportion. What was the matter with her?

"So then. A plan."

Gathering her wits with difficulty, she asked, "You spoke to the groom—the one who was with us when . . . in the carriage?" Fiercely, she commanded her cheeks not to flush.

"Yes. He seems a trustworthy fellow. He's been with my mother for some years. When we rested the horses at the White Hart, an ostler brought him a mug of beer. It must have been laced with something, and they tampered with the harness while he was drinking it. By the time we set off, he was too befuddled to notice the cut."

Emily leaned forward. "If we find that ostler . . ."

"I've inquired. No one seemed to know who I meant."

She sank back, disappointed.

"A dead end, though it does tell us that a watch is being kept."

"Someone followed us to Hampstead. And to the park that day." Emily shivered. It was unpleasant to think of spies observing one's movements.

"You really believe you saw someone push that urn?"

"I can't be sure. It was so quick—a movement in the corner of my eye." An idea struck her. "We might hire watchers of our own, to see who is following you."

Richard smiled slightly. "To watch the watchers?"

"Yes."

"I don't wish to become the head of a circus parade."

"But . . ."

"I can keep an eye out as well as anyone. If someone is following me, I will discover them." He seemed to read Emily's doubts in her face. "I have been stalked for three days running by a jungle cat. I can spot a human hunter. But why am I being hunted?" he murmured. "That is the real puzzle."

"An enemy?" ventured Emily.

He frowned. The old Lord Warrington had certainly made enemies. He had probably offended most of the *haut ton* at one time or another. Some of them may have wished him dead for the insult or slight, but they were hardly the sort of men to plan actual attacks. Besides, he had been out of that world too long. "None that I can think of."

"A quarrel?" wondered Emily. "Someone you bested at . . . something?"

"I have certainly had disagreements and rivalries. But none that warrants murder."

"Your cousin Donald inherits your title," she pointed out.

"Donald lives happily and distantly in Yorkshire."

"He might have hired these ruffians we have heard of."

"I admit I don't know him well. But all reports make Donald a kindly country-loving man." He shook his head. "No, I do not believe in him as the adversary."

Emily reserved judgment on this point. "Who would wish to kill you?"

He shook his head. "I do not imagine myself a paragon of virtue, but I have never offended anyone so deeply, I would vow. My past holds no ruined gamesters or spurned lovers or jealous husbands."

Emily looked down at her hands.

"A paltry record, really." The old Warrington had been a paltry fellow. "A life without high drama."

"Yet you do have an enemy."

"Yes. Peculiar. And a bit heartening? Perhaps I wasn't such a negligible fribble after all."

She gave him an odd look. "It is not a joke."

Richard let out a breath. "No. But it is far more diverting than I thought London would be."

The look he gave her then made Emily's pulse flutter.

"You are as fascinated as I," he added almost teasingly.

"I am concerned . . ."

"Nonsense. Why should you care anything about me? We had barely met—indeed, we hadn't even met—when this began. The mystery of it draws you."

He was right, she thought. Curiosity, the challenge, had driven her into this search. But then, oddly, it seemed there was something else. She couldn't quite grasp it.

"Admit it," he insisted.

Emily nodded, unwilling to delve further into this slippery subject.

He smiled. "We are alike in that."

He gave one satisfied nod, and his eyes smiled into hers for a moment. Their hazel depths were mesmerizing. Emily felt a strange little lurch, the sort of tremor she'd felt when looking down from a great and precipitous height.

"So. You will speak to your friends, and I will keep a sharp lookout for these watchers."

"Perhaps you should find out if anything went on while you were away," Emily suggested.

"Went on?"

"You were out of the way," she reasoned slowly. "And someone clearly wants you out of the way. Why?"

"You are suggesting it might not be personal?"

"You said you have no enemies. If not, then it must be something else."

"What?"

She shrugged.

Richard rose. "A question for another day. I must go. I promised my cousin I would take her driving in the park to observe the smart set."

Emily stood also. "Mrs. Farrell?"

He nodded.

"Is she making a long visit?"

"I hope so," was the fervent reply.

He took his leave, and Emily returned to the armchair. She had been so despondent earlier when she'd feared he had come to end their connection. Why didn't she feel better now?

Tᴏ Eᴍɪʟʏ'ꜱ ᴀꜱᴛᴏɴɪꜱʜᴍᴇɴᴛ, Daniel Fitzgibbon readily agreed to see Richard. Indeed, he offered to take him to meet the Bruiser at his earliest convenience. He really didn't wish to remain in contact with the fighter and his circle, she realized, which made her a bit wary about the whole matter.

The difficulty arose not over Richard, but when Emily herself insisted on coming along. "You shouldn't be acquainted with no one like the Bruiser," Daniel insisted.

"But I am acquainted with pickpockets and confidence men and ladies of . . . of dubious reputation . . ."

"Never mind them. They don't hurt nobody. Not really hurt them."

"And the Bruiser does?"

Daniel looked torn. "It's not him so much. I mean, he beats coves bloody in the ring, but that's the game there. It's the people he knows. They ain't so particular about where they put their fists."

"But we aren't meeting them."

"No." He drew the word out dubiously.

"I promise you I have no intention of doing so." He shook his head.

"You have no objection to taking Lord Warrington to meet the Bruiser, however? Because he is a man, I suppose."

"Seems he can take care of himself," Daniel declared.

"How can you know that?"

"Fought his way through a jungle full of tigers, they say."

"You've heard of that?" asked Emily, too curious to correct the zoology.

"It's talked of in the pubs."

"Oh." She took this in before returning to the real topic. "I am going," she told Daniel. "I am working with Lord Warrington on this matter, and he never would have found the Bruiser without me. I won't be shunted aside."

"He'll forbid you to go," asserted her father's old friend.

"Forbid me?"

"What sort of man would let his promised bride risk herself that way?"

"The sort who is confident of her abilities," she responded automatically. But as soon as she spoke, she suffered a qualm of doubt. If the question were put to Richard, would he want her to come? Would he side with Daniel against her?

In the end, it was Sarah who convinced her father that it would be grossly unfair to exclude Emily from a scheme she herself had made. Sarah threatened him with various forms of retribution until he gave in, with poor grace, and agreed to escort both of them to a rendezvous with the fighter.

She wouldn't tell Richard of his reluctance, Emily decided on her way home. In fact, she would tell him that Daniel would only do this favor if she were along. There was no sense having the argument all over again. The second time, she might lose.

TWO DAYS LATER, Richard sat in a hack facing Daniel Fitzgibbon as it wove its way through some of the seedier streets of London. Emily, beside him, was silent. She didn't seem the least bit intimidated, however, as the neighborhood grew less savory and the noise outside the vehicle more raucous.

Richard occupied himself by examining Fitzgibbon. He would have wagered a good deal that the man hadn't always been a dancing master, and even more that his career included some shadier endeavors. Why else was he using a false name? How did Emily know him so well? No doubt her father had something to do with it.

"Here we are." Fitzgibbon struck the roof to signal the driver to pull up before a tall narrow house in a bit better shape than others on the street.

Richard opened the cab door and stepped down, turning to offer Emily a hand. She held up the skirts of her gown as she climbed down.

"The Bruiser doesn't like to leave his own part of town," repeated Daniel.

"So you have said." Richard surveyed the area. In broad daylight, it didn't appear actually dangerous. He wouldn't have cared to come here at night. A mocking laugh drew his attention. There were two burly ruffians leaning against the wall across the way. One of them pointed at Emily and sniggered. Richard caught his gaze and held it. After a moment, the man jerked his head and urged his companion away.

"Come on," said Daniel. "No sense hanging about outside here."

He was nervous, Richard noted. Fleetingly, he wondered if the man was leading them into some sort of trap. Were they to be robbed in this shabby place? But no, it was much more as if Fitzgibbon didn't want to be anywhere near here himself.

"It's a decent boarding house," he said, his tone confirming Richard's instincts. He sounded as if he were reassuring himself.

They went upstairs, and Fitzgibbon knocked on a door near the back. It was opened at once by one of the largest men Richard had ever seen. He stood well over six feet, and his heavy frame was overlaid by slabs of muscle, particularly in the arms and shoulders. His head, which looked rather small in contrast, showed scars from his bouts in the ring, and he had the horny hardened knuckles of a fighter. His hair was carrot red, and when he smiled—with surprising sweetness—large gaps showed in his teeth. "Mornin' Daniel," he said, gesturing them in.

Richard glanced at Emily, who looked a bit wide-eyed. Apparently, her father's eccentric circle of friends had not extended quite so far as this.

"This is Lord Warrington," Fitzgibbon was saying. "And . . . and Miss Crane."

The extreme reluctance with which he spoke the last words roused a sudden suspicion in Richard's mind. *Who* had insisted that Emily come on this expedition? Perhaps it hadn't been Fitzgibbon after all.

"Yer lordship. Miss." The giant moved uneasily. "I only got the one chair."

It was a poor room, Richard acknowledged. There was an iron bed that scarcely looked as if it would support the man's weight, a rickety table with one straight chair, and a broken down wardrobe which presumably held all his possessions. He gestured Emily to the chair. "You know why we are here?"

"Daniel said someone's after you. Asked me to put my ear to the ground, see what I could find out."

Richard nodded. "And were you able to find out anything?"

"Oh. Like I tol' Daniel, a couple of coves ha' been talkin' about a job they got, and the money comin' to 'em when it's done."

"A job?"

The Bruiser grinned, but the effect was far from humorous. "That's what they call it. When they're out to do harm."

"And what made you believe this had any connection to me?" Richard wondered.

The fighter looked confused.

"Was my name mentioned?"

"Oh. No names, yer lordship. They're not as stupid as that."

"Then why do you think they meant me?"

"They bragged as how it was a swell they were to do."

That was probably unusual, but it was a slender connection. "I don't suppose they let on who hired them."

The Bruiser shook his head.

"No, they wouldn't be that careless."

"Afeard some other cove would take the job from 'em," the fighter elucidated.

"Like you, perhaps?" Richard was a bit impatient.

The fighter shook his head slowly. "I don't do none of that," he stated firmly.

Emily leaned forward. She didn't look the least bit intimidated, Richard saw. "What is your name?" she asked.

All three men stared at her.

"Your mother didn't call you Bruiser," she added, with a smile that softened the question.

The huge man ducked his head. He was flushing, Richard noticed incredulously. "No, miss. She called me Jerry. Jerry Jenkins is my name."

Emily nodded, still smiling.

Her smile encouraged the man to further confidences. "But it don't sound well, for a fighter, you see. Jerry Jenkins. It's too . . . light-hearted, like, for the ring. So I started callin' meself the Bruiser." He cocked his great fists and scowled.

"Very effective," pronounced Emily, earning another grin.

The fighter turned back to Richard. "You a member of the Fancy, my lord? Look like you'd strip right well."

"No." He had had no interest in boxing before leaving London; and after the rigors of his journey, he had even less. Fighting for no purpose but money and attention seemed a ridiculous waste after fighting so many months for his life. "Is there anything else you can tell us?"

The Bruiser frowned.

He had either never had quick wits, or they had been pounded out of him, Richard concluded. "Who are these men you spoke of, the ones doing the 'job'?"

"Oh. Bob Jones and Ralph the Thumb, me lord."

"Ralph the Thumb?" echoed Emily.

Richard tried to imagine any other granddaughter of an earl brightly asking such a question, and failed.

"He bit off Ikey Reynolds's thumb in a fight six year ago. So they started callin' him Ralph the Thumb. Ikey put it in a flask of brandy. He shows it for a penny."

"What?" Emily asked.

"His thumb."

At this she finally looked a bit green, thought Richard with satisfaction. "Perhaps we should talk to, er, Bob and Ralph," he suggested.

Daniel Fitzgibbon looked horrified. The Bruiser

shook his head in his deliberate way. "They'd cut you as soon as look at you." Thoughts seemed to move ponderously through his brain. "And if they're after you, me lord, then it wouldn't do to meet them."

"And present yourself to be killed," added Emily tartly.

"I suppose it won't do," acknowledged Richard. "But you could talk to them," he said to the Bruiser. "Buy them some blue ruin, get their tongues wagging, see if you can learn more."

"They're partial to the bottle," the fighter allowed.

"I would pay you to do this," said Richard, trying to be very clear.

"I could use a bit of rhino. Ain't gettin' the matches I used to, these days."

"You'll do it then?"

"I'll try me best, me lord. Bob's a mean, close-mouthed cove. Ralph might let somethin' slip, if he was far enough under the hatches."

"Perhaps you should concentrate on him, then."

The Bruiser frowned uncomprehendingly.

"Perhaps you should get Ralph off alone and fill him with gin," Richard explained.

"That's right clever." He nodded in appreciation.

Richard's hopes, never high, sank a notch. "The important thing to find out is who hired these men and who is their target."

"And you must be very careful," said Emily. "It sounds as if they are dangerous."

Fitzgibbon looked startled, but the Bruiser seemed positively astonished. "You worrin' about me, miss?"

"You are taking a risk to help us. Of course I am concerned."

She really was, Richard thought. He looked at the Bruiser in a new light. The man seemed totally at a loss for words. He was staring at Emily as if she were a creature wholly outside his experience. Undoubtedly, she was. She was rather outside his as well.

"I'll do my best for you, miss," said the Bruiser, with the fervency of a convert.

"Thank you, Jerry." Emily rose and offered the giant her hand. "I'm sure you will do very well."

The Bruiser held her fingers as if terrified of breaking them. It took Richard a moment to recover from the sight. Then he took out a sum he judged sufficient and passed it over to the fighter, along with his card. "You will send word when you have news?"

"Yes, me lord."

"A note will fetch me any time."

"I don't write so good. I'll get the landlady's boy to go."

"Very well."

They moved toward the door, but Emily stopped before going through. "Do you like being a fighter, Jerry?"

The man grimaced. "I used to, miss. But I ain't so quick on my feet now, and my fams ache in the wet so it's hard to mill like I did."

She looked blank. "Fams?"

"Hands, miss." He flexed them. The horny calluses on his knuckles cracked.

"You need some other employment."

"Ain't none for such as me." He frowned. The effect was daunting. "Or none I'd take."

"Nonsense. I'm sure something can be found."

Richard's heart sank at her thoughtful expression. He was not surprised when she turned a speculative eye on him. "We must go," he said quickly.

"Yes, but . . ."

"We will talk later."

She hesitated a moment longer, then went out. Richard followed with the sure knowledge that he had only postponed the inevitable.

ELEVEN

SINCE THE CRANES did not insist on a house in the most fashionable part of London, they found lodgings without much delay. The house included space for a studio for Emily's father, which sweetened his temper considerably.

Her mother bustled into her chamber. "Do you need anything?"

"I don't think I can fit all my things into my trunk," she admitted. Her aunt had expanded her wardrobe even more than she'd realized until she tried to pack it.

"I'll borrow another from Julia." Her mother started out again, then hesitated. "I've arranged with her to continue chaperoning you. You were promised a whole season, and you shall have one."

Her mother suspected something, Emily knew. She had sensed an oddity about the engagement, though she hadn't quite put her finger on what it was. "I'm surprised Aunt Julia agreed," she said as a diversion.

Her mother smiled. "I made it the price for our leaving her house."

"But . . ."

"Your father was insisting on going, but Julia didn't know that."

Emily laughed. "We've been a great trial to her."

"It's good for her to be shaken up a bit. I'd forgotten how complacent she is." She gave Emily a searching look. "Was I mistaken to send you to her? We might have found some other way to . . ."

"She is very kind to me. I have learned a great deal from her."

"Um." Her mother didn't look entirely satisfied. "I'll go and see about the trunk."

When she was gone, Emily sat on the bed, a half-folded chemise in her hands. She and her parents had never communicated well, she realized. They talked, and her parents were solicitous when they noticed there was some difficulty; but remarks on both sides seemed to veer off in incompatible directions, never quite hitting the mark. How had she turned out so different from them?

IN THE NEW HOUSE Emily had far more freedom than before, and one of her first acts was to invite Sarah Fitzgibbon to tea. The great pleasure she found in this simple act showed her more than anything else had done the constriction she had felt at the duchess's.

"We haven't had a proper talk in ages," said Sarah when they were sitting together over the tea tray. "Now we can say what we like."

"Yes."

"So why don't you tell me what's really going on between you and this Lord Warrington."

Emily's cup wobbled in her hand, though she managed not to spill any tea. "What do you . . . ?"

"I remember when you were wild about the second assistant curate at the cathedral in Winchester. You aren't acting anything like that."

"That was five years ago! And a case of calf love. This is entirely different."

"Why?"

Sarah had always been blunt, Emily recalled. "I am older now," she hedged, uncertain whether to tell her the truth.

"And wiser," mocked her old friend. "And so? You've decided to settle for money and position after all."

"He hasn't any money," Emily replied before she thought.

Sarah stared. "None at all?"

"I don't care about money."

Sarah's answering look was penetrating. "We used to imagine the sort of men we'd marry. Remember our lists?"

"Yours was very long," said Emily with a smile.

"I'm particular. You always said that all you wanted was the sort of love your parents have."

Her smile fading, she nodded.

"Well, I beg your pardon, but your . . . connection with Lord Warrington doesn't look like that to me."

"You can't tell that," she protested half-heartedly.

Sarah merely continued to look at her.

Her regard was irresistible. And it would be a relief to have a friend who knew her true situation. "You must swear not to tell a soul."

"Haven't I always kept your secrets?"

Taking a moment to gather her thoughts, Emily told the whole story, beginning with Richard's appearance at her house in the country and omitting nothing, not even the night they spent in the hay. "So we will break it off when we have discovered the truth," she finished. "*I* will, I mean."

Sarah gave a soft whistle. "If it weren't you telling me, I'd have trouble believing such a rigmarole." Her eyes gleamed. "You really got to meet the Bruiser? I've begged to do so, but my father always refused."

"He didn't seem at all dangerous. His real name is Jerry." Sarah's answering grin made Emily feel that they were children again, conspiring over some forbidden treat.

"So it's not love, but an adventure."

Even as she nodded, Emily felt an irrational tug of sadness. But that was exactly what it was.

"He's a handsome man, though," added Sarah. "And he must be brave, getting out of the jungle like he did."

"Yes." Some part of her enjoyed hearing these compliments, though of course they had nothing to do with her.

"He's worried about his mother. He doesn't like her going to Herr Schelling. Can't say as I blame him," Sarah went on. "Most of the women—and nearly all who come are women—just stay a few sessions, get what they want, and go on. But a few keep coming, and those tend to be, I don't know, shaky."

"What do you mean?"

"Like they've lost their confidence or something. They can't break free."

"You mean Herr Schelling plays on their weakness?"

"No." Sarah wrinkled her nose. "Well, he does. But it's not that. It's like . . . something happens to them, and they never move on and get back to the way they were." She shook her head. "And the strange thing is, he didn't even die."

"Lord Warrington?"

"Right. She was all to pieces when she thought he was gone. You'd think with him back, she'd be set right. But she comes to Schelling's little shows same as ever, and she still seems shaky, like I said. Her son sees it, too. I could tell."

Emily felt as if she had gotten a glimpse into Richard's heart. It felt clandestine, and all the more thrilling because of that. She was filled with a sudden desire to do something for him, to help. She wanted to repay him, she realized, for accepting her family as no one else had ever done. Ideas racing, she examined Sarah. "Why do you work for Herr Schelling?"

"It annoys my dad," was the quick response. But at Emily's look, she shrugged. "Well, it does. He always assumes I'll do whatever he thinks I should."

"Do you like Schelling?"

"He's all right. A businessman, you know?"

"He does seem to take advantage of people's sorrow."

"I've seen churchmen do as much. Get the money for a new window in the church or a fine monument from the grieving relatives."

"I suppose."

"I probably won't stay with him much longer," she confided. "But the thing that really drew me in— it's like the plays we did in Dad's troupe, but it's real. The people come in, and they tell their stories, and they're full of emotion, you know. The things that have happened to them are as amazing as in the plays, but they really happened."

Her expression was intense, and Emily didn't interrupt.

"I used to feel—well, I still do sometimes—like my life was all made up. We wandered around, doing the plays. We had no house or anything . . . real. So when I watch these people at Herr Schelling's, it's as if that's all reversed. I'm on the other side."

"But you're still . . ."

"I'm still performing," acknowledged Sarah. "I'm not part of it. But I understand it better, almost so I could go off and do it myself."

"It?"

"Real life," explained Sarah. "A regular life, like most people have."

Emily stared at her, feeling a strong echo of what

she meant in herself. Where did one find that confidence in life, that contentment? How did you know that you were doing it right?

"I'll be moving on soon," repeated Sarah.

"To what?" Emily leaned forward a little, waiting for her answer.

"That's what I'm figuring out." Smiling, Sarah added, "Perhaps Herr Schelling will give me the answer from the Great Beyond."

Emily smiled back, but her mind was still busy. "If you are really going to leave his employ," she began.

Sarah raised her eyebrows.

"Would you help get Lady Fielding away from him?"

Inquiry turned to surprise on Sarah's face.

"If we could think of some way to discourage her from seeing Herr Schelling . . ."

"Nothing easier. I know how all his dodges work."

"Then you'll do it?"

"You're dead keen on this, aren't you?"

Emily drew back. "I'm simply trying to help a . . . an acquaintance."

"Ah, that's what it is, is it?"

"What else?" Emily took care to meet her gaze squarely.

After a moment, Sarah grinned. "What indeed? Sure. I'll do it. Easy." She snapped her fingers.

Emily was overcome by gratitude too intense to be examined.

RICHARD MADE a small elegant bow and put out his hand to lead Emily into the dance. He'd been a bit surprised to see her arrive at the ball, chaperoned by the duchess as before. But at the first sight of her, his spirits had risen. "I didn't expect to see you," he said as they began the waltz.

"My mother insisted, and she blackmailed Aunt Julia into bringing me."

Emily appeared to be watching her feet, so he couldn't see her expression. "Blackmailed?"

She nodded, though all he could see was the top of her head. "She promised to remove Papa from my aunt's house as long as she continued to take me about."

"Ah." He tightened his arm slightly, and they turned at the end of the room. He thought he felt her slender frame tremble very slightly. "Is anything wrong?"

At last, she looked up. "No." Her gaze dropped again.

Richard said nothing, and the silence lengthened. "Nothing further has happened?"

"No."

Another couple moved clumsily into their path. Holding Emily closer, he swung out of the way. She gave a little gasp at the quick movement, and he suddenly became aware of the suppleness of her waist under his hand and the grace with which she danced. Her ballgown left her pale shoulders half-bare, and ringlets of hair brushed her white skin as one's lips might. The image was electrifying. It filled his senses until he was conscious of nothing else in the room but her. The rhythm of their dance faltered briefly.

"I'm sorry," said Emily. "I haven't actually waltzed before. I mean, I've practiced, but I've never . . ."

"So I am the first?"

"Yes."

She met his eyes, and it seemed to Richard that she was as conscious of him as he was of her. Their clasped hands seemed to pulse with heat. Muscles clenched involuntarily in his other arm, seeming eager to draw her tight against him. He remembered the feel of her nestled close in the hay. Shadows shifted in her gaze, and her lips parted slightly. His body was urging him to take them for his own.

This wouldn't do at all, he thought. This hadn't been part of the plan, and desire had no place in their arrangement. He clenched his jaw. Would the music never stop?

"Did I make a mistake?" asked Emily.

"Possibly," he muttered.

"Did I step on you? I didn't think I had . . ."

"You dance beautifully, Miss Crane." He could move to the side of the room and suggest they stop. But somehow he didn't. He kept holding her, turning in the dance, her flowery scent clouding his senses.

When the music finally ended, they were both breathing rather quickly, as if the waltz called for great physical exertion. They stood together as the couples moved off the dance floor, still linked by the fever they'd roused.

Richard realized that they were attracting amused glances. He offered his arm and led her out of the ballroom into an adjoining chamber. "A glass of champagne?" he said.

Emily put a hand to her flushed cheek. "Thank you."

When he returned with their glasses, she was composed once more. Indeed, she appeared determined to ignore the past quarter hour. "I don't suppose you've heard anything from our friend Jerry?"

"No." She looked more than ever like a Botticelli, Richard thought. She was drawn on such delicate lines, and her face had that blend of the sensuous and ethereal that made a man want to . . . "There's scarcely been time."

Emily nodded and drank from her glass. Groups of guests chattered around them, but it was somehow as if they were quite a distance away. She took a deep breath. "We must find some job for him."

"I sensed you would expect me to do so." His voice sounded caressing, Richard realized. This must stop at once. "I don't see why," he added in harsher tones.

"He is helping us."

"And being paid for it."

"But it is so sad, the way he has been treated."

"The world is full of sad cases."

Emily looked at him as if he had disappointed her. Richard felt a pang, but the important thing was to break this unforeseen current of attraction. It complicated matters most damnably, and threatened to take him in directions he had no intention of going.

"Perhaps on your estates somewhere. Surely there are many tasks Jerry could do."

"You think he'd like to herd sheep? Or farm?" answered Richard mockingly. "Or are you imagining him as a footman? I suppose he would be handy for ejecting unwanted callers."

"You're teasing me, but—"

"I have no intention of employing the Bruiser." His reward was a startled, hurt glance, quickly averted. He tried to take satisfaction in it.

"There you are."

Lydia Farrell came up to them, and Richard greeted her with relief. The dance had been a bizarre aberration. Something in the air, or the music. It wouldn't happen again. "Hello, Cousin."

Lydia's tone was rueful. "I'm afraid your mother sent me to fetch you."

"To detach me, you mean?"

They exchanged an understanding smile. "Well, yes."

"I'll go and speak to her. If you'll excuse me, Miss Crane?"

Emily looked mortified. That was probably all to the good, Richard thought as he walked away. In fact, it certainly was. Things must be kept on a clear footing.

"I beg your pardon for sending Richard away," said Lydia.

She used his first name with practiced ease, Emily thought, as if she had done so for uncounted years. "It is of no consequence." She started to excuse herself.

"We've had so little time to talk," objected Lydia. "And we will be members of the same family. More or less."

The last phrase made Emily raise her eyebrows. But Lydia didn't explain.

"It was quite a whirlwind romance, I understand.

You'd been in town only a few weeks before the engagement was announced?"

"Yes."

"Charming. Like a fairy tale."

Something in her voice made Emily examine her. Would Richard have confided the truth to this intimidatingly beautiful cousin? Emily found that she hoped not.

"When is the wedding to be?"

"We haven't decided."

"Oh, you must set a date. You have no idea of the planning involved. Your mother . . . but she might not realize either, I suppose."

Emily choked back a gasp. This reference to her parents' elopement was in the worst possible taste.

"My dear," said Lydia, laying a hand on Emily's arm. "Families have no secrets."

Of course Lady Fielding knew all about it. What else had she expected?

"I would be happy to help with the wedding plans. I do love a wedding. It would be such fun."

If there were going to be a wedding. Richard must not have told her. Emily's spirits rose. "It's kind of you to offer."

"You may call on me at any time."

The look in Lydia's dark eyes was intent. Emily didn't know what to make of it.

If she were truly engaged, she would ask her to convince Lady Fielding that the Cranes were not demented. As it was, she simply smiled and thanked the woman. "My aunt will be looking for me," she added.

Lydia looked as if she were going to speak, but then she just smiled back warmly and nodded. When

Emily saw her a bit later in the evening, bent close to Richard laughing over some unknown joke, she wondered whether Lydia had told him of their conversation. But it looked as if they had quite enough to say to each other without that.

TWELVE

AS EMILY WAS walking home from the
Fitzgibbons' house a few days later, still smiling from
her visit with Sarah, she was suddenly overtaken by a
sense of foreboding. It was so abrupt and unexpected
that it stopped her in the middle of the pavement. It
wasn't late. Though she had once again slipped out
without the maid she was supposed to bring, she
wasn't foolish. She looked around.

Everything looked perfectly normal. Emily started
walking again, but she couldn't dismiss the uneasi-
ness, and she decided to find a cab for the rest of the
way home. It was all very well to get a bit of exercise,
but one thing her parents had taught her was to heed

the promptings of intuition. She gazed up and down the street. No hacks were visible. Walking faster, she kept an eye out.

She saw nothing more unusual than a cat leaping from a tree branch to a windowsill. But the sense of oppression didn't lift. When no cabs materialized, Emily walked faster still. She wouldn't come out alone again, she vowed. Not ever. Just let her get home today, and she . . .

There was a loud report from somewhere behind her. Before Emily could react, she heard a whine like a wasp and something pinged on the stone wall of the house beside her. Chips exploded from the stone, hitting her skirts and cutting her arm. She heard a shriek and a man shouting.

"Are you all right?" someone asked.

"Of course she is not all right, Harold," replied a woman. "You can see she's bleeding. Where is your handkerchief?"

A cloth was applied to Emily's arm.

"Find a hack," said the authoritative second voice.

There was an indistinct mumble.

"I'm all right," said Emily, raising her hand to her forehead.

It was pushed aside with surprising gentleness. "Your arm is covered in blood. The wound is superficial. I can see that. But I am surprised you don't feel dizzy."

She did feel a bit dizzy, Emily thought, but she wasn't going to admit it.

"Where do you live?"

She gave the address, and wished fervently that she was there now, or that she could at least sit down.

After what seemed like a very long time, hoof-beats approached. Emily was bundled into a cab over the driver's protests about her condition. Assured by her formidable rescuer that she wasn't anywhere near dying, he finally slapped the reins and started off. In a few minutes, which passed for Emily in a daze, Harold was helping her down and knocking sharply at the house her parents had taken.

The housemaid who opened it screamed. Harold abandoned her at once, slipping back to the cab and away. Emily tried to reassure the girl, and keep her quiet, but it was already too late. Her mother came running from upstairs, and her father started to bellow from the back. Perhaps she could faint, Emily thought. She closed her eyes and tipped her head back. But her consciousness remained stubbornly alert.

"Be quiet, Nan," said her mother to the maid. She took Emily's uninjured arm and led her into the front parlor, pushing her down on a sofa. "Get some water and soft cloths," she told the servant, who ran to do so. "What happened?" she demanded then.

"Something hit a wall I was passing. Bits of stone flew out and some struck me. It's really not . . ."

"Hit?" The maid returned, and Olivia began bathing her arm.

"I didn't see what it was." Which was true, Emily thought woozily, though she had a pretty good idea.

Though Olivia was concentrating on her task, it didn't prevent her from giving her daughter a searching look. "Were you out alone again?"

"Yes, but—"

"I have *told* you . . ."

"I will never do it again, Mama."

Her tone appeared to convince Olivia. She finished bathing the wound and began to bandage it. "I still don't understand how this can have happened." Completing her work, Olivia sat back. "We should have a doctor look at you."

"I don't need . . ."

"You will do as I say."

Emily blinked at her tone of command, which she had heard only a few times in her life. "Yes, Mama."

Olivia continued to gaze at her. "I cannot imagine how such an accident might have occurred. And I have a very good imagination."

"I should have asked the people who helped me." She should have questioned them, Emily thought. "I was too shaken."

Her mother responded to the genuine chagrin in her voice. "Only natural."

"I didn't even get their names." She couldn't believe she had been so heedless. "Well, the man was called Harold, but that is not very useful. I'll never find them again."

Her obvious bitterness had puzzled her mother, she could see.

"I . . . I didn't get a chance to thank them properly," she added.

"Nor did I." Olivia shook her head. "It is too bad."

Emily sat up straight, only to be urged back onto the sofa. "You will lie still for the rest of the day," commanded her mother. "In fact, I think you should have your dinner on a tray." She left unspoken the true reason for this—preventing an outburst by her father. Emily understood it immediately, however, and agreed to be helped up to her room and put to bed.

Someone had shot at her, she had absolutely no doubt of that. They had followed her—she'd felt their presence—and then tried a shot. She shuddered when she thought of the whine passing her ear. A tiny deviation, and she would be dead. The certainty made her feel cold, and she pulled the covers up under her chin.

It didn't make any sense. Richard was the one in danger. Had he been targeted as well? Was he all right? Sitting bolt upright, Emily reached for the bell-pull, then she drew back. Jumping out of bed, she got writing materials. With shaking hands, she wrote a note and sealed it before finally ringing.

Nan appeared at once, looking worried. "Would you have this delivered to Lord Warrington's house? And have the footman wait for an answer."

Emily tossed and turned for two hours before receiving a reply. Lord Warrington was well and thanked her for her inquiry. Emily smiled in relief as she read this, and in amusement as well. Obviously, her vague note had puzzled him considerably. She savored the thought as she settled down to sleep. He imagined he knew everything, but he didn't.

In the morning, she evaded her father over breakfast, then endured the attentions of an imposing doctor recommended by her aunt. She wasn't entirely surprised to hear a knock on the door in midmorning and be brought Warrington's card. She was very glad he had come, she realized. There was no one else she could talk to so freely.

RICHARD CAST A generally approving eye over the neat entrance hall of the house the Cranes had hired. It was well proportioned, and it appeared there was more room than showed from the street. The hallway stretched back a good distance. There was a faint smell of gum spirits in the air. No doubt the older Cranes were already at their easels.

He smiled slightly. It seemed such a simple way to find contentment—a piece of canvas and some brushes. But it hadn't been simple at all, of course. It had meant giving up the prerogatives of birth, the support of family, everything, in fact. He should keep that in mind.

The maid returned and ushered him into a small parlor. Emily rose to greet him, but the words froze on his lips when he saw the bandages on her arm. "What happened to you?"

Emily made an airy gesture. "The most foolish thing. It was quite diverting, really."

Richard stared at her. What could be diverting that required bandages? Then he heard the parlor door close behind the servant.

Emily took a breath. "Mama will be down in a few minutes. I haven't told her . . . anything."

"You will tell *me*."

"There is no one else I can tell."

Richard sat down, feeling oddly unsettled by her

apparent reliance on him. She could tell him what she told no other? He was puzzling over that fact when her next words drove all thought from his brain.

"Someone shot at me."

It was like a whip cracking overhead. He couldn't believe he'd heard correctly.

"I was out . . . walking. I began to feel uneasy, and then I heard the shot." She put her fingers on her bandaged arm. "It knocked splinters of stone from a building. That is what cut me."

Richard's throat was choked with surprise and apprehension.

"I was stupidly shaken, and I didn't even get the names of the people who helped me." She shook her head as if she had made some silly social error. "I don't know why I couldn't have . . ."

"You are absolutely certain of this?"

She blinked, touching her bandage again as if to ask if he questioned its reality.

"You're sure it was a shot?"

"Oh. Yes. The ball buzzed just past my ear."

"Just past . . . you speak of it as if it were a shuttlecock. Are you entirely out of your mind?"

Emily looked offended. "No. It was an unpleasant experience, but . . ."

"Unpleasant? Coming within an inch of death was unpleasant?"

"Well, you talk of it in much the same way," she accused.

He scarcely heard her. "Why in God's name would anyone shoot at you?"

She leaned a little forward. "That is what we

must discover. I have been puzzling over it ever since. We thought it was only you being attacked. But do you think the carriage incident might really have been aimed at both . . . ?"

Richard couldn't concentrate on anything but the bits of cotton wool affixed to her arm. If she had heard the bullet, it had barely missed. It might very easily have snuffed out her life.

"I was thinking we should have asked the Bruiser . . ."

"You were a target because of me. Because you are associated with me," he reasoned. "The engagement, perhaps. It was publicly announced."

"Why should someone who wishes to kill you care about that?"

"To frighten me?" he wondered, hardly heeding her. "But what could that accomplish?"

"I think we should . . ."

Richard rose, unable to sit still a moment longer. " 'We' shall do nothing further. This supposed engagement must be broken off at once. We will not be seen together again." He began to pace. The prospect was surprisingly distasteful. But it was necessary, of course. A shudder went through him. He could almost hear the bullet whizzing by her.

"You are abandoning me now that I have been attacked?" said Emily.

"I am not abandoning . . ."

"Not seen together again?"

She said the words as if they were an insult. "Your association with me has put you in danger. I cannot in conscience . . ."

"So you think. But you don't know."

Richard didn't understand how he had made her so angry.

"It might be because I have been extremely helpful in the search for the attacker. Where would you be without me?"

"I . . ."

"Well, dead," she went on. "Drowned in the pond behind our house." She brushed this aside with a gesture, as if he had brought it up. "But that isn't what I meant."

"I cannot see you put in danger," he declared.

"I already am," she pointed out, as if speaking to a simpleton. "I was shot at."

"But if you were no longer connected with me . . ."

Emily sat up very straight, her chin in the air. "I see. You don't wish to be burdened with any other problems when you are trying to save yourself. It doesn't matter. I can manage perfectly well on my own."

"That is *not* what I meant." He had a fleeting desire to shake her. "You are willfully misunderstanding me. I don't want to see you hurt!"

This silenced her. She met his eyes almost timidly, it seemed. She looked—not frightened, but wary—of what he didn't know. "Do you really think I would be safer on my own?" she said quietly.

"If you had not gotten involved with me, you would not . . ."

"You may be right. But now that I am . . . involved, do you think whoever is behind the attacks will simply forget about me?"

He stared at her lovely face, a sinking sensation spreading through him.

"I helped discover certain things," she continued. "If the plot succeeded and you were killed, do you think this person would want anyone knowing anything about it?"

Her voice was so calm, so reasonable as she set out this terrifying case. Slowly, reluctantly, he shook his head.

Emily stood. "If you wish me to break off the engagement, I will do so."

For such a small, delicate creature, she had a great deal of dignity. He was deeply struck by it.

"I can take care of myself. I have been doing so all my life." A melancholy smile curved her lips. "If I can manage my parents, I can manage anything!"

Richard was struck by a memory of their first meeting. She had scared off his assailants with her dogs, half-carried him home, and then dealt with her volatile father with marvelous finesse. She did have surprising resources. "All your life," he murmured, trying to picture it.

"Well, since I was quite small." She wrinkled her nose. "I remember offering the local vicar's wife a pansy when I was about three. It just prevented her from beating my father about the head with her umbrella." Emily nodded to herself. "He would have hit her back, you know, which she didn't expect, and then . . ." Her gesture left the ensuing chaos to his imagination.

Richard smiled. But his amusement was nearly submerged in some other emotion. "A big responsibility for a child."

She glanced at him almost as if he had frightened her, then quickly away. When she spoke again, her tone was brisk. "So, what are we to do?"

"It appears we must leave things as they are, for now."

"I am sorry."

"For what?"

"That you are in such an . . . uncomfortable position."

Richard shrugged. "That is the fault of this villain of ours."

She started to answer, then stopped.

"You are not to go out walking again," he added, making it a command. "You are not to go anywhere unless I am with you."

Clearly, she had a reply to that, but before she could make it, her mother came into the room and greeted him. "I hope you have convinced her, Lord Warrington. I do not understand just how this . . . accident happened." She looked at him as if to judge whether he knew more.

Richard attempted a façade of amiable innocence.

She rejected it with a look. "The important thing is to prevent any similar episode."

"Exactly." This time he met her gaze with no qualms. "I shall do everything in my power to prevent it."

Olivia seemed to approve of his tone. "That will be sufficient, I would think."

"I'm still here in the room," said Emily.

"Of course you are, dear. You should sit down. I expect you are still a bit weak." Olivia took a seat and waved Richard into another. "Nan is bringing a tray. You ought to offer guests some refreshment, Emily."

Richard nearly laughed at the look this roused. Emily was not used to being lectured on manners by her mother, he saw. "You have set up your household very quickly," he commented.

Olivia's smile was impish. "Julia was a great help. She even lent me servants and some bits of furniture."

"She would have given you all her best plate to get us out of her house," said Emily.

"My dear, you mustn't give Lord Warrington the wrong impression about our family."

He had to stifle a laugh at Emily's incredulous expression. When he caught Olivia's eye the next time, he began to suspect she was teasing her daughter. It was a family like no other.

THIRTEEN

SITTING OPPOSITE his mother and Lydia Farrell in the former's fashionable barouche, Richard watched other members of society parade through the park in the daily display of the season. The stream of carriages, showy hacks, and carefully dressed walkers reminded him of a circus. There were the trainers of dangerous animals—duennas escorting rapacious young debs; the jesters—dandies padded and pomaded into ludicrous shapes; the jugglers—those who had staked every cent on some precarious social scheme. And himself? Some days he felt like a tightrope walker, teetering on a thin line between various sorts of disaster.

"There is Jane Townshend," said his mother. "Look, Richard. In the carriage with the wheels picked out in red."

Automatically, Richard looked. A thin dark girl sat beside an older, stouter version of herself in the carriage.

"A lovely girl. And they say she has four thousand a year, at least."

"Which makes her even lovelier," murmured Lydia Farrell with a sardonic look.

"Drive over that way, Ben," Lady Fielding urged the coachman. "I will introduce you, Richard."

"No thank you, Mother. Ben, stay as we were."

The team swung back into line, and the barouche moved on, passing the Townshend carriage at a distance.

"You are being thoroughly exasperating, Richard," commented his mother. "If you have made up your mind to marry, you should take some thought for . . ."

"That matter is settled." He was already weary of this argument. It would be a great relief when his engagement to Emily was ended. His mother would be delighted. But somehow, the thought didn't comfort him.

"Speaking of which," said Lydia. At her companions' questioning looks, she pointed.

Richard's spirits rose at once. "Pull up, Ben. There is someone I wish to speak to."

"Richard!" objected his mother. But he stepped down from the barouche without responding.

Emily, he was pleased to see, was walking with

her mother. When she saw him approaching, she smiled, and Richard's mood lightened further.

"You see I am following everyone's advice," she said when he reached them. "I have not taken a step out of the house alone in three days."

"Commendable." Richard made his bow to Olivia Crane, who carried a sketch pad under her arm. "You are going to draw the parade of fashion."

She made a face. "No. I thought I would do some studies of the flowers, until Emily goes mad with boredom, that is."

"Mama! Of course I am happy to sit while you sketch."

"You know you find it horridly tedious." She turned to Richard. "I have never understood how Alasdair and I could have had a child so utterly uninterested in painting. We got her a watercolor box when she was three, you know, and she—"

"There is no need to tell that story again, Mama."

"But I would like to hear it," Richard said. And it was true, he realized. He was curious about the youthful Emily.

"She ate them."

"I did not!" Emily gazed at her mother in laughing exasperation. Olivia raised her eyebrows. "One," conceded Emily. Now, she turned to Richard. "The colors looked just like some candies I had seen in a shop window. Papa did *not* explain what they were for when he gave me the box."

"He thought you would know instinctively," put in her mother.

"It tasted quite nasty." Emily looked wistful. "I would have liked some of those candies."

Richard couldn't contain a laugh.

"You, of course, have never been a disappointment to your parents," Emily accused.

"I . . ."

"Well, until now," she added, with a look that told him she was referring to his connection with her.

"You are not a disappointment," declared Olivia, whose gaze had begun to roam over the flowerbeds nearby. "You know your father thinks the world of you, as do I."

"I know, Mama." The look Emily gave her was fond and forgiving.

"Those roses are rather fine. The color!" She wandered off the path toward the spill of blooms.

"Perhaps Miss Crane could walk a little with me while you draw?" said Richard.

Olivia agreed with a wave of her hand. She spread her shawl on the grass and sat down on it, pulling a pencil from her reticule, already lost to her surroundings.

"It is providential that they found each other," said Emily. "Can you imagine how unhappy a conventional man of fashion would be with my mother?"

Richard gazed at Olivia, settled on the ground, her pencil busy, oblivious to the stares and snickers of passersby. "I would find it rather . . . challenging myself."

The look Emily gave him was incandescent with emotion. He couldn't read it all; gratitude seemed to be part of it, and relief. But there was more than he could grasp in a fleeting instant. Nonetheless, the intensity of it shook him. "And your father," he said as a diversion.

Emily laughed. "Aunt Julia wanted to murder him after only two days in the same house."

"Perhaps two such spirits were bound to come together."

She looked surprised; which was no wonder. He was surprised himself. Where had those words come from? He offered his arm. "Would you care to walk?"

"*Not* to the Grecian temple."

"Indeed not." He smiled back at her, feeling an unexpected twinge of something very like joy.

They strolled along the gravel path in silence for a few minutes. The sun set her hair afire, Richard thought. It made her skin glow like pearls. He needed to say something before he lost himself in . . .

"I have arranged something I hope you will like," said Emily. "I think you will."

Richard dragged his thoughts from the grace of her form with great difficulty.

"It's about Herr Schelling."

"What?"

"I know you don't approve of him and . . . and you wish your mother would not go there."

She had his full attention now.

"I believe I have a way to stop her."

"You? How?"

"Sarah Fitzgibbon, Daniel's daughter, works for Herr Schelling. And she has agreed to help."

Richard was having trouble taking this in.

"She needs to speak to you about some of the . . . details." Emily faltered a little under his fixed gaze. "If . . . if you wish her to do this," she stammered.

"This was your idea?"

She nodded uncertainly.

"You persuaded Miss Fitzgibbon to go along?"

"She didn't need much persuading."

A tightness in Richard's chest kept him silent.

"I . . . I saw that you disliked your mother's association with Schelling," Emily hurried on. "Well, Sarah noticed it, too. And so, since she is there and knows all his shifts and she is going to be leaving anyway, I just thought . . ."

"You concocted this whole scheme for me."

Emily gazed up at him, looking a bit apprehensive.

"You saw my distaste for the man, and you put yourself out to do something about it," he marveled.

"I didn't really . . ."

"You had no obligation to do anything."

Emily had flushed a little. "It seemed a simple service for a . . . a friend."

He couldn't take his eyes from her face. He felt an unsettling mixture of gratitude and excitement and disappointment. "A friend? Of course."

"So you will see Sarah? So she can set it up?"

"Of course," he repeated.

"Good. I'll speak to her and tell you the day." She moved slightly, tugging on his arm.

They had stopped walking, Richard realized. They were standing stock-still in the middle of the path, forcing others to go around them and drawing amused or irritated glances. He moved on at once.

"Wherever did you meet the Fitzgibbons?" he said with an attempt at lightness.

Emily's smile was wry. "My father is always bringing home some . . . unusual acquaintance."

"Ah." Where would Alasdair Crane draw the line? he wondered. Capital crimes? Convicted felons?

They turned a corner in the path and walked back the way they had come. "Oh, dear," said Emily.

"What?" He followed her gaze and found that Olivia Crane had attracted a small group of onlookers. As he watched, one of them pointed to her drawing and made a comment.

Emily walked faster. "She hates that."

"No doubt."

When they reached her mother, she was gathering her things. "I can't work here. These people are incredibly rude and will not move on."

Richard wondered if she would expect him to disperse the crowd. Her husband would set on them with his walking stick, he supposed.

But Olivia said only, "Let us go."

"You selling that picture of the roses?" asked a man nearby. "It's dashed good." Olivia was looking slightly less annoyed, when he added, "My little girl could color in the lines."

Olivia drew herself up. Her lack of height didn't detract from the impression of freezing dignity, Richard thought. "You may wish your daughter to be a mindless copyist," she declared, "but I will not be a party to it."

The man goggled at her. Gathering Emily with a glance, Olivia walked away, every inch an aristocrat. If she had chosen the stage rather than the brush, she would have been a sensation, Richard thought, moving to catch up.

There was little conversation up to the gates of the park, where he saw them into a hack and on their way. When they were gone, Richard looked about for his mother's carriage, but as he expected, she had departed as well. He would walk home, he decided. He got little enough exercise here in London.

Strolling down the busy streets, watching the clerks and shopgirls and servants on errands hurry past, Richard's eye was caught by the display in a confectioner's window. There was a box of multi-colored candies lying open to tempt passersby. The reds and blues and greens were as brilliant as paints. He looked at them for a long moment, then went into the shop, bought the box, and directed that it be sent to Emily at home. When he came out again, he was smiling.

A different, but perhaps related impulse stopped him at an elegant shop a bit farther along. He examined the display rather longer this time before moving on.

THE MEETING OF Richard and Sarah was soon arranged, but as the hour approached Emily found herself unexpectedly nervous. Richard had reacted so strangely when she told him the plan. And she wasn't at all certain how the two would get along. What if they disliked each other?

As agreed, Sarah arrived first.

"Is it all set?" Emily wondered.

"Lady Fielding's due tomorrow night," was the cheerful response. "We'll be ready."

"Thank you," said Emily, meeting her friend's eyes.

"Can't have your betrothed unhappy," Sarah teased. "Who'd send you sweets then?"

Emily felt herself flushing. The box of candies had been an unexpected, and unexpectedly affecting, gesture.

"Good ones, too," added Sarah.

The parlor door opened, and the maid appeared. "Lord Warrington," she announced.

Emily and Sarah rose as he walked into the room. "Good day," he said, surveying Sarah with obvious curiosity.

"This is Sarah Fitzgibbon, Daniel's daughter," Emily said quickly. "Sarah, Lord Warrington."

"I've seen you at Herr Schelling's," Sarah declared.

"Yes." Richard examined Sarah more closely. She returned the favor. Emily sank down on the sofa again.

"I understand I owe you my thanks," Richard said. "I hope you are not jeopardizing your . . . position." His tone made it clear what he thought of her line of work.

"I'm not staying with Schelling much longer anyway," replied Sarah. "I've learned all his tricks."

"Going to set up on your own, are you?"

Emily bristled at his tone. "What do you know about it? Sarah is—"

"Not likely," interrupted Sarah. "I expect I'll go back on the stage."

"I thought you disliked it," said Emily, startled.

"Not traveling players. Something here in London." Sarah grinned again. "Perhaps I'll join Flora at Covent Garden and become the next Mrs. Patrick Campbell."

"Laudable."

Emily frowned at Richard's drawling response.

"But before you make your debut . . ."

"Right." Abruptly, Sarah was all business. "There's a few things I need to know before tomorrow night."

Richard looked surprised at the change in her.

"This Sir Walter Fielding we're supposed to be contacting—what was he like?"

Richard looked at the carpet, frowning. "He was a good man," he said finally.

"He spoke like you, I suppose? His accent, I mean?"

"Yes."

Richard didn't look as if he was enjoying this, Emily thought.

"Were there any expressions he used often?" asked Sarah. "Pet names about the house?"

"Why must you know such things?" demanded Richard, looking revolted.

"We want to make it as convincing as possible, before we blow the gaff," answered Sarah.

His mouth hard with distaste, Richard said, "He called my mother 'dear heart.' And he often said 'by thunder.' "

Sarah nodded. "Good."

"This is intolerable," he burst out. "This kind of deception and trickery . . ."

"It's for the last time," Sarah pointed out. "If you'd rather Herr Schelling pulled the strings . . ."

"No." Richard looked grim. "What else?"

"That will do for me." Sarah rose. "I've got to get back before they miss me. And to see to some things." Her smile was wicked.

Richard stood also. "Thank you," he said stiffly.

Sarah gave him a mock salute.

"I'll see you out," said Emily. She wanted a word with her friend.

"No, no. I wouldn't want to separate an engaged couple." Sarah went out, leaving the engaged couple looking self-conscious.

Silence fell over the room. Emily's pulse speeded up, and her mouth felt a little dry.

"An unusual young woman," Richard said finally.

"I think she's splendid."

He held up a hand in defense. "No doubt you're right. It was certainly kind of her to offer to detach my mother from . . . her employer."

"She is only working there because . . ." Emily broke off, not wanting to betray any of Sarah's confidences.

"I'm sure she has her reasons."

Silence descended again. Stealing a look at Richard, Emily couldn't interpret his expression. He looked very handsome this morning. His simple blue coat and buff pantaloons set off his athletic figure to perfection. And the bronze of his skin was striking against his snowy neckcloth. She had first imagined him as a gladiator, she remembered suddenly, and flushed. "Thank you for the candies," she said to erase this image.

He smiled. "I thought they looked like the watercolors your mother spoke of."

Her answering smile came without conscious bidding. "They did. But they tasted much better."

"I'm glad."

Their gaze held as the smiles slowly faded. Emily looked away first. "I'm sure Sarah will do the thing just right."

"She seemed very capable."

They were repeating themselves, Emily thought. Why didn't he take his leave? He had gotten what he came for, hadn't he?

"You've known her a long time?" he asked, in the tone of someone making polite conversation in difficult conditions.

"Most of my life. We used to see each other every year when the Fitzgibbons' acting troupe came to our town." She smiled reminiscently. "They always came—wherever we lived."

"You moved about a great deal?"

"Papa is always looking for new places to paint. And escape from irate neighbors. We were rarely more than a year in any one spot."

He frowned.

"It was great fun," lied Emily. "I got to see all sorts of country."

He made no reply. Another silence fell. She would just say she had an appointment, Emily decided. But she didn't move.

"I have something else for you."

She started slightly.

Richard drew a small box from his waistcoat

pocket and handed it to her. It was covered in dark blue velvet. Emily held it, gazing at him.

"Open it," he commanded as abruptly as before.

Her hands trembling, she did so. "Oh." Inside was an exquisite ring set with a sapphire flanked by two smaller diamonds. "Oh," she said again. "I can't . . . you shouldn't . . ."

"It is the expected thing," he replied stiffly. "Several friends have been asking me what sort of ring I meant to get you."

"But you . . . we aren't . . ."

"Try it on."

Emily knew she shouldn't, but the ring was so lovely. She drew it out, fumbling a little, and fit it on her finger.

"Too loose?" he asked, as if there were nothing strange about any of this.

"No. It's just right."

"Ah." He nodded as if satisfied. "I thought the blue stone would suit you."

She slipped it off. "I can't take it."

"Why not?"

"You must see that it is impossible."

"It fits with our . . . plan."

"Pretending to be engaged. That does not mean you must spend large sums of money on the—"

"I didn't spend anything," he interrupted, sounding bitter. "It is the ring my father gave my mother when they were engaged. She put it aside for my future wife."

"Then I certainly can't accept it." She tried to hand it back.

"You don't care for the ring?"

"It's lovely, one of the most beautiful I've ever seen. But your mother will . . ."

"She will do as I say." His voice was steely.

"There is no need to carry our charade to such a length." Emily retrieved the box and held out the ring to him.

"I don't wish people to start to doubt it," he answered in quite a different voice. "The only way I can offer you my protection is if we are known to be engaged. If anyone suspects the truth . . ."

He broke off, but Emily had no trouble finishing the thought. If her true role were known, the mysterious attacker would bend every effort to eliminate her.

"Put it on," he said.

She slipped the ring on again. It really was exquisite. When she raised her eyes, Richard was watching her with an odd expression. His hazel eyes seemed almost soft.

"It becomes you."

She swallowed.

His short laugh was derisive. "I was once a veritable pink of the *ton*. My advice was sought after on all matters of dress and decoration."

Richard stood. "Wear it," he commanded. And without another word, he strode out of the room.

Emily remained sitting on the sofa. Her eyes kept straying to the ring. She held out her hand finally, spreading her fingers to admire its rich glitter in the sunlight. She had never had anything so beautiful. Her throat ached with a threat of tears. She cleared it, and dropped her hand to her lap.

The ring had been lent to her. She would return

it to Richard when their quest was complete. She mustn't think of it as hers.

She cleared her throat again. It was something precious she was guarding for a friend. She would take very good care of it for the short time it remained with her. Unconsciously, Emily's right hand crept over to cup the other. It was no more than that, she reiterated. It meant nothing, really. Nothing at all.

FOURTEEN

"THERE IS A BOY asking to see you," Henley
told Richard very early the next morning. The butler's tone made it abundantly clear that he did not
approve of the individual in question. "He insisted
you would wish to know he was here." He waited for
Richard to confirm his doubt of this.

"Where have you put him?" asked Richard, laying aside a letter to his estate agent and rising from
the library armchair.

"He is waiting in the kitchen." Henley's face had
gone impassive at this distressing reaction.

Richard nodded and started for the back prem-
ises.

"I will have him brought to you, my lord!"

"No need."

Leaving Henley to recover from the shock, Richard went down the backstairs to the brick-floored kitchen. Suspecting the identity of his caller, he thought the boy would be more comfortable there than in an upper room.

His entrance roused a flurry of exclamations and fluttering aprons. With a smile for the cook, whom he had known since he was in short pants, Richard went over to the raggedly dressed boy who was twisting his cap near the outer door. "I am Lord Warrington," he said.

The boy looked relieved. "T'Bruiser sent me."

"He has news for me?"

"Aye m'lord. He asked, could you come and see him."

Richard started to ask for more information, but realized the boy was unlikely to have any. "Tell him I'll be there at two."

The boy's relief increased. He nodded and put on his cloth cap. When Richard handed him a coin, he goggled at it, then looked deeply gratified as he slipped out the door and up the area stairs.

He would have to send word to Emily, Richard thought as he returned to his correspondence. But he set the letter aside again when it occurred to him that perhaps he should not. She really oughtn't visit the Bruiser's neighborhood.

She would be furious if he went without telling her, he mused. Oddly, the idea made him smile. There was something inexplicably enjoyable about quarreling with Emily.

He would go without her, he decided, and tell her the outcome later on.

He took up his pen and tried to frame a few more sentences to his estate agent. It was damnably difficult to know what to say to him. Even if Richard managed to convince the man that he was serious about restoring the land, what could he offer? Nothing could be done without money, and there was no money. It was damnably depressing.

Richard frowned, wrote a bit more, then stopped again. Something was nagging at him. Had he forgotten to tell Taft anything important?

No, that wasn't it.

He re-read the letter. It seemed as clear and sensible as he could make it. Taft would very likely doubt him, but . . . it wasn't the letter. He put it aside once again, scowling at the library wall.

He didn't want to go and see the Bruiser without Emily, Richard realized. The expedition would lack a vital . . . spark. It would become a duty instead of a foray into mystery. Emily added something indefinable to any outing.

Ridiculous, he told himself. He valued Emily's insights; that was all. She had encountered unusual people and circumstances in her unconventional life, and her unique point of view was very helpful. He simply wanted to take advantage of it.

Richard took out a fresh sheet of notepaper and scrawled a few quick sentences on it. When he had dispatched it to the Crane house, he felt much better.

EMILY GRIPPED THE SIDE of the seat as the carriage clattered over a rough stretch of pavement. Her ring glinted in the sunlight, and she was startled yet again by the sight of it on her hand. Stealing a glance at Richard beside her, she found him intent on guiding the vehicle through the narrowing streets. He had been quiet since taking her up, and didn't seem to share her anticipation of the Bruiser's news. She wanted to ask him if anything was wrong, but she couldn't, quite. The presence of the groom and husky footman perched behind was inhibiting.

"It's odd that the Bruiser won't venture out of his own neighborhood," she said finally. "It seems he wouldn't be afraid of anything."

"Difficulties in Mayfair are seldom solved with one's fists."

She blinked. The sentiment, and the abrupt tone, were unexpected. "You mean he feels out of his element elsewhere?"

"Undoubtedly."

"We should have invited him to our house. Papa would put him at ease."

A short laugh escaped Richard. "I daresay he would."

"I'm sure he would like to paint him," continued Emily meditatively. "You know, that might be a step in finding Jerry employment. I don't suppose you have thought . . . ?"

"No."

"I'll speak to Papa," she decided.

"How will you account for your acquaintance with a prizefighter?" Richard asked.

Emily couldn't resist. "I'll tell him you introduced me."

"Indeed?" He threw her a look. "Is your father a good shot?"

"Rather good. Why?"

"Because it will be pistols at dawn if you say that. I just wondered about my chances."

She laughed. "He might call you out. But when you met, he would be distracted by the mist on the grass or the color of the clouds and forget to shoot you."

"It almost sounds as if this has happened." The amusement in Richard's voice dissipated the constraint she had noticed earlier.

"It did. One of our neighbors challenged him once. But then Papa wandered off as the seconds were pacing the ground to watch some willow leaves floating in a brook. When he shot them—"

"The leaves?" interrupted Richard incredulously.

"Yes. He was framing the composition, you see, and he forgot he had a loaded dueling pistol in one hand. I understand they go off at the least touch."

Richard made a choking sound.

"The duel was called off. Our neighbor decided he was mad."

"You seem to know a great deal about the occasion."

"I was hiding in the bushes."

"What?"

"I was only nine, and I wanted to see a duel." She paused, remembering. "I was worried about Papa, too."

"That he let you find out . . ."

"Well, he shouts. One can't help but overhear."

"I would have thought your mother . . ."

"Oh, she was . . ."

"What?"

"Never mind."

"She was there with you, wasn't she?"

Emily hesitated, but he looked very certain. "She wanted to make sure he was all right. I think she meant to throw a rock and spoil both their aims."

Richard burst out laughing. "That is outrageous."

"She said the squire had no business offering a challenge. Papa hadn't meant to insult him."

"I doubt that."

"He hadn't. Papa's insults are very . . . straightforward."

Richard gave another snort of laughter.

"And he only said he didn't wish to paint a portrait of the squire's wife."

"That's all?"

Emily wrinkled her nose. "Well, he did tell him that he couldn't because his life was devoted to the pursuit of beauty. But he didn't mean it as an insult."

"No, indeed."

"He didn't. More of an abstract judgment."

Richard pulled up the horses in front of the Bruiser's boarding house. "One can see why the squire might take it personally, however."

"He was not a connoisseur of art."

As he helped her down, Richard smiled in a way that made Emily feel quite euphoric.

THEY FOUND THE BRUISER sitting in his room, as before. "What happened to your face?" Emily exclaimed, distressed by the discoloration and swelling all along his cheek and over one eye.

"Sparring with some of the hopefuls," was the obscure response. "One lad looks promisin'."

He seemed oblivious to his injuries, indeed almost to approve of them, she thought in bewilderment.

"You have some news for us?" asked Richard.

"Aye. Bob and Ralph the Thumb have gone."

"Gone where?"

The fighter shrugged his massive shoulders. "No one knows. They packed up and left."

"Left London?" Richard demanded.

"Well, they ain't anywhere people knows of. And Ralph owes Sam Pierce ten quid." His expression suggested that this should tell them something important.

"Sam collects his debts?" ventured Richard.

"Regular," replied the Bruiser, looking solemn.

"I wonder where they can have gone?" Emily frowned. "If they were indeed behind the attacks . . ."

"They was after somebody in foreign parts," put in the Bruiser.

"Foreign . . . ?"

"You mean, in another part of London?" asked Richard.

The fighter nodded, waving his huge hand. "Off away west."

"And you have heard nothing of where they went when they disappeared?"

"Disappeared's the right of it. Nobody knows where they are." He shook his head. "Sam has friends in foreign parts."

Richard looked at Emily. "It sounds as if they have left London."

"But why?"

"To keep them from being questioned, perhaps."

"Someone found out we were asking about them?"

"It seems likely." Richard gave the Bruiser a side-long glance, as if to say that he was not the most subtle questioner.

"So the attacks will end?"

"These men will no longer be involved," he corrected. He frowned. "They must know something useful, or there would be no need to get rid of them." He turned to the Bruiser. "See if you can find out where they went."

"Right."

"And keep your ears open. If anyone else is offered their job in 'foreign parts' send word to me at once." He rose to go.

"Do be more careful," Emily said, making no move to follow suit. "Do you have something to put on those bruises?"

The fighter stared at her. "Had a beefsteak on my eye yesterday all right and tight."

"A . . . ?"

"A customary remedy," Richard put in. "I believe it's quite helpful."

"I'm going to tell Papa," she said. "Would you like to pose for a painting, Jerry?"

The Bruiser looked uncertain, and apprehensive. "Painting?"

"A picture. Of you. In your . . . fighting clothes, I imagine."

"Like the ones of Cribb and Molyneaux?" answered the fighter.

Emily looked to Richard for guidance.

"Two famous champions," he explained. "Their bout in 1810 was epic in the world of the Fancy. I believe it has been painted several times."

"A little like that," Emily said. "But you would have to come to Papa's studio in, er, 'foreign parts.' "

The fighter scowled, struggle evident in his face.

"He would treat you well," Emily assured him. Her father was kinder to his sitters than to his aristocratic kin.

"Your dad?" said the Bruiser, and Emily couldn't tell if he found the connection reassuring or intimidating. She simply nodded. "I dunno."

"He's a right one," said Richard. Both Emily and the Bruiser looked at him. "Nothing toplofty about him."

The Bruiser looked half-convinced. Emily felt a rush of emotion at his endorsement of her father.

"Mebbe," allowed the fighter.

She left it at that, wanting to speak to her father before making definite arrangements.

"We should go," said Richard.

Emily rose and offered Jerry her hand.

As she and Richard walked back down the stairs to the carriage, she couldn't help but say, "Thank you."

"For what?"

There seemed too much to say. For not thinking my family bizarre, for not deploring my father's eccentricity or my mother's lack of ceremony. For taking them as they are and, seemingly, liking them.

"Is it so important to you that the Bruiser be immortalized?" he asked, amusement in his voice.

"I would like to help him," she managed.

"And you think this is the way?"

"Papa will pay him a little, and then perhaps we can find something else for him to do."

"Is that how your father gained so many unusual friends? Does he paint them, and then find them employment?" His amusement seemed to have faded to curiosity.

"Sometimes. Not always."

They climbed into the carriage and started off. Richard was silent for a few minutes, and Emily wondered what he was thinking.

"I'll see what I can find for the . . . for Jerry," he said then.

"I thought you didn't want to . . ."

"I changed my mind."

His tone didn't encourage questions. He must have been affected by the fighter's battered face, Emily decided, as she had certainly been. Men disliked admitting such sympathies. Which was silly, but that was how they were. She felt a moment's warm cordiality toward the entire male sex. They needed their little ruses and evasions. "It has gotten quite hot, hasn't it?" she asked, and was gratified to see the expected relief in his expression.

RICHARD MANEUVERED the carriage through a narrow gap left by a curricle and a wagon full of vegetables. He didn't even notice the approving looks from the other drivers for his steady handling of the reins. He was contending with a tangled mass of feeling that the expedition with Emily had evoked.

He'd given her the ring because he wanted to, he admitted to himself. It wasn't really a necessary part of the charade. He'd become aware of this the moment she settled beside him in the carriage this morning, ring on her finger, and looked up at him with a confiding smile. He had a sudden image of her face when she had first taken the ring from its box and held it out. There had been a glow in her eyes, a softness to her mouth.

His jaw hardened. This wouldn't do. He had to stop it at once. Richard's fist closed and his face reddened. She had engaged herself to him because of the thrill of the chase. There was nothing more between them, and he had been profoundly relieved to find that this was so. Profoundly relieved, he repeated silently. He had important things to think about, a whole life to reshape for himself. He couldn't afford errant impulses of . . . sympathy.

That was it, he decided. He had felt sorry for her, with her gypsy existence, her unsettled youth, not to mention parents who might be amusing, but clearly did not devote themselves to her comfort.

He had wanted to give her a treat, he thought, as one would a child. The candies were clear evidence of that; the ring had been merely an extension of the same whim. Excessive, he acknowledged, even foolish perhaps, but no more.

Reassured, Richard guided the carriage into his mother's stable yard and handed the ribbons over to a groom. He seemed to have developed a somewhat maudlin tendency during his sojourn in the jungle, which was odd. Perhaps enduring hardship had made him more sensitive to others' trials? He shook his head. He would have to curb the inclination, which had already committed him to finding work for a broken down prizefighter. He hadn't time for such things.

Striding into the library, he took up the letter he had been drafting to his estate agent Taft. He needed to get it off. It was time to act, to take control of events. He couldn't waste time chasing an illusory enemy or feeling sorry for individuals he encountered. He had enough to do just hunting down himself. But even as he took up the pen to work on the letter, his eyes grew distant, and he forgot matters of business as he lost himself in the memory of Emily's exquisite face.

SARAH PUT HER FINGER to her lips, signaling silence. Emily nodded, and her friend led her through a door and into a narrow space defined by a wall on one side and a thick velvet drapery on the other. She could hear people talking quietly beyond the curtain. This was the room where Herr Schelling did his spirit calling, she realized. Sarah had explained to her that it held a number of secret spaces, from which various effects could be created.

The man was a total fake, she thought. Of course, she hadn't believed he was really contacting the dead, but having the tricks explained made it more distasteful. She was very glad they were going to get Richard's mother away from him.

Chairs scraped on the other side of the drapery. Sarah touched her arm and pulled her a few steps to show her a tiny hole in the fabric. Setting her eye to it, Emily could see a round table with a single candle burning on it. Herr Schelling was facing her, and he seemed to be looking right at her. She drew back quickly. He couldn't possibly see anything, she told herself, and peered out again.

Richard was there. His strong profile was stiff in the dim light. His mother sat next to him. Strangers occupied the other chairs. Her gaze drifted back to Richard. He looked so stern, and so handsome. Emily felt a thrill of excitement and nerves run through her.

Herr Schelling raised his hands and the circle stirred with anticipation. Schelling moaned and chanted. "We seek Walter, beloved husband of one of our circle," he concluded.

Emily saw Richard's mouth jerk. His mother looked anxious and hopeful and distressed.

"Bring him hither my messengers," continued Schelling. "Azrael. Phileto. Bring him!"

Beside Emily, Sarah pushed at the heavy curtain so that it billowed and swished. There was a low sound from high up in the corner of the room. This came from a henchman stationed on a set of wooden steps, Emily knew. Sarah had explained that this fellow—an actor who had fallen on hard times due to a propensity for drink—would provide the voice of Sir Walter Fielding, which would seem to come from above.

"He is coming!" intoned their host. "He is near."

The man on the steps let out a long "Ahh."

"Walter?" said Lady Fielding shakily.

The man gave something between a sigh and a groan.

"Is it you, Walter?"

Emily watched Richard's face. He was obviously having difficulty controlling himself.

"Dear heart?" said the actor in a muffled voice, as if from far away.

A small shriek escaped Lady Fielding. Richard scowled.

"By thunder, is that you?" added the actor.

"Walter. Oh, Walter, I have missed you so."

This was cruel, Emily thought, letting people imagine that they could reach loved ones who were gone. She turned to Sarah with some reproach, but her friend was gone. She had slipped away to carry out the plan.

Swallowing her outrage, Emily did her part, keeping the curtains moving so that Schelling would not notice Sarah's absence.

"And I you, dear heart," continued the actor. "You are always . . ." The man broke off with a startled exclamation.

"What is it, Walter?" cried Lady Fielding. "Are you all right? Are you . . . happy where you are?"

"I am serene. Here on the other side . . ." He stopped again, with an audible curse. Sarah was doing her part, Emily thought with a smile. She made the drapery billow more wildly.

"What is the matter?" cried Lady Fielding. She started to rise from the table.

"There is some disturbance," began the actor. Then, with a whoop, he tumbled from the steps that Sarah had pushed over and fell through the velvet curtains out into the room. "Devil take it," he grumbled as he flailed at the folds. It was clearly the same voice as "Sir Walter's," and just as clearly the man was half-drunk. Sarah had counted on that.

"It's a fraud," declared Richard, standing. "It was all a trick, Mother."

Lady Fielding was staring at the actor. Bewilderment slowly gave way to understanding, then to outrage, in her face. She drew herself up very straight. "How dare you pretend to be my husband?"

The man looked at her indifferently, then shrugged, gesturing toward Herr Schelling as if to say, "It was all his idea."

Richard's mother turned and faced the turbaned German.

Schelling spread his hands. "My dear lady, this is some dreadful mistake. I promise you, I never . . ."

Lady Fielding's glare cut him off. "All of it a fake. What else is behind these curtains?" She gestured as if she would pull them down. Richard stepped forward to restrain her just as Emily felt a touch on her arm. Sarah was there, indicating that they should go. Emily had to agree, though she very much wanted to see the rest of the scene.

Sarah led her to a room at the back of the house where they put on their wraps and slipped out. Sarah had a portmanteau as well. "That's that," she said as they walked along a back street in search of a hack.

"You aren't going back?"

"No, I'm done with Herr Schelling." She laughed shortly. "I expect he's about done with London as well."

"Good riddance. It was despicable, the way he deceived people."

Signaling to a cab, Sarah agreed. "Though most of them were eager to be deceived."

"Even worse."

They climbed into the hack and directed the driver to the Fitzgibbon house. "Dad will be pleased that Schelling's out of business," continued Sarah.

"Aren't you?"

"Oh, yes. But there are worse folk about, Emily. He gave some of his 'clients' a deal of comfort."

"False comfort."

Sarah shrugged.

FIFTEEN

"I DON'T THINK SO," said Emily in response to one of Lydia Farrell's questions. The woman always had a lot of questions. And she was nearly always in evidence when Emily and Richard encountered each other at a *ton* party. Had Richard's mother asked her to interfere with the match? Emily examined the handsome older woman more closely. She looked guileless.

"Of course, Richard knows more than I about fashion," Lydia said.

Emily couldn't decide whether she meant to be cutting, but it didn't really matter, because Richard wasn't listening. He seemed fascinated by another conversation entirely.

"A madman," one of the exquisitely dressed gentlemen behind him was saying. "He's built some sort of mechanism that runs along a rail. Belches smoke and steam and makes an ungodly racket. He thinks people will want to ride in the thing!"

"Madness," agreed his companion.

"Worse than that, he expected me to put up three thousand pounds to lay rails across my land. As if I would soil my hands with such an investment."

"The gall!"

"Fools," muttered Richard.

Lydia gave him a sharp glance. "Do you think so?"

The two exquisites moved down the room still shaking their heads.

"They were talking about the steam locomotive," Emily said. "We saw . . ." Seeing Richard's expression, she broke off.

"Locomotive?" drawled Lydia. "What a very curious word." She looked Emily up and down. "Don't tell me you are interested in such things, Miss Crane."

Out of the corner of her eye, Emily saw Richard wince. It seemed he was right about the *ton*'s contempt for new inventions and change. Raising her chin, she said, "Very. I find them extremely interesting."

"How prodigious unfashionable of you," murmured Lydia mockingly.

Richard shifted from one foot to another.

"Locomotives will revolutionize the transport of

goods," Emily replied, recalling some of the things Richard had said when they viewed the new mechanism.

He turned to look at her.

"Laying the rails is a large expense, of course," she added.

"Why, Miss Crane, it sounds as if you have made a study of the subject," jeered Lydia.

"No. Merely listened with interest to people who really know. Steam power is changing all sorts of manufacturing, I understand."

"And fomenting riots among the weavers," retorted Lydia Farrell. "Do you care nothing for poor men's livelihood?"

"That is exactly why men of wealth and influence should be interested in such matters. Particularly those who care about their tenants and dependents. They can make certain the new inventions are used wisely." Richard was staring at her, she noticed uneasily. Probably she had made some mistake in what she said. She really knew next to nothing about steam power or anything to do with it.

"What a very novel idea," said Lydia coldly. She seemed displeased with the entire conversation.

"Every day I hear of some new device that will ease men's labor and aid their work," put in Richard quietly.

"Or put them out of work altogether," commented Lydia.

Replying, he spoke very slowly. "Not if it is done properly."

He looked astonished, Emily thought, as if he had

been struck by a notion so vast that he could hardly contain it.

"I wouldn't expect utopia just yet," was Lydia's sour reply.

Unexpectedly, Richard laughed. His cousin appeared to take this as an insult. "Would you excuse me?" she said. "I think your mother wants me."

Emily scarcely noticed her departure. She was transfixed by the joy and excitement in Richard's face. "What is it?"

"You. You are the most amazing creature."

The light in his hazel eyes shook her. She had to swallow before she could say, "What?"

"A few words, a phrase, and you cut through weeks of pondering and confusion."

"I . . . I don't understand." She couldn't think; she could hardly breathe with him gazing at her in that way.

Richard laughed again. "I know. That's the true beauty of it."

"Of what?" She had to smile, but she was also impatient to understand him.

"I will show you that," he replied with the same maddening obliquity. "In time, I will show everyone."

"Couldn't you just tell me now?"

"I haven't got it all worked out." His smile was tender. "Perhaps *you* should tell me."

"Lord Warrington!" But her protest was cut short by the arrival of the duchess, who was ready to depart.

EMILY JOINED HER AUNT in the carriage feeling exhilarated and bewildered. What had Richard meant? What had she done to make him so happy? She very much wanted to know that, she realized. She very much wanted to repeat the thing, whatever it was.

She opened her hands and looked down at the exquisite ring. She had no business wanting any such thing. Their engagement was a sham. This ring was a deception and would soon go back to him. She shouldn't be thinking this way.

"It is a lovely piece," said her aunt.

Emily started out of her reverie. Aunt Julia was also gazing at the ring.

"Perfect for your coloring," she added. "And very suitable." She looked regretful. "You know, I am sorry, Emily."

"Sorry?"

"I intended to find you a great match—brilliant even. I did everything I could." She looked bewildered. "Things just somehow . . . slipped out of control."

"It was not your . . ."

"Alasdair wasn't even here," murmured her aunt. "I just don't understand how it went so wrong."

You aren't taking into account the interference of a killer, Emily thought.

The duchess was gazing worriedly at Emily. "Lord Warrington is quite different since he returned to town. Not nearly so arrogant. Handsome, too." She grimaced. "But Emily, how will you live?" The last words came out almost as a wail.

Emily saw real concern in her aunt's eyes. For a

moment, Emily was tempted to tell her the truth. But she couldn't. "I am accustomed to a . . . gypsy existence," she said, trying to offer some comfort. "I've never had all the luxuries you take for granted. What you might see as hardship will not be so to me."

"But to have no assured income . . ." There was fear in the duchess's face.

"Well, I never have," answered Emily, suddenly feeling she understood her aunt better. "Never any significant amount, anyway. I'm used to dealing with the bailiffs."

"I always knew Olivia was mad," whispered her aunt.

Only the horror in her tone kept Emily from taking offense. "She's quite happy, you know."

"That's what I mean. I would be worrying every moment, terrified that . . . that everything would be at an end."

Emily felt an instant's true sympathy with her aunt. She had had such moments. But she had dealt with the fears, and they had passed, leaving her the stronger for it. She patted her aunt's hand. "You are in a far different position." She searched her mind for a distraction. "You never told me whether Lady Sefton granted vouchers to that girl you mentioned?"

The duchess appeared to gather herself. Her customary blend of dignity and reserve returned to her features. "I doubt it. The chit wore a silk ballgown cut down to her . . . ahem."

For just a moment, her aunt looked much more like her mother than usual. Emily smiled at her, and received a slightly sheepish smile in return. "If only she had had you to advise her, she would have been quite all right."

Aunt Julia looked surprised, then touched. "Do you think so, my dear?"

"Oh, yes."

The duchess cleared her throat. "Thank you."

RICHARD PACED from one end of the library to the other, his whole body vibrating with energy. It was as if every part of him had come awake. He would be one of those men Emily had described, part of the legion who helped a new age to be born. He wasn't wealthy, true. But he was intelligent, knowledgeable. He could persuade those who had money to use it wisely and well. He could bring the inventions he found so fascinating into the world in ways that made sense for the people already living there. It was the thing he had been searching for—a mission that could consume him.

Richard was flooded with gratitude to Emily. Somehow she had brought it together for him. In a few words, with her honesty and lack of pretension, she had made it all clear. She would understand, as no one else could, exactly how he felt now and the plans that were unfolding so quickly in his mind. He would go and see her, he decided. He longed to tell her everything, to exchange ideas and see the future opening out in this exciting new shape.

He was halfway to the door when he realized that he was picturing their meeting all wrong. He wanted to sweep her into his arms. He wanted to thank her in ways that were out of the question. He had been seeing the future as something they shared, something that involved far more intimate matters than inventions.

Some of Richard's excitement drained away. He stood in the middle of the room for a moment longer, then went to the desk and sat down. This wouldn't do. Emily Crane had never intended to be part of his future; and even if she had, he could give her nothing but genteel poverty and an empty name.

There was the thrill of a changing world, he argued silently. But that was his vision, not hers. Asking her to give up so much for an idea . . . Richard shook his head. That would be offering her the same sort of life her parents had given her. She deserved far more than that.

She deserved everything, Richard thought. She should never have to worry again.

His fists clenched, and the muscles in his jaw hardened. He had let things get out of hand. *Things?* inquired a sardonic inner voice. Richard clenched his teeth. He had let *himself* get out of hand. He had drifted somehow into . . . into feeling things he should not feel and thinking things that could not happen.

With a great effort of will, he relaxed, placing his hands flat on the surface of the desk. He must put Emily from his mind, and certainly from his plans for the future. His gaze encountered his never-finished letter to Elijah Taft. He needed to make some decision about his estates. Taft had sent a note saying as much, and suggesting he come down to Somerset and observe for himself.

He would do that, Richard decided. Though his true interests lay elsewhere, he couldn't neglect his inherited obligations. And it would be a very good idea to get out of town for a while, to put some distance between himself and a woman he could not have. A woman who had never said she wanted him. Yes, it was time to go away.

"SOMERSET?" said his mother when he informed her that evening. "I can't bear that house. Besides, it must have tumbled to pieces by now."

Richard pressed his lips together, suppressing a bitter comment.

"But you cannot go now, when Lydia is so stupidly insisting on leaving."

"My husband wants me home," said Lydia.

"I won't be left all alone," Richard's mother wailed. "After that dreadful scene at Herr Schelling's and . . . everything."

"You could come and visit us in Wales," Lydia suggested.

"Wales?" She said it as if the word were foreign to her.

"The countryside is beautiful at this time of year," offered Lydia.

"But the Season isn't half over," objected Lady Fielding.

"You can certainly stay for it," Richard assured her.

"But you will not," she accused.

He shook his head.

"I don't know what is wrong with you. You haven't shown a particle of interest in society since you returned." His mother looked from his face to Lydia's. The corners of her mouth turned down. "I think you are both extremely disobliging."

Lydia gave her a compassionate smile.

"Well, I *will* go to Wales then." She said it as if someone had dared her not to. "But Richard, you must escort us. I will not travel across the country all alone."

He might have mentioned the servants who would be with her, or the post boys and outriders. But he would concede this much. He could have a look at his property in Wales before going on to Somerset. It was out of the way, but if he meant to set things in order, that property must be included. "Very well. When do you want to go, Mother?"

Lady Fielding's mouth fell open.

Lydia looked surprised. She couldn't seem to accept the idea that he was a changed man.

"You will go?" his mother asked.

"I will escort you down to Wales. I shan't stay long."

"But you . . ."

"We have plenty of room," said Lydia.

Richard didn't bother to mention that he would be staying on his own acres. It would only provoke another protest from his mother.

"When will we leave?" wondered his mother. Now that her request had been granted, she seemed at a loss.

"You will have to pack," replied Lydia. "What about Wednesday?"

"Two days! I would never be able to . . ."

"I'll help you get your things together," Lydia soothed. "I know just what you'll need."

His mother looked stunned. Was she regretting her decision to abandon the delights of the Season? "Very well," she said. "Wednesday."

Back in his study, Richard drafted a new letter to Taft, detailing his travel plans and assuring the man that all would be settled when he came to Somerset. After that, there was nothing more to do but resolutely suppress his regret.

"He didn't mean anything by it," Emily told the cook.

"He called my ragout of beef a 'glutinous mishmash,'" countered the stout older woman, hands on her hips.

Emily wished, for perhaps the hundredth time in her life, that servants did not so relish repeating her father's intemperate remarks. If they had not told the cook . . .

"What is 'glutinous?'"

She wasn't about to answer that.

"And he overturned a perfectly good dish of oyster fritters."

And rather enjoyed seeing them rolling around on the tablecloth, Emily suspected. "He is an artist, you see. His feelings, er, run away with him. But he does not mean . . ."

"It's not what I'm used to."

Emily was sure it wasn't. She was a good cook,

highly recommended by Aunt Julia. No doubt she had worked only in calm, regulated households. "I know my father thinks your cooking splendid. He has said so." She hurried over this small white lie. "When his painting goes badly, he is out of sorts, you see. He needs to . . . to grumble. But he does not really mean it."

The cook considered this.

Emily watched her, hoping she wasn't going to give notice. "You know how gentlemen are," she ventured.

The cook sighed.

She was going to stay, Emily saw. She made a mental note to get her mother to compliment the dishes at dinner.

"I suppose they all have their little ways."

Emily nodded, though it was difficult to imagine other gentlemen with "ways" like her father's.

"We just have to get used to them."

"Thank you."

"I'd best be getting back to the kitchen." The cook turned, and gave a wordless exclamation at the sight of a figure looming in the doorway.

"They did not tell me you were occupied," said Richard, stepping farther into the parlor.

That was another thing, Emily thought as she rose and the cook sidled out. Their housemaid had picked up her father's free and easy manners, and let anybody in whenever they knocked.

"A domestic crisis?"

How long had he been standing there? "A misunderstanding merely."

"Ah."

He had been there a while, she concluded. She offered him a chair and sat down again herself.

Richard seemed about to speak, but he didn't.

Emily tried to think of something to say. She could ask a question about railroads or steam engines. But somehow, with him sitting across from her, handsome in his blue coat, she couldn't think of any.

"I came to tell you that I am going out of town," he said.

"Oh." She hadn't expected this.

"My mother has formed a desire to visit Wales. I am taking her to stay with my cousin there."

"Mrs. Farrell."

He nodded. "I have some business in the area as well. An estate my stepfather left me."

A fine excuse to spend more time with a relative he obviously found fascinating, Emily thought.

"I believe you will be quite safe in my absence," Richard added. "The attacks have stopped, and the culprits have apparently fled. You will continue to take care, of course."

"You seem eager to get away." The remark had escaped her lips before she knew it.

"It will be pleasant to see the countryside," was the bland reply.

Emily wanted to protest, but she had no grounds. Richard was not really her promised husband, despite the ring on her finger. She had no claims on him. "Wales is very beautiful, I understand."

"So they say." Before she could answer, he was rising. "I must go. My mother has all sorts of commissions for me."

Emily stood. "How long will you be gone?" she couldn't help asking.

"I'm not sure."

In other words, it was none of her affair, she thought. Stung, she did not offer her hand. "I hope you have a pleasant journey."

"Thank you." He hesitated a moment, then bowed and went out.

He would have all the time he wanted to talk with Lydia Farrell. Staying in the same house, they would naturally form an even closer connection. She had a husband, Emily thought. But from what she had gathered during her brief time in London, that often made no difference whatsoever.

OVER THE NEXT FEW DAYS, Emily found that she had completely lost interest in London. When her aunt offered to escort her to a ball, she could scarcely muster the energy to refuse. The streets seemed dirty and the amusements pallid. Despite the hordes of people, there was nothing to do in town. One sat about waiting for something to happen, but it never did. She would almost have welcomed a sign from Lord Warrington's attackers, but of course there was none.

Was the threat really over? Had Richard's obscure enemy given up and called off the vendetta? It seemed so. Nothing even slightly suspicious had occurred in days. When he returned to town, she would give him the ring back, and announce to the world that their engagement was at an end, Emily decided.

There was no reason to delay. And then . . . then she would get on with her life. This resolution provoked a small nod. It was very important that she get on with her life at once.

"Are you quite all right, Emily?" asked her mother at breakfast the following morning.

"Yes."

"Feeling well?"

"Perfectly."

"I thought you seemed rather silent."

"I don't really have anything to say just now, Mama."

Olivia Crane seemed pleased rather than disapproving of this bad temper. Indeed, the look she gave her daughter held equal parts of relief, gratification, and compassion. "When does Lord Warrington return to London?"

"I have no idea."

Another mother would certainly have reprimanded her offspring for impertinence. Olivia hid a smile instead.

Emily rose from the table and went into the front parlor, where she took up her station for another day of boredom. Her parents would be laying out their palettes, she thought. They would soon be deeply engrossed in their painting. What was she going to do? She must make a plan. She never had a proper plan. That was her problem.

But her mind remained blank when the question of the future arose.

She turned instead to the book she had gotten from the circulating library on new inventions and industries. The subject matter was more interesting than she had expected. She might have enjoyed reading it, except for the fact that every paragraph reminded her of Richard. She put the volume aside without regret when she heard the bell ring, followed by footsteps in the hall.

Sarah Fitzgibbon hurried in, waving aside the maid who would have announced her. "I must speak to you."

"Of course. I'm so glad to see . . ."

"There's something wrong."

Emily blinked. "Your parents? What . . . ?"

"No. They're fine. It's the Bruiser. He sent a messenger to Lord Warrington. When he found he was gone, he came to Dad."

"Sit down and tell me," commanded Emily.

Her friend sat. "The Bruiser heard that those two men, the ones you suspected of being the attackers, have gone into Wales. And they went in the company of someone very frightening."

Emily sat back, shaken. "Frightening to London toughs?"

"It's very odd," agreed Sarah. "But he heard it from one of their, er, lady friends. He seemed quite sure." She hesitated, biting her lower lip. "Lord Warrington went to Wales, didn't he?"

All Emily's faculties were painfully alert. She nodded. "When did they go?"

"That's what I don't know."

"It was today you heard this news?"

"Just now," replied Sarah. "I came right over, though Dad didn't want me to."

Emily sprang to her feet. "What if the killers are lying in wait for him?" Emily moved toward the door.

"I must get word to Lord Warrington at once." She hesitated, turned, then turned back again. "I must go after him."

"What could you . . . ?"

"We are working on this matter together!"

Sarah looked startled at her vehemence. She drew back slightly when Emily grabbed both her hands and added, "Thank you for telling me this. If only it is not too late."

"I don't think you should be—"

"Forgive me, I must go," Emily interrupted. "There is so much to do."

Sarah was beginning another protest as Emily swept out of the room. She stood still for several moments, frowning. Then she seemed to come to a decision. She contemplated it, nodded once, and also left the room.

EMILY FOUND HER FATHER in his studio. By great good luck he was not immersed in a painting, but rather was setting up a still life on a tabletop. He was humming, too, which was a good sign. "Papa," she said, rather loudly.

"Eh? Oh, yes, my dear? What do you think of these figs?" He held one up with the tips of his fingers. "That purple sheen along with the . . ."

"Very nice, Papa. But aren't you tired of painting fruit and flowers? And you have so little room here."

He acknowledged it with a look around the cramped studio, then put a hand on his heart. "I would make any sacrifice for my daughter's happiness."

"But I am not happy, Papa."

He looked astonished. "You aren't?"

Emily felt a twinge of guilt. Papa was so very easy to manipulate. But it was for a good cause. "I don't like London."

"You don't?"

She shook her head.

"I don't like it either."

"I want to go back to the country."

"But I thought . . . Olivia told me you should attend all these balls and other idiocy so that you could . . ."

"They're so dull, Papa."

Her father looked at her with pride. "Exactly so. I knew you were too much my daughter to like that sort of thing. We'll pack up and go home at once."

Emily gave him a brilliant smile. "Oh, thank you, Papa. But, I've been thinking, I should like to see some really dramatic country—to get the cramped streets of London out of my head."

"Dramatic?" he echoed, his attention truly caught now.

"I have heard that Wales is very beautiful. Mountain crags and torrents. Ancient trees and rock."

Her father's eyes grew distant. One could almost see pictures composing themselves in his head.

"Waterfalls," said Emily.

"We must go to Wales," declared her father. "At once. Today. I shall tell Olivia . . ."

"I'll tell her." She didn't want to risk a diversion. "I'll go right now."

"Good girl." He started putting tubes of paint in a wooden case. "Mountain crags," he muttered.

If Emily had expected opposition from her mother, she soon discovered her mistake. Olivia Crane seemed positively gleeful at the idea of packing up all their possessions and moving them on an instant's notice to the wilds of Wales. In any other mood, Emily would have noticed the sidelong looks and knowing smiles her mother gave her. But all of her faculties were concentrated on one goal—reaching Richard and saving him from whatever plot the killers had hatched.

SIXTEEN

RICHARD WATCHED the flames rise and fall in the wide kitchen fireplace of Morne. The kitchen was one of the few habitable rooms. He had a passable bedchamber as well, but the rest of the old house was barely furnished. Lydia had sent some of her servants over to scrub out the dust and cobwebs, all the while urging him to join his mother at her far more comfortable house.

He listened. There was the crackle of the fire, the rustling of a breeze outside, an occasional creak of ancient boards. But no human voices, no chattering or demands for attention. That silence let something inside Richard relax, let a tension he had scarcely

been aware of ease. He had grown accustomed to solitude in the jungle. He had regretted it most bitterly
then, but it had set down roots. He would need occasional doses of it from now on. He took a deep breath,
feeling as if his spirit had expanded to its full extent.
Here in this house he had neglected and ignored, he
felt a measure of content.

Here was something about the man he had become. Here was one trait to mark down as his own.
He savored it.

Then he smiled and rose to add wood to the fire.
These philosophical ruminations weren't much like
the old Richard either. Of course, the old Richard
wouldn't have spent half an hour in this primitive
place. It was hard to imagine what circumstances
would even have lured him to Wales.

Richard walked through the other rooms. The
walls and roof were tight; the windows, small and
mullioned, still kept out the weather. He suspected
that the old man who lived down the hill had kept an
eye on the place and made repairs. The way he had
spoken of Morne showed that he loved it.

Opening the front door, Richard looked out over
a narrow valley and the crags of mountains beyond.
Morne sat on the knee of another such range with a
view that went on for miles. It was beautiful, but not
the sort of land for anything other than sheep.

A rider approached along the rough lane that me-
andered up from the valley floor. Squinting against
the afternoon sun, he recognized Lydia. She waved,
and he lifted an arm in response, trying not to resent
her appearance. She was just trying to play the good
host.

"Hello," she said as she dismounted and looped her horse's reins around a post. "I just wanted to make sure that you were settled in all right."

"Very well. Will you come in? I can offer a mug of cider, if nothing else."

Looping up the skirts of her riding habit, she followed him into the kitchen. "Betty brought you supplies? If you need anything . . ."

"She did, along with offers to come round every day and cook them. I am perfectly satisfied with the arrangements."

Lydia looked around the nearly bare room. "You're certain?"

"Completely."

She gave him a rueful smile. "Well, you've said I mustn't bully you any more about staying with us, so I won't. But you know that any time you wish to . . ."

"I know."

"Yes." She put her riding crop on the long wooden table in the center of the kitchen, then picked it up again. She walked a few steps toward the fireplace, then turned back restlessly. "Actually, I came to talk with you about something."

He gestured toward one of the three wooden chairs, but she didn't notice.

"William and I have been thinking about it for a while."

Richard waited, curious. Lydia's husband had seemed to him a bluff, hearty man who thought very little.

"We wondered if you would sell this place to us."

The unexpectedness of the offer kept Richard silent.

"Now that you have had a chance to see it again," Lydia continued, "you must have realized that it is not particularly productive. But it borders our land, and we could use the extra grazing. We do not need another house, of course." She looked around the shabby room. "Another buyer would want a place to live." Her tone implied that Morne would never be livable.

"I hadn't thought of selling."

"You don't visit or pay the least heed to the place."

"I haven't," he acknowledged.

"Cash is always useful," she added diffidently.

There was no denying that. He could use the money—though he didn't expect it would be any great sum—to improve his Somerset acres. But his stepfather had left him this place. It was the only legacy he would ever have of the man he should have revered as a father. The only sign of respect he could show now was to value the gift. And on this visit he had found himself drawn to the wild landscape and the silences. "I don't think I want to let the place go."

Lydia looked surprised, and predictably displeased. "Why not?"

"I didn't properly appreciate it before. I want to get out into this country, explore."

"You could do that on any visit to Wales. There is no need to burden yourself with an estate."

"True. But as I said, I am beginning to like the place."

"I see."

"If I ever should decide to sell . . ."

"You will think of us, I hope." Her tone was brusque, and she moved toward the door as if impatient to end this conversation. Lydia strode out to her horse. She waved aside Richard's help and mounted at the block. She looked down at him for a moment before departing. "You're quite sure?"

He nodded.

Lydia flicked her horse with the riding crop and set off down the hill at a brisk pace. Watching her figure grow smaller with distance, Richard wondered at the visit. She had made rather a long ride to ask a question she could have put to him at any time during their journey. But she had wanted him to see Morne. She had thought he would be repelled at the dilapidation.

And so he would have been, not long ago. Lydia still thought of him as Lord Warrington, pink of the *ton* and perpetual annoyance. He wondered how long it would take for her to see that man was gone.

Richard stretched and breathed in the clear cool air. He decided to go out riding himself. The slant of light across the crags was golden and alluring.

EMILY RODE up the rough lane toward the low, steep-roofed house that she was almost certain must be Morne. This place matched the description she had been given in all particulars. She had meant to arrive in early afternoon, but the innkeeper's directions had failed her more than once today, and she had been thoroughly lost for more than an hour. She looked more closely, and didn't see any lights in the windows. What if Richard wasn't home?

Weariness weighed her down. There had been the hurried packing and the long jolting journey by coach. Settling on an inn had been the usual chaotic process, with her father ranging up and down stairs criticizing the accommodations. Then she had gone to Lydia Farrell's house, only to be told by a servant that Richard was not there. At least she had avoided encountering Lydia and Richard's mother, she thought as she reached the small yard before the house and found the mounting block.

There were no lights. Evening was blurring the edges of things, and she couldn't see a place to stable her horse. It was growing cool here in the mountains.

Emily rubbed her forehead. No doubt her father had discovered her absence by this time and was wreaking havoc in the village. She had no idea how to find her way back in the dark.

With a sigh, she pulled the long skirts of her riding habit over her arm and went to the front door. As she expected, there was no answer to her knock. She waited a moment, then knocked again. The only response was the call of an owl. Emily tried the latch. The door opened on a small entryway. "Lord Warrington?" she called.

There was no reply. But she did see a glimmer of light through a doorway at the back. Following it, she came into the kitchen, where the embers of a fire glowed and there were signs of habitation. Pulling off her gloves, Emily put logs on the fire and lit an oil lamp, filling the room with warm golden light.

She unpinned her hat and laid it on the table

beside her gloves. She was extremely hungry, having had nothing since the bread and cheese she took from the inn this morning. Searching the pantry, she found half a ham, some dried apples, a loaf of bread, and a crock of pickles. A jug of cider sat on the table. Emily put the apples in a pan of water on the hearth to soften and proceeded to make a meal with the rest. She was just thinking that it was too bad there was no sugar or cinnamon to put in with the apples when she heard sounds outside.

A male voice cursed as something fell with a clatter. A horse snorted. She had to find somewhere to put her horse, Emily thought, starting up guiltily. She would be hungry, too.

Old hinges creaked, and then there was the sound of footsteps behind the house. Somehow, they sounded angry. The back door burst open. Richard stood silhouetted in it, lamplight gilding his face and figure. He stared at her as if he couldn't believe his eyes. "What the devil are you doing here?"

Emily took a step forward. "There is something I must tell you."

Richard scowled. "I took the wrong trail coming back and was nearly lost in the mountains overnight. I'm tired. I'm hungry. My horse needs attention. You'll have to wait."

Years of dealing with her father had taught Emily that this wasn't the time for argument. Instead, when Richard lit a lantern and went back outside, she fetched her horse and led it around to the shed where he was tending his own mount. She was struggling to pull off the saddle when two strong arms suddenly enveloped her and lifted it from her hands. "Go in," he said roughly. "I'll be there directly."

Once again, she obeyed. In the kitchen, she cut ham and bread and poured a mug of cider. Checking the apples, she found them palatable and set them out in a bowl. Life with her father had also taught her that gentlemen listened much better when their stomachs were full.

Dinner was a silent affair. Emily had a bit of apple and bided her time. She could almost feel Richard's irritation fading with the food and the firelight. He even began to show that expression she had seen so often on her father's face—a mixture of sheepishness and stubbornness that meant he was sorry but wasn't going to apologize.

"What are you doing here?" he said finally.

"I came to warn you."

Richard frowned.

"Sarah came to me after you had left London and said those ruffians had gone to Wales."

His frown deepened.

"You aren't safe here," she insisted.

"You came all the way from London to tell me this?"

"I didn't want them to catch you unaware."

"You didn't come alone?"

"With my parents. Have you understood what I . . . ?"

"Where are they?" He looked around the kitchen as if someone might be hidden in the room.

"The killers?"

"Your parents."

"Oh. In the village, at an inn."

"Even they would not allow you to go out alone after dark."

"It wasn't dark when I left. I got lost. What do you mean, 'even they?' "

Richard stood. "I'll take you back there."

"Why aren't you listening to me?"

"You've told me nothing of consequence. Come along."

"Sarah is not a fool, and she thought it important."

"And did she tell you to come haring down here rather than sending a message?" Richard came to stand over her. "If there is danger here, all you have managed to do is put yourself in the middle of it. And then you ride out alone, lose yourself, generally behave like an idiot."

He was really angry, Emily saw. His hazel eyes glittered with it. Mustering all her dignity, she stood. He loomed over her, very large, and very close.

"You had promised not to go wandering about alone," he accused.

"That was in London."

"It applied to everywhere!"

"I was only thinking of warning you. I . . . I forgot."

Richard grasped her upper arms, his fingers digging into her flesh. He shook her slightly. "Forgot?"

"The attacks in London had stopped."

"So you came down here where you think they will begin again."

"You were here!" The words came out with such emotion that Emily herself was surprised. They seemed to stun Richard. He stared at her. She could

hear him breathing. His grip on her arms tightened.
And then he pulled her closer and kissed her, hard.

Emily was too shocked to react for a moment. He
had been shouting at her, and now suddenly his lips
were crushing hers. She pulled back. But even as she
thought to struggle, the kiss changed. It grew softer.
His mouth moved on hers, coaxing, instructing. The
demand was still there, but it beguiled and taunted
her, sought to lure her into matching it.

Richard's hands slid down to her waist. He pulled
her against him, every hard line of his body joining in
the kiss somehow, which went on and on overwhelming her senses. Emily found her hands slipping under
his coat and along the fine fabric of his shirt over his
ribs. She gave herself up to the strength of his embrace, melting into the contours of his body so naturally it amazed her. She hadn't understood that a kiss
could be so wildly intoxicating.

She felt his heart pounding to match her own.
Her fingertips explored the muscles of his back, her
lips parted under his coaxing and her senses swam.

Richard raised his head and looked down at her.
He blinked as if dazed, then grimaced. "Oh, God."

She wanted him to kiss her again, Emily realized.
She pressed closer, and he groaned. "We are engaged," she murmured.

He gave a little laugh. Then, as if he couldn't
help himself, bent to capture her lips again. Emily
gave herself up wholeheartedly to the kiss, following
where he led. His mouth was warm and sure. His
hands evoked promises of delight she had never
dreamed of. She felt weak with yearning and charged
with energy at the same time. He had stirred a sense

of sweet urgency that felt likely to carry her completely away.

Richard ripped them apart. "No," he said.

Emily's hands were reaching for him. She pulled them back.

"This won't . . . do." He was breathing hard.

So was she, Emily noticed. Her knees were trembling, too.

"I have to get you out of here."

Without conscious thought, Emily took a step toward him. Her feet tangled in the long skirts of her riding habit, and she stumbled. Richard caught her, off balance, and they both went down in a flurry of broadcloth.

She landed on top of him, clinging. And then he was kissing her again, crushing her to him as if afraid she would escape. She surrendered to his lips gladly, shifting so that her knees rested on the floor to either side so that she could press closer. When she felt his hands through the cloth running up her thighs, she shivered with pleasure.

But they closed on her waist to lift her away from him. He thrust her upright, then stood himself, moving around the kitchen table so that it separated them. "I'm going to saddle the horses."

"We'll never find the way back to the inn in the dark," she pointed out breathlessly.

"Yes, we will." He moved abruptly.

In the same instant the window behind him shattered and a bullet whined between them to explode in the plaster wall. Richard dove, catching her in his arms as he hit the floor just as the other window erupted, showering them with bits of leaded glass.

Richard started to crawl along the floor, pulling her with him. They wormed their way into the windowless hall, where he stood, yanking her upright.

There were voices outside. Emily couldn't tell how many, though it seemed like more than two. And they seemed to come from all sides of the house.

Richard ran to the front door and dropped a wooden bar into place across it. "Not that it will keep them out," he muttered. His face showed intense concentration, and perhaps anger, but not a trace of fear.

The hinges of the kitchen door creaked, then immediately fell silent. Richard put an arm around Emily's waist and swept her silently down the hall and into a room at the opposite corner of the house. At a window he listened intently before pushing the casement open. Emily heard branches scrape softly as it moved.

Richard listened again, then leaned out the window. In the next instant he was pushing himself through it, his shoulders sticking briefly in the small opening. Once out, he turned and practically lifted Emily through. He pushed the casement shut and crouched beside her.

They had come out into a thicket of some kind. In the moonlight she could see that the bushes had grown into a mound, and dying branches in the center had broken off to leave a sort of vegetative cave.

Richard grasped her shoulder and pointed. Emily nodded and started to crawl in the direction indicated. She stopped briefly to hike her long skirts out of the way. Richard's fingers encircled her ankle as she did, sending a thrill through her despite the danger. And then they were both moving on hands and knees through a dark tunnel of underbrush away from the beleaguered house.

There were occasional shouts behind them. Once, a flurry of shots made Emily falter. But the sounds gradually faded as they drew farther away. And though her knees were being lacerated and her hands torn, she didn't consider stopping. It was obvious the killers had struck again, and there was no doubt about the outcome if they found them.

SEVENTEEN

CROUCHING IN A tangle of underbrush in the darkness, Richard listened for sounds of pursuit with all the intensity he had learned in the jungle. He heard a hunting owl, a whisper of breeze, the trickle of water in the gully below. He heard the rapid breathing of the woman kneeling next to him. They had been working their way steadily uphill, as fast as they could manage under the circumstances, and it had been taxing.

He listened. He didn't hear voices, or hoofbeats. It seemed that they had eluded the attackers for now. But they had to get farther from the house before daylight, and confuse the trail.

They began to move cautiously along the slope. Emily made no protests, thought Richard; no sign of tears or the fear she must be feeling. He hadn't been wrong about her—pluck up to the backbone, someone to count on.

He was shaken by a tide of feeling that kept him motionless. He had tried to run. He had put the width of a country between them. When he had felt the bond with her deepening in London, he had fled. It was the only honorable thing to do. Their sham engagement must be ended, his internal judge pronounced. He had to let her go before things became even more complicated.

But she had come after him, he protested silently. She had worried about him. Of course he hadn't been able to resist. No man could have resisted that tone in her voice, the delicate glory of her hair and eyes and that delectable body.

He heard echoes of her soft murmur—they were engaged. Engaged in chasing assassins the judge replied, and nothing more, as he well knew. Taking advantage of their agreement was not the act of a gentleman, even if her response had been so warm and eager that it nearly drove him mad to remember it.

Emily stopped and waited. No doubt she was looking back at him, wondering at his stillness. Richard started after her.

He steered downward now, with a ridge between them and the house. Near the bottom, the gully grew steeper, and he signaled for Emily to stop. Worming his way forward, he came to an overhang that dropped sheer to the small stream running through the bottom. The moon was fully up now, and its gleam on the water showed him only empty countryside. There was nothing to do but risk it.

He swung over the lip of the overhang and hung by his hands briefly. When he let go, he fell only a few feet to packed sand. Emily was already looking down at him. He made a motion and held out his arms. With only a moment's hesitation, she jumped into them.

It was like catching an armful of steel and velvet. He held her against his chest for a moment, relishing the feel of her slender strength. Then he set her down on the sand and bent to whisper in her ear. "We need to obscure our trail. We'll walk in the stream."

She nodded. The moonlight frosted her hair and gave her skin a pale sheen. She looked directly back at him with a clear confidence. She was relying on him to get her out of this. She seemed to have no doubt at all that he would. That was far more daunting than simply saving himself had ever been.

She went over to the stream and Richard used a branch to sweep away their footprints as he moved after her. The water was shallow, fortunately, but lined with rocks and pebbles. They would have to wear their boots, and soak them. There was no other way to navigate such treacherous footing.

Richard prepared to step in, then noticed that Emily was holding up the trailing skirts of her riding habit with one hand. The extra cloth would hamper her damnably if they had to run. He knelt beside her and began to cut away the hem with his penknife, trimming the skirt well above her ankles. After one small sound, she turned to allow him to reach the other side.

When he finished, he rolled the cloth into a tight cylinder and shoved it into his pocket with the knife. It wouldn't do to leave it for their pursuers to find. Then he retrieved the branch broom, which would also alert hunters, and stepped into the stream.

The water was cold seeping through his boots, but not icy. They could probably manage it for quite a while. Waiting for Emily to go ahead where he could keep an eye on her, Richard scanned the walls of the gully once more. They were visible here, and vulnerable. But he still heard nothing other than natural sounds. By daylight, he intended to be far away, leaving no track to follow.

They moved through the night, splashing as little as possible, following the meanderings of the streambed. Richard estimated that two hours had passed when the gully began to narrow and the sound of falling water came to his ears. A little way ahead, the stream fell about ten feet to a pool before continuing.

He surveyed the dim scene. The gully widened and flattened, offering less cover. The moon was descending; soon their light would be gone. It was time to go to ground.

He held out his hand. Emily took it without hesitation, her fingers small and cold. Yes, he thought, she would have fought at his side through the jungle. She would keep going without complaint until she dropped of fatigue. He squeezed her hand in reassurance. She smiled up at him, and his heart faltered momentarily before beating faster. He let go.

Taking advantage of the slanting rays of the moon, he picked a way across the stony incline that caused the waterfall. It steepened ahead, suggesting the possibility of caves, which riddled this country-side. The moon had nearly set before he found one, and it was a shallow cup above head height in the rocky wall. Not ideal, Richard thought, but it was going to have to do. Deep darkness was just ahead and Emily must be exhausted.

Reaching up, he hooked his hands over the rim of the cave. He groped for a foothold in the cliff and heaved himself up. The depression was scarcely ten feet deep, he saw then. But it was dry, and there were no signs of animal inhabitants. Also, it faced west. Sunrise would not reveal its recesses to the world. He knelt at the edge and held out his hands for Emily's, half-pulling, half-balancing her as she made her way up. "We'll stay here till dawn," he murmured.

She nodded and sank down inside the cave, her shoulders drooping and her head down. After a few moments, she tugged at one of her wet boots.

"Let me." He knelt and pulled off first one, then the other. "We should try to get your stockings dry, at least," he said very softly.

Emily half-turned away from him, embarrassed he thought, and reached under her skirts to unfasten the stockings. She slipped them off quickly, shivering a little at the night air on her bare feet.

Richard took the cloth torn from her skirt out of his pocket and began to dry her feet. With a small sound of protest, she pulled the cloth away and did it herself. He picked up the wet stockings and hung them over a projecting bit of stone, knowing that they wouldn't actually dry by daylight

"Shall I help you with your boots?" she murmured.

Wild laughter bubbled up in Richard's chest, almost impossible to choke back. She had sounded so matter-of-fact—as if they often removed each other's boots in the dead of night, in the back of beyond while men stalked them with murder on their minds.

"Are you all right?"

"Yes," he managed. He pulled off his boots and stockings, hanging them next to hers. He took the piece of cloth and dried his feet. She had tucked hers under her skirts, he saw, rather envying the source of warmth.

"What will we do in the morning?" she asked quietly.

"Figure out where we are, and head for the nearest house or village, someplace with enough people to make an attack impossible. My cousin's house, by choice."

"We're lost now, aren't we?"

"In the dark, yes. But by daylight, I can get my bearings." The problem was, it was several miles to any safe place, and their pursuers would certainly be mounted. "See if you can sleep a little."

"Are you going to sleep?"

"I'll keep watch. I'm used to it."

She was silent. After a little while, she leaned back against the wall of the cave and appeared to relax.

Richard watched the slope below and listened. The moon was gone now, and there was little to see.

But he could hear night sounds. He could test the breeze for scents. There was no danger on the wind just now. He thought Emily had dropped off, and was fighting his own drowsiness, when she suddenly spoke very softly.

"When you were first lost in South America, were you frightened?"

He turned toward her voice, but he couldn't see her in the dark. Briefly, he debated his answer. He didn't want to make her feel any worse. But he couldn't offer Emily anything but the truth. "Terrified," he replied. "The closest I'd ever been to wilderness was a foxhunt."

She gave a little spurt of laughter, quickly stifled.

"I'd never even been in at the kill," he added, remembering the old Richard with something near disbelief. That man had receded so far that he seemed even less than a memory.

"Were you wet?"

The question made him smile. "Soaked in salt water and cursing my fate. I spent most of a year wet. In the jungle, it rained every few hours." He heard her small shiver. "It was hot, though, so one didn't mind as much. Are you cold?"

"A little."

They seemed doomed to huddle together outside the confines of civilization, Richard thought wryly. First a shed full of hay, and now this. They were coming down in the world. He didn't know how he would bear being so close to her, but he couldn't let her shiver alone. Shifting, he slid an arm around her and pulled her to his side.

Emily nestled in as if she had done so a thousand

times. Despite the rough surroundings, and their peril, Richard's body began to demand things he had no intention of giving it. He could control himself, he insisted.

Emily's head burrowed into his shoulder. He could feel the curve of her breast like soft flame on his ribs. She trusted him, he thought, with her honor, with her life.

The mixture of fear for her, self-doubt, and determination that Richard felt then was more intense than any emotion he had ever suffered. He wanted more than anything to deserve that confidence. The thought of failure was intolerable. Failure meant that Emily Crane would disappear from the face of the earth.

She stirred a bit, like a cat getting comfortable. Her breathing grew more regular. She had fallen asleep in his arms. She had given herself up completely to his vigilance.

The determination strengthened, filling his consciousness, steeling him against the voice of doubt. He would see her safe. He would do whatever that required. And any man who stood in his way . . . would regret it to the end of his days, which might be brief indeed.

Emily sighed in her sleep. She turned, and her arm fell across his chest. He wanted her, Richard thought. He had never wanted anything half so much. But that was irrelevant. He could keep his desires in check. His right hand, resting on the cave's stone floor, clenched.

At least sleep was out of the question, he thought sometime later. The unceasing demands of his body were keeping him wide awake on his watch. He dared a feather touch on Emily's hair. But the result was enflaming rather than soothing, and he stopped at once. He must think about tomorrow, plan their moves. He wouldn't rescue her by sheer desperate longing.

With a massive effort of will, Richard shifted his attention to the future, and ways they might evade their attackers and find their way out of the wilderness.

DAWN ARRIVED by imperceptible stages, a slow diffusion of pearly light. Mist pooled in low places and drifted in veils among the crags. It would hamper their attackers, Richard thought, but it was a disadvantage for them as well. It would be much harder to get their bearings or travel in a consistent direction. Sound would be deceptive, too, difficult to pinpoint.

Emily woke. After a moment's disorientation, she smiled at him in a way that made his pulse jump. Part of him wished fiercely that she had never come here from London, but another part exulted in her presence by his side. "Are you all right?" he asked quietly.

The smile turned rueful. "I'm hungry."

"I'm afraid the servants have neglected to set out breakfast."

"How careless of them." She reached up and took her stockings from the stone, wrinkling her nose as she felt them. "Still damp. But I suppose it is only what one should expect when one is being chased by murderers."

Richard smiled. "It doesn't lend itself to luxuries." He watched her check her boots. "Are you ever afraid?"

Her azure eyes met his directly. "I'm terrified right now. But I've found it doesn't help in the least to give way to emotion on these occasions."

"Having been so often chased by murderers?"

"They were usually after Papa," she admitted. "But it's hard to tell the difference when you're small. Perhaps there isn't any."

Some weeks ago, he might have laughed at this. This morning, he couldn't. Indeed, he felt an unaccustomed tightness in his throat.

"Not that most of them would have actually murdered him," Emily added softly. "Well, maybe one or two."

"You haven't deserved the life you've had. You should be given every luxury. You should be cared for and cosseted, and never have to worry."

Emily didn't seem to know what to say. Her cheeks flushed, and she gave him a doubtful look. "I'd settle for a cup of hot coffee," she replied finally.

Richard called himself to order. Turning away, he put on his stockings and boots and let himself down from the cave into the mist below. It swirled about his shoulders, completely obscuring the ground. "We'll have to get above this," he muttered.

"What?" Emily's head appeared in the opening.

He gestured for silence, then helped her down. Keeping a hand on the cliff face, Richard moved away from the sound of the waterfall.

It was rough going at first. They couldn't see their feet, or obstacles that tripped them up. But finally the ground began to rise and the mist to recede. Richard judged that they had been walking about an hour when they reached the top of a ridge and looked out over a sea of fog broken by similar heights. Very conscious of their exposure, he led her down a little, until they were mostly hidden, and then went over his sketchy mental map of the area.

"Do you know where we are?" whispered Emily.

"We left the house going east," he told her softly. "The stream flowed northeast. We are still on my land, I believe. My cousin's estate borders it on the north, so that is the direction we want. The difficulty will be keeping to it in this weather."

"How far?"

"Six or seven miles." In a straight line, he added to himself; not taking into account the mountainous nature of the country.

"That isn't far." She attempted a cheerful smile. "And it will be hard for them to find us in the mist."

"As long as we're quiet."

They set off at the best pace they could manage and were soon struggling down slopes into narrow ravines and up the opposite sides. Now and then, one of them would send a stone rattling into the depths, making him wince. His only consolation was that their pursuers would have the same problem. At intervals, he stopped and listened intently, but the morning passed without any sign.

Around noon, the fog began to dissipate. Richard left Emily resting beside a trickle of water and climbed up to reconnoiter. He didn't stand on the peak this time, but crouched among some boulders to take bearings.

He could see the country spread out now, mist covering only the lowest places. Some of the hills would be landmarks to a native, but they told him next to nothing. All they could do was continue going north. When he judged that they had gone far enough, he would cast about for the Farrells' house. He made his way carefully back down. But when he reached the place where he had left Emily, it was empty.

Richard had to bite back a cry. His first instinct was race down the ravine shouting her name. It took him a long moment to control it, and to quell the panic surging up inside. Clenching his fists, he mastered his fear.

He knelt, searching the ground. It was stony and showed no footprints. However, the vegetation wasn't disturbed. There was no sign of a struggle. Nor was there evidence that anyone had forced his way through the bushes upstream. Setting his jaw, he walked down, all his senses straining.

He found her barely ten yards away. A curve of rock had hidden her, and she was standing still, making no sound. She turned as he approached and started to speak. "Look at this . . ."

Richard grabbed her upper arms and shook her. "Don't ever move from the place where I've left you," he hissed.

She blinked, startled. "I only . . ."

"And keep your voice down!"

Emily took a breath, her eyes wide on his. "I only went a few steps," she whispered.

He couldn't help shaking her again. "You are to stay exactly where I put you."

"But it was . . ."

He started urging her upstream. "I chose a spot sheltered by an overhang and concealed by bushes. If I had been taken above, you might have stayed hidden."

Emily looked uneasy. She struggled in his grasp. "I'm sorry. But I noticed this odd . . ."

"It doesn't matter what you noticed."

She jerked away from him and took a step back. "My observations are worthless?"

Richard's anger was ebbing now that he knew she was safe. "No. But you shouldn't go off alone. If we were separated, I couldn't protect you . . ."

The stubborn look didn't entirely fade from her face, but it moderated. "All right. The next time I will wait until you come back."

He nodded. His pulse had returned to normal. "We should move on."

"Look at this first." She led him back a bit and pointed to the wall of the ravine.

Richard looked, frowned, and moved closer. Reaching up, he broke off a loose piece and rubbed it in his hand.

"Isn't that coal?" Emily asked. Her reading had not been entirely in vain.

"It certainly looks like it."

"It gets wider as it goes down the hill." She pointed to the broadening seam of dark rock.

He walked a little way, seeing that she was right. Farther along, most of the cliff face was black—here, on his own land. He reached up again to verify the evidence of his eyes. Coal was the lifeblood of the inventions that so fascinated him.

"Do you . . . ?"

A clatter of stones sounded in the distance, followed by the whinny of a frightened horse. All of Richard's faculties focused in an instant, calculating the direction of the noise, the terrain, the nearness of the threat. Demanding silence with a savage gesture, he scanned the stony ground. They had left no sign.

He moved quickly downstream, drawing Emily along with him. A man called out, too far away for Richard to catch the words. Using every ounce of skill he had gained as a castaway, Richard guided Emily north.

EIGHTEEN

EMILY TRIPPED over a scatter of rocks and staggered. Richard caught her arm and urged her on. They had been moving fast and quietly down a series of gullies for what seemed like hours. There had been no further sounds behind them. They didn't even know if the one they'd heard was their attackers, Emily thought. But they couldn't afford to assume it wasn't. She was coming to the end of her strength, but didn't dare ask that they rest.

She watched Richard moving ahead of her like a wild creature. In the last few hours something about him had changed.

He turned to check on her. His hazel eyes seemed

exultant as well as intent, lit with a kind of triumphant determination. He frightened her a little. Since they had fled his house together, his presence had seemed to guarantee safety. Until now.

"We must keep going," he said.

When Emily nodded, he took off again with the loping stride that looked so effortless and was so hard to match. Emily followed as best she could. The sun was past noon, and the air had grown unseasonably warm as the last of the mist burned away. She had taken off the snug jacket of her riding habit, but even carrying it over her arm, she was hot. Her blouse clung to her back, and her still damp boots were a penance.

Up ahead, Richard had stopped. He was listening again, she saw. She heard nothing but natural sounds—birds, the rustle of leaves. By the time she reached him, he was moving again. It had been that way all day. He drew ahead, waited for her to catch up, and then set off again, having had a rest, Emily thought resentfully, while she never got a moment's respite. A trickle of sweat ran down her neck. It was as if some other personality had taken over in him.

She stumbled again, this time knocking two rocks together with a sharp crack. Richard whirled, crouched for battle. His eyes took in every shadow. His lips were drawn back in something very like a snarl. Emily went dead still. For a moment, she was convinced that some terror menaced her from behind.

He straightened slowly, then he came back to where she stood. "I . . . I kicked a stone," she admitted as he loomed over her.

He bent toward her. Emily swallowed. But it was the old familiar Richard who said, "You're tired, I know. I'm searching for a place where we can rest." He gestured at the open valley around them. "This is too exposed."

"I'll be more careful." She got a glimpse of compassion in his face before he moved off again.

Emily trudged on, watching where she put her feet and taking particular care around stones. The sun started down the western sky. The emptiness in her midsection made her a bit dizzy. She had never been so hungry in her life.

At last, she had to stop. She would sit for just a few minutes. She looked ahead for Richard, to signal her intention, and saw nothing but empty landscape.

She rubbed her eyes. The valley was narrowing. There were walls of stone on either side, a few trees and brush ahead. But it wasn't so thick that she couldn't see clearly to the end of the declivity. Richard was gone!

Emily's heart began to pound. Her mouth went dry, and her legs trembled. She hadn't known what fear really was until now, she realized. Richard's presence had been sustaining her in ways she hadn't begun to understand.

How could she have lost him? She turned in a circle. There were no side trails. He couldn't have turned off without her noticing. Had he fallen? Was he hurt? Frantically, she ran forward, glancing left and right, watching for a hidden obstacle, something he might have fallen into or behind. There was nothing. Had he been captured? Were their pursuers waiting to pick her off as well?

Emily stopped and listened as she had seen Rich-ard doing. She heard nothing helpful. Clasping her shaking hands together, she tried to think what to do. Keep searching, she thought. She had to find him.

Some sound made her look up. Richard was standing not five yards from her, gesturing for her to come along.

Emily gaped at him. One minute, she had been alone; the next he had reappeared like an apparition. She must be going mad. Relief and bewilderment overwhelmed her. Her legs gave way and she sank to the rocky ground, shaking.

Richard rushed over. "Have you hurt yourself?"

She managed to shake her head.

"I've found a place to rest." He took her arm and pulled her up.

Leaning against him, Emily walked. This was how they had met, she thought fuzzily; only then she had supported him.

"It isn't far," he assured her.

His arm was steady around her. Emily let herself relax.

They were heading straight for the wall of the valley. It towered over their heads at this point and was nearly sheer. Had he climbed that cliff, and then somehow jumped down when she wasn't looking?

"This way." Richard guided her right up to the wall of rock, around a projecting bit, and *into* the cliff. "Turn sideways. It's narrow."

There was a crack about two feet wide through the whole mass of stone, Emily realized. You couldn't see it unless you stood in exactly the right spot behind a thicket. The fissure seemed to go very far back. She couldn't see the end.

"How did you find this?" she murmured, astonished.

"An unlikely coincidence. A wren flew in just at the moment I was looking that way," Richard told her. "No one will find us here."

The opening was just wide enough to allow passage.

Stone scraped Emily's back.

"This is the narrowest part. You have to squeeze through."

She wriggled a bit, and was through. Richard had more difficulty, but he was soon behind her again. Emily saw light ahead and walked faster. When she emerged from the dimness of the fissure, she gasped at the scene that opened before her.

The crack widened to form an oval the size of a ballroom. Trees grew thickly around the edges, shading a small pool in the center fed by a spring trickling over a slab of stone. Shafts of sunlight gilded the leaves and glowed in the water. The earth was cool and carpeted with ferns.

"Help me move this," said Richard.

Turning, Emily saw that he was pushing a boulder toward the opening. She lent a hand, and it rolled into place, blocking the way. Richard picked up a smaller rock and set it on top. She helped him make a small pile, and soon they had the passageway effectively closed.

"The trees hide us from above," he said. "But we must be very quiet. If we are heard, they can find their way here."

She nodded, already walking under the trees toward the water. Cupping her hands, she drank from the spring. Then she splashed the clear liquid over her face and neck, sighing at the wonderful feel of it. She pulled off her boots and stockings and sat on a rock at the edge of the pool to dangle her feet in it. It was heavenly. But it wasn't enough. Emily turned to see what Richard was doing.

He was watching her with a smile. "Go ahead," he said. "I'll sit here." And he sat on a rock with his back turned, facing the blocked entry.

Emily hesitated, but the lure of the water was irresistible. With another look at Richard's back, Emily began to unbutton her blouse.

She shed her clothes quickly and slid into the pool. The water slid over her skin like silk, washing away the dirt of the journey and even, it seemed, some of the aches and bruises. It made her feel charged with energy, as if she could swim for miles, leap like a salmon, or flip like an otter.

She ducked under and shook out her hair under the surface. Coolness enveloped her head. She spread her arms and swooped back up, breaking the surface in a scatter of golden droplets. An even brighter glint drew her eye to Richard's ring on her finger. It was the only thing on her body at this moment.

She glanced quickly at him. He sat as before, turned away. Emily experienced an odd qualm of disappointment, immediately dismissed. She swam a few strokes to the edge of the pool, turned and swam back. It was as if they had entered another world through that narrow passage in the cliff.

Something touched her foot. Emily gave a startled cry and jumped onto a rock slanting into the pool. Gazing into the water, she saw a glint of tiny fish, and felt foolish.

"What is it?"

Emily looked up to find Richard on his feet, facing her, poised for rescue.

The universe seemed to stand still. Emily didn't feel the slight breeze on her body or the water dripping from her hair. She couldn't move. She was conscious only of Richard a few yards away.

The tension in his face and stance slowly drained away. His hands dropped to his sides. His eyes stayed on her as if he was helpless to shift them. She couldn't read the expression in them. She had never seen it before.

A bird called. Emily started and grabbed her skirt, holding it up before her like a curtain. "It was nothing," she stammered. "A fish. It startled me."

Richard turned his back. He stood there, rigid, giving no sign of what he felt.

She had spoken too loudly, Emily realized, not to mention standing there like a stick without anything on.

Richard folded his arms. Every ounce of his attention appeared to be focused on the pile of stones blocking the entrance. He was keeping watch, the pose seemed to say, not squeaking at shadows and possibly bringing their enemies down on them.

Emily yanked on her creased, stained riding habit. It had been a silly mistake, she acknowledged. But she wasn't accustomed to bathing outdoors. There was no call for him to be so superior about it.

She marched over to Richard. "Your turn," she

whispered. "I'll keep watch." She would show him that she could be as responsible as he.

He stared down at her, his hazel eyes hot.

Emily took a step closer. He moved quickly back. "Go," she murmured. Commandeering the rock, she sat down in his place, facing the cliff.

There was a period of silence. Emily was acutely aware of his gaze on her back. At last, she heard him walk away. There was another silence, which seemed very long, before she caught a quiet splash and knew that he had gone into the pool.

Emily felt a brief glow of satisfaction. He had succumbed to this small indulgence. He wasn't immune. She heard water ripple against rock, the sound of swimming. Unbidden, her imagination began to build a picture. It grew more and more detailed, filling her senses until she was conscious of nothing but the liquid sounds behind her and the images in her mind. Her cheeks reddened. Had he done this when she was in the water?

Without realizing it, she had inched around on the rock. She was perpendicular to the cliff now. Shocked, she started to turn back. But splashing stopped her. Emily bent her head, letting her damp hair hang down along her face. Twisting her head slightly, she sneaked a look at the pool.

Richard had just climbed out. He stood at the edge, shedding water like dripping gold. His body was dappled with shadow from the overhanging trees, and it was gloriously formed—broad shoulders, lean muscled arms and legs, a deep chest that narrowed to . . .

He raised his head and caught her looking.

Heat flooded Emily's face, washing down her neck to prickle over her whole body. She was transfixed by his unwavering stare. Even if she turned now, pretended she had been looking in quite another direction, it wouldn't matter. He knew. And she didn't want to turn away. She wanted to keep looking. She wanted to memorize the contours of his body. Remembering his kisses at the beginning of this journey—so long ago it seemed now—she realized she wanted even more.

Richard simply stood there. He didn't reach for his clothes. He didn't seem to breathe, though Emily's breath was rapid. It was as if he was waiting for a sign. She had the sudden sense that he would follow whatever lead she gave. This moment, full of portent, was in her hands.

She found herself on her feet, facing him, unclear how she had gotten there. Her body seemed to have made the decision on its own. She walked to the opposite side of the pool from where Richard was standing, following her with his eyes. Quickly, she slipped off her riding habit once again and stepped into the water. Her pulse was pounding. Part of her was silently shrieking at her temerity. With the water softly lapping about her shoulders, she looked at Richard again. A tremor of nervousness shook her. What if he . . . ?

In one swift movement, he returned to the pool. In another instant, he had her in his arms, his lips warm and urgent on hers, nothing between them but a film of water.

The flood of sensation was dazzling. Emily felt him along every inch of her skin. His kiss made her dizzy as they floated together. His hands on her back made her shiver. Her arms crept around his neck as his mouth coaxed and enflamed hers. They sank slowly beneath the surface, hardly noticing the water close over their heads.

The kiss was endless. It took her breath away even more than the liquid atmosphere. It seemed that she had never experienced physical sensation before. Nothing that had happened to her body up to now had had this intensity, this irresistible demand.

With one kick of his powerful legs, Richard brought them up again. When they broke the surface, he pulled Emily toward the rocks at the edge of the pool. But she slipped out of his arms and dove, twisting around behind him, touching the back of his knee fleetingly before darting away.

He came after her at once. In the small pool, they circled and danced. He caught her once from the back, letting his hands slide up and cup her breasts, pulling her back against him so that she felt his arousal unmistakably. His fingers teased her into gasping before he let her go again and arced away through the water. She pursued him then, slipping up from below to brush along the length of him, evading his hands by an inch as hers moved featherlight over his skin.

At last, though, he caught her and crushed her to him in another shattering kiss. Emily gave herself up to it completely, and it carried her to a level where she ached for more. As if he knew, Richard lifted her out of the pool and carried her to a shaded bank of ferns. Sinking down beside her, he began to drop soft kisses over her whole body until she vibrated with longing.

She pushed her fingers through his brown hair and down over his wide shoulders. Tugging at his arm, she brought the kisses back to her lips, holding him close, reveling in the things he was making her feel.

His knee slid between hers, and his hand moved upward along the tender skin of her inner thigh. It stopped a bit above her knee, and his kiss deepened. She was drowning in it when his hand moved a little farther, then stopped again. Emily trembled with anticipation so intense it astonished her. Richard's lips strayed to her neck, her breast. He made her gasp again. Then his hand moved up a little, and stopped.

She shifted to encourage him. He gave a low laugh and captured her lips again. She pleaded with her body, curling one leg around his, pressing closer. And at long last, his fingertips caressed the aching center of her desire.

Emily went rigid with pleasure. His kiss, his strong body against hers, the overwhelming sensations he was drawing from her, all of it combined into an urgency like nothing she had felt before. She would have cried out if he had freed her mouth. But he kept it for his own as he drove her wild with longing.

It built and built until she knew nothing but him. They were rising; he was carrying her into unimaginable places. It built to the unendurable. And then shattered into glorious pieces blinding as lightning flashes.

Richard shifted, and she felt him inside her. She clung and moved with him, still caught in the waves of passion he'd evoked. He took her lips again, moving faster. She felt the urgency driving him and exulted. She had the same power as he; she could wipe out the universe for him as well. He reached a crescendo, crushed her in his arms for heartbeats, and relaxed against her.

Emily listened to his breath rasp. She felt the pounding of his heart and the sheen of sweat that coated them. She felt her pulse gradually slow and the world seemed to slow with it. The sun had dipped behind the cliff to the west, throwing their refuge into shadow. Above, the sky was still blue, but the ferns wore a cloak of evening. Birds called in the trees. A pungent green scent rose from the ferns crushed under them.

Tired from days of unaccustomed exertion, Emily nestled into Richard's arms and dozed.

RICHARD RAISED HIMSELF on one elbow and looked down at Emily, sleeping innocently as a wood nymph in a bower of ferns. Her skin glowed in the fading light. He allowed himself a lingering gaze along her legs, the curve of her hip, the lovely arc of her breasts and creamy shoulders. Her face was peaceful, a fringe of copper lashes hiding her eyes. Her lips were slightly parted, and it was all he could do not to bend to them and coax her to wakefulness and passion once again.

But he slid carefully from her side and rose. He gathered her clothes and put them beside her, then slipped briefly into the pool again before donning his own. These mundane tasks gradually pulled him back into the reality of their situation.

He had strayed from it somehow. When he had felt her eyes on him at the edge of the water, the very atmosphere had seemed to thicken and change. Thought had given way to something more primitive. Caution had—not disappeared—but retreated, perhaps, to the further reaches of his consciousness, leaving only Emily in the foreground.

What fire she had. He looked at her pale form under the trees. He had been wanting her for weeks, he admitted now. Resisting had taken all his strength. And now he'd lost the battle. Richard smiled slightly in the gathering gloom. He ought to feel remorseful about that, he supposed. On the contrary, all he wanted was to do it again.

He turned away. They had to reach safety, but after that, with the altered circumstances . . . his smile broadened in anticipation.

A breath of cooler air touched his skin. Emily should dress before she took a chill. Richard wondered if he dared make a fire, and decided that would be tempting fate. He walked over and bent to touch Emily's bare shoulder. When she started, he said, "It's getting cold."

She sat up, looked around as if dazed, then reached for her clothes. Richard strained to make out her expression, but though there was still light in the sky, darkness had come to this hidden place. He could see only her pale skin being obscured by the darkness of clothes. She might not feel as he did, he realized. He had not been too entranced to notice her inexperience. "Are you all right?"

"Perfectly." She stood.

Saying the wrong thing loomed suddenly as a fearful risk, one Richard had never faced before. He considered a whole spectrum of remarks. This was ridiculous, one inner voice declared—inexplicable.

Emily took a step closer. "Is something wrong?"

Yes, Richard wanted to say. I've become a tongue-tied idiot. "No."

"You sound . . . odd."

"The circumstances are . . . unusual," he managed, then cursed himself for a fool. He had never in his life sounded so stiff. But the emotion that seethed below the surface seemed to translate into paralysis.

Emily gave a breathless little laugh. "If my aunt knew of *this*," she murmured.

It wasn't a moment when he wanted to recall the duchess.

"You'll have to marry me now, or I am quite ruined."

Richard felt a surge of resentment. Was this all she could think of? "As I told your cousin, I'm a man of honor."

Emily pulled back. "I know that. I . . ."

"So you needn't worry." He turned away. Her first thought had been for the proprieties—not for the way he knew he had made her feel, not for any bond their caresses forged. She had not engaged herself because she cared for him, Richard reminded himself. She had never said that she did. They had agreed that their association was purely practical. And then he had broken the agreement.

Emily had enjoyed their lovemaking. He was certain of that. But who knew better than he, Lord Warrington, that such physical pleasure could mean little else?

She wanted a haven after her—what?—her brief lapse under the strain of their flight? He set his jaw. "We should get some rest," he added in a hard voice. "We'll move at dawn." Taking out his penknife, he began cutting ferns to cushion the rocky ground.

Emily said nothing. He could feel her gaze on him as he worked, but she made no sound. When he had accumulated a good pile of vegetation, he said, "You can sleep here." Moving off a little way, he started cutting again. He heard the rustle of the ferns as she lay down on them. And why not, he thought bitterly. She had gotten her assurances. No doubt she would drop off at once, while he was certain that he would be awake for hours yet—if not all night.

His bed of fern complete, Richard sat down beside it. In the morning, he would climb the nearest peak and take bearings. It couldn't be much farther to his cousin's house.

Emily stirred, and all his senses came alert. But her even breathing didn't change. It was the worst fate he could imagine, Richard thought—to be so attuned to a woman who wanted nothing more than the protection of his name.

He made himself lie down, but turned restlessly. Memories of the silk of Emily's skin, the scent of her hair, plagued him. Try as he would to push them aside, he kept hearing the gasps of pleasure he had drawn from her. His body betrayed him, hungering for things his mind denied.

She belonged to him now, a sharp inner voice

insisted. She had made the bargain clear. He had no reason to deny himself. Or she to refuse him.

Richard rose in one swift movement and went to where Emily lay. Her face was a blurred white oval in the darkness. Kneeling beside her, he slipped his hand under her skirts and ran his fingers along the skin of her leg.

"Richard?" she murmured, waking.

He caught her lips in a hard kiss, not wanting talk, and pulled roughly at buttons and fasteners. He stripped the cloth away, and ran his hands over her lucent contours possessively.

She murmured his name again.

"Don't speak," he commanded.

He cupped her breasts, let his hands wander down over her skin. He could see every inch of her clearly in memory, dappled with the shadows of leaves, the sparkle of water. The feel of her under him was driving him to a fever pitch of desire.

He pushed her knees apart with his own and freed himself from the encumbrance of breeches. He was rock hard and aching for release, and he would have it. She was his to take, a glow of warmth and surrender in the dark.

She lay still. She said nothing. The last time, her body had begged for his touch.

Something like anger flashed through him. Something like pain. Richard was assailed by a savage need for her to beg for his touch.

Fighting his own pounding demand, he set out to make her beg.

He ran his fingertips lightly up her inner thighs, pausing just long enough to tantalize before moving over her hipbones and along the curve of her waist. He teased her breasts until he elicited a breathy gasp, then let one hand slip down again to rouse her. He touched and caressed until she was straining against his hand.

When she cried out softly, he felt a flare of satisfaction. He took his own pleasure with a hard, driving rhythm that surged through his body like storm surf. The tempo rose and rose, and exploded in a wave that slammed through every nerve and fiber with an intensity that left him panting. She was his, declared his scattered thoughts. His.

Emily's hands moved gently on his back. He pulled away from her and stood. There was no way to see her expression in the dimness, and he didn't care about it anyway, he told himself. He strode over to the pool and stripped off his clothes, finding a grim satisfaction in the fact that he hadn't taken off his boots during the encounter. The cool water damped the remains of his fever, soothing him toward sleep. He staggered over a stone once going back to his bed of leaves, and once there, he felt exhaustion dragging at him. He gave himself up to it gratefully, falling into a bottomless pit of black.

Insensible, he dreamed. He was running, not away, but toward some unimaginable reward that continually eluded him. The harder he searched, the more it receded. He despaired, dreaming, of ever finding the thing that he sensed would make his life complete.

Birdsong woke him at first light. The sun was still below the clifftop, and the air was cool and damp with dew. Richard sat up, his gaze drawn to Emily, who slept in a tangle of clothes and bright hair. He felt a pang, and rejected it. He had to concentrate on getting them out of here.

Leaving his coat on the pile of ferns where he'd slept, he moved silently off toward the wall of stone he meant to climb.

NINETEEN

EMILY OPENED HER EYES on a dazzle of leaves and the cry of a jay. The morning was golden and green. She was lying in a nest of her clothes, mostly covered by them, and she was alone.

How did she know that? Raising her head, she looked at the spot where Richard had slept. Only his coat was there. She surveyed the ground around the pool. There was no sign of him.

She didn't know if she was glad or sorry. Yesterday had ended in such a muddle. She hadn't known how to speak to him, and her feeble effort to joke had obviously gone wrong. Her mind was dizzy with memories of his touch, worry that she had made a fatal mistake.

She sat up, her hopelessly crumpled riding habit sliding away. She clutched at it, then she let go; there was no one to see. Though the morning was cool, she made her way to the pool and slipped in to bathe. The water was comforting. She glided back and forth, letting it soothe aching muscles. It was quite a while before she climbed out again, refreshed, and stood at the edge.

Waiting a moment to dry before dressing, Emily had the sudden sense that she was being watched. She turned quickly. The hidden glade was empty. The pile of stones at the entrance was undisturbed.

There was nothing, no sound to betray a watcher. Yet the feeling remained, and she was suddenly convinced it was Richard, silently back from wherever he had gone.

Her heartbeat accelerated. A pulse of heat passed through her body as if she'd been dipped in flame. It was partly embarrassment. But it was also something else that she didn't recognize. That something directed her hands as she slowly picked up her underthings and slid them on. It informed her fingers as she buttoned her blouse languorously, hands lingering on her own skin. It arched her back as she lifted her skirt and dropped it over her head. By the time she was fully dressed, Emily's breath was coming faster, and she was thoroughly astonished at herself.

There was no sign of the audience she had been certain was there, and she was glad now to think that she had been imagining it. What was wrong with her?

Events of the last few days seemed to have scrambled her brain.

Memories of Richard's touch rose up in sharp contradiction. Emily went to sit on a rock and catch her breath.

"Good morning."

She jumped and nearly fell off. Richard had materialized out of nowhere and was bending to retrieve his coat from the pile of ferns.

"I've been up above getting bearings." He spoke as if yesterday had never happened, as if they were back in the first hours of their flight together. "If we move quickly, we can reach my cousin's house tonight."

Emily stood, brushing down her skirts to mask her nervousness. "That's good," she managed. He was intimidating this morning. It seemed this couldn't be the man who had come so close to her in the dark.

Richard went to the entrance and began removing the stones they had piled there. She moved to help.

"Quietly," he warned.

Emily reached for a rock, and their hands brushed, making her tremble. She thought his hand jerked a little. He grasped a larger stone and turned to set it aside. When it came time to move the boulder out of the way, and they had to push side by side, he gave no sign that he noticed her nearness. Emily was torn between wanting to put her arms around him and wanting to give him a thundering setdown. She settled for silence.

At the outer end of the entry, they paused for some time while Richard reconnoitered. Finally, he signaled with a gesture, and they started out along the rough ground. It was much more difficult than at the start of their journey together, Emily thought. She was deeply tired and terribly hungry and confused. Her feet kept wanting to stumble.

Richard led them to the end of the valley and then up a tumbled incline to a ridge masked by trees. They followed this north for most of the morning, and when it veered off in another direction, they made their way down into a gully that ran in the right direction.

Clouds began gathering at noon, and it was soon clear that rain was on the way. Emily concentrated on taking one step after another.

"There," Richard said, pointing.

Emily looked, and saw a manor house on the side of a hill beside a stream.

"We'll have to take particular care from now on," he added. "They must have suspected we'd come here."

The shots in the night seemed to have happened ages ago. "That would be sensible of them," she acknowledged.

He gave her a quick glance. Something flickered in his hazel eyes, and it seemed for a moment that he would speak, but he didn't.

It started to rain.

Richard led them behind the crest of the ridge, staying out of sight of the house. As they worked their way along it, rain muffled their footsteps. The skirts of Emily's riding habit dragged at her legs. Cold drops pelted her scalp and shoulders. She trudged along, boots squelching, feeling a kind of misery descend. The strain of being hunted was weighing on her. But as she watched Richard through the rain, she knew it was more than that.

"We'll work our way around to the back, and come down on the house from the heights," Richard said softly. "It's farther. But I don't want to arrive until it's dark anyway. It's our best chance to avoid being seen."

"I know." Water dripped onto her face from the pine boughs above. She wiped it away. Picking up her heavy sodden skirts, she started walking.

"Emily."

She froze in the middle of a step then turned to him. It was the first time he had used her name.

He was looking at her as if he needed to tell her something important. She thought she glimpsed a yearning question in his face. But even as she responded, it vanished. His chest rose and fell in a deep breath. "This way," he said.

The disappointment she felt then was so sharp that she told herself she'd been mistaken. She was probably becoming delirious from hunger. He had only wanted to tell her that she was going the wrong way. He was not going to explain why he scarcely looked at her now, after he had touched her in a way that . . .

Emily banished these thoughts. She was not going to stumble over this rough country soaking, starving, and weeping like a watering pot. She could do nothing about the first two, but she could . . . she could damn well control the third, she thought defiantly. "Damn well," she muttered, savoring the phrase.

Richard heard it. She didn't know whether she'd meant him to or not, but the utter astonishment on his face was so satisfying that she was glad. It buoyed her up for some time as they plodded on.

Emily lost all sense of where they were, or how much farther they had to go. Thus when Richard said, "This will do," and stopped, she bumped into him before the words sank in.

He reached out and steadied her. She leaned against him. After a moment, his arm encircled her waist and remained there.

"The house is below," he whispered close to her ear. He took her hand and led her through the dark, sodden woods. He seemed to know where he was going, and she tried to match his steps and avoid obstacles.

After what seemed hours, Emily made out a light in a window high above their heads. They came to a wall. Richard put a hand on it and moved left until they came to a gate. There, he stopped to listen.

Emily could hear nothing but dripping water. Then there was a soft rattle.

"Bolted," Richard murmured in her ear.

In the light from above, she watched him take hold of the top of the wooden gate, pull himself up, and swing over. A moment later, the bolt slid back and the gate opened for her. Richard left it unlocked behind them.

The windows in this part of the house were dark, and securely locked. Richard moved along the building to another gate and into the kitchen garden. Here, the house showed more signs of life, and a back door.

Richard strode over to it, listened at the panels, then tried the latch. He made a sharp beckoning gesture. When she reached him, he threw the door open and surged inside. On his heels, Emily hurried in, and came face to face with a trio of startled servants sitting around the kitchen fire. "Fetch your mistress at once," Richard said.

The young man jumped to his feet, looking as if he intended to defend the two women servants—one older and one young as himself.

"I am Mrs. Farrell's cousin," Richard told him. "I must see her at once. Privately."

The young man eyed them suspiciously.

They must look like vagabonds, Emily thought, drenched and exhausted and dirty.

"He brought his mum here," said the girl. "That Lady Fielding."

Richard nodded. The young man seemed unconvinced.

"We mean no one any harm. But I must speak to Mrs. Farrell."

"I'll fetch her, Sam," said the girl. She picked up a lighted candlestick and slipped out of the kitchen looking excited.

The other two servants stared at them. Richard offered Emily a chair, and she sank into it gratefully. They had done it, she thought. They had reached safety. Magistrates would be summoned, the countryside scoured. It was over.

A scent, a glorious intoxicating scent captured her attention. Turning, she discovered a loaf of bread on a board and a round of golden cheese on a plate. Beyond politeness, she reached for them.

Seeing her move, Richard turned. He picked up a knife to slice the bread, and Emily nearly snarled at him before realizing that he meant it for her. When he handed her a thick sandwich, she tore into it before he could cut another for himself. Oblivious to the stares of the servants, they ate like the starved creatures they were.

Footsteps approached. The door swung open, and Lydia Farrell entered the kitchen in a rustle of silk. "Richard! Miss Crane!" She looked stunned. "You can't be here. Come with me." Taking the candle from the servant, she gestured urgently for them to follow her. Emily snatched the bread from the table as she obeyed.

"Don't go near a front window," Richard commanded as they moved down a corridor.

Lydia looked upset. "Come," she repeated. Opening a door, she revealed a staircase. "Down here."

They descended quickly into a large brick-walled cellar. The light of a single candle did not reach into its corners. "This way," said Lydia. She strode across the floor. Opening a thick wooden door, she added, "You'll be safe here."

Richard went through it. Emily followed. The door thumped closed behind them, cutting off all light. There was the sound of a key turning in a lock, and then silence.

Emily clutched her loaf of bread to her chest. "What . . . why did she . . . ?"

Richard cursed.

"I don't understand," said Emily.

"It appears that we have made a mistake."

RICHARD SAT on the stone floor of what he took to be a storage room. He had explored the perimeter, reaching as high as he could, and found only brick walls, without windows. Five paces square, with a sturdy plank door and a lock in sadly good repair. It was pitch black and silent, assuring him that sounds made here were unlikely to carry beyond the basement.

"Couldn't we talk a little?" said Emily. "It's so . . . oppressive in here."

Her voice wavered a bit, and Richard felt a pang of guilt. He had shouted at her when they were first shut in, furious with himself and the situation. "There doesn't appear to be anything else to do," he acknowledged.

"There's no way out?"

He shook his head, realized she couldn't see it, and said, "Just the door."

Richard listened to the silence. It felt thick, like a blanket draped over him cutting off the air.

"Mrs. Farrell . . . you don't think she's . . . ?"

"She wants my land," Richard answered. "She tried to buy it from me."

"Because of the coal?"

"I suppose they discovered it some time ago. No doubt the seam runs through the Farrells' estate as well."

"And they want it all for themselves."

"Yes." He felt like a fool for not having seen it.

"So, you think . . . they hired those men in London?"

Richard sighed. "Hired them, and when they failed, Lydia came up to town herself to see what could be done." His short laugh was humorless. "She settled in my own house, made a friend of my mother, who is now her hostage, and persuaded me to come to Wales where I could be more easily disposed of."

"But if you were dead . . ."

"The estate would pass to my mother as nearest kin. I never made any other provision. I'm sure Lydia thinks she can bilk her of it." It was almost unbearable—to have been so deceived, to have failed to see any signs of Lydia's true thoughts and purpose. He still couldn't quite believe it. He'd thought he'd developed keener instincts.

"That is . . . difficult," Emily said in an oddly tentative voice.

"It's damnable."

The silence returned. Richard found that now he couldn't tolerate it. He had a sudden desire to see Emily's face. "Are you all right?" he asked instead.

"You mean, aside from being wet and cold and shut up in the dark? Probably about to be killed?"

Despite their circumstances, Richard smiled. Nothing they had endured, not even imprisonment, had broken her buoyant spirit.

"I stole the loaf of bread," she added.

"Prescient of you."

"You don't think it will attract rats?"

"I don't think we will give them time to notice it."

"Oh." She didn't sound comforted. "Would you like some now?"

He wasn't particularly interested in eating. But he wanted to be closer to her, to feel her as a real presence rather than a voice out of the dark. "Yes," he said, rising.

Emily's skirts rustled.

"Stay where you are. Just say something, and I will come to you."

"Uh . . . do you think perhaps there are no rats, since this room is empty?"

Following her voice, he found her sitting against the opposite wall. It was a great relief, somehow, to sink down beside her and feel her shoulder warm on his. When she handed him a piece torn from the loaf, he realized that he was still hungry. He ate it, and then they finished off the rest between them.

She shivered, and Richard pulled her close without even thinking. She nestled in the curve of his arm. "It's so dark."

He said nothing. There was no cheering answer to this.

"What will she do with us?"

Richard considered various vague answers. But he knew Emily wouldn't believe them for a moment. "I suppose she is sending for her hirelings, to put us in their hands."

"The ones who shot at us?"

"Yes."

She assimilated this silently. He had never met a woman with such courage, Richard thought. Or a man, for that matter. She took each catastrophe as a new obstacle to be overcome. She would continue fighting right to the end of her strength. A fierce protective anger blew through him. He had to find a way to get her out of this.

"What was your favorite game when you were a child?"

"What?"

"Mine was making villages. I would clear a patch of grass and build houses of twigs, with leaves for the roof."

Her voice was meditative. She was searching for a distraction. It wasn't a bad notion.

"There were streets of pebbles, and usually a little square. A delphinium blossom makes a splendid church steeple."

"Does it?" Richard could see her, suddenly, a small girl with bright hair bent over, placing a blue flower at the peak of her creation. The vision made his throat tight for some reason.

"Of course, in a day or two, it would wilt. But that didn't matter because I wanted to keep working on it, making it better. Once, I dug a whole little river—coming out of a stream—to run through my village, with a bridge and a waterfall. That was the best one."

Her voice was beginning to soften toward sleep.

"What was your favorite game?" she asked again.

Richard considered. "When I was very small, we lived in Somerset. Before my father died."

She made a sympathetic sound.

"I liked the usual sorts of games." Richard suddenly remembered something he hadn't thought of in years. "I liked to build things, too. Not villages."

"What?" she murmured.

Her head had come to rest on his chest, and he felt her voice there. "Machines." A self-deprecating laugh escaped him. "That's how I thought of them. They weren't, really."

"What do you mean?"

"They were mechanisms, made of things I found around the place—bits of wire, gears from a broken clock—but they didn't do anything."

"And a machine must do something."

"Yes. That's the beauty of it."

Emily raised her head as if to look at him. In the thick darkness, she sank back again at once. "Beauty?"

He groped for the thought. "It begins as an idea of how to accomplish some task. And when the machine is manufactured, the idea comes to life. It works. It must be such a thrill when you start up something you have conceived, and it goes, it succeeds."

Emily said nothing. Richard suddenly felt self-conscious. He had never talked to anyone like this.

"Why did you stop?"

"What?"

"Why did you stop building your 'mechanisms?' "

He'd not only stopped, he'd forgotten all about them. "My father got me a pony," he remembered. "And he was teaching me to fish and . . . other things I was supposed to do. There wasn't time any longer."

"Supposed to," she echoed.

"Yes." Richard grimaced in the darkness. "A country gentleman has no interest in machines. Still less a man of fashion."

"Your father wished you to be a man of fashion?"

"No. That was my mother. He would have settled for a country gentleman, I believe."

"As he was?"

Richard tried to remember his father's face. "I don't really recall. I was very young when he died."

"That must have been hard," said Emily softly.

"I missed him. But I was small. All I knew was that we were moving to London to my grandparents' house. I'm sure it was much harder for my mother." He'd never thought of that before, he realized. She must have been frantic, with the abrupt loss of a young husband, debts left behind, a child.

"Everything suddenly changing," said Emily, echoing his thoughts.

Almost the way his life had shifted when he was shipwrecked, though they hadn't had to eat grubs, he thought with a smile. "You know what that's like," he said, recalling things she had told him about her own childhood.

"But both my parents were always there."

"Very much so," he joked.

She nodded against his chest. Richard felt a kinship vibrate between them. Their lives hadn't been alike in the particulars, yet the end result was similar.

A sudden certainty descended on Richard. She was the only kind of woman he could admire now. He would never tolerate a partner without her unique blend of courage and sensitivity and humor.

Ideas opened out in his mind, one after the other, like curtains parting to reveal a wide vista. Perhaps the things that had pushed them toward an engagement—for he had been pushed—weren't mere convention or accident. Perhaps it was larger, more portentous, than that. "We're meant to be together," he murmured.

She made no reply, and Richard was shaken by a dread that she didn't feel this, that it was a delusion he'd woven of longing and fatigue. The idea was so bleak he couldn't speak for a moment. And then when he could, he didn't know what to say. Why didn't she answer him?

The silence was heavy and lightless. The brick storage room seemed to close around him, the walls drawing in to stifle.

"Emily?" he managed at last.

There was no response but her even breathing, the weight of her head on his chest. It was another few moments before Richard realized that she had fallen asleep.

Relief coursed through him, and he didn't know whether it came from the explanation of her failure to answer, or the knowledge that she hadn't heard his admission in the first place.

She stirred, nestling closer to his side. His body responded with a jolt of desire and a confusion of emotion. He could taste her lips, feel her skin in his fingertips.

Richard closed his eyes and rested his head against the brick wall, fighting the images in his mind and the echo of sensation demanding repetition. It was far too dangerous, in several senses, to give way.

TWENTY

RICHARD WOKE to a dim filtering of light, yellow green along the brick of the walls. There were narrow slitted openings near the ceiling of the room, closed with glass and overgrown with vines. They were well out of reach.

Carefully sliding away from the still sleeping Emily, he rose and surveyed their prison. The room was nearly a perfect cube, and it was perfectly empty. There wasn't a scrap of metal or a bit of lumber he might use as a weapon. And the brickwork looked solid. By the time he could pry one loose and break a window, it would certainly be too late. Nonetheless, he took out his penknife and began scratching at a line of mortar.

Emily sat up. Putting her hands to her hair, she pulled out pins and held them in her mouth while she tidied the unruly mass. Richard couldn't take his eyes off her as she pinned it up again. When she smoothed it back and looked up, he looked quickly away.

"I wish we hadn't eaten all the bread," she said.

Richard laughed.

Bracing one hand against the wall, she stood. "At least we're dry." She brushed at her skirts. "Though covered with dust."

Richard watched her examine the room. He could almost hear her coming to the same conclusions he had reached himself. She went over to the door and tried the lock, rattling it quietly.

"Mrs. Farrell keeps her house in annoyingly good order."

"An estimable housekeeper," he replied dryly.

Emily turned to him. "Will they come for us this morning?"

"I imagine so. Lydia probably had to search the hills for her hired killers."

"I hope they were out in the rain all night!"

Another laugh escaped him. Richard felt a kind of irrational joy bubble up. He wished with all his heart that she was safe elsewhere, but if he had to face death, he couldn't think of anyone he would rather face it with.

"When we hear them unlocking the door, we can hide behind it and grab them," she suggested.

"I'm afraid it opens outward."

"Oh." She examined it again. "If we pressed ourselves against the bricks right beside it"—she demonstrated—"they wouldn't see us at first. Perhaps we could surprise them."

"We will certainly try that."

"But you don't believe it will work."

"They'll have guns, I imagine. And Lydia will most likely keep them from rushing in."

"She leaves a great deal to be desired as a family member," declared Emily severely. "It is enough to make one glad not to be well acquainted with one's family."

"I imagine it is. I am scarcely well acquainted with Lydia, however."

Emily stared at him. "You seemed such good friends."

"She took care to make it seem so," he answered ruefully. "I might have suspected something, since I had met her only once before."

"Only once?"

"When I was fifteen," Richard replied, and then wondered why she cared.

Emily turned away from his gaze. "We will escape," she said staunchly. "The men she hired are incredibly inept."

"They haven't been clever." He thought back over the attacks. They would have better direction this time, however.

"We'll outwit them."

He didn't want to discourage her.

"A distraction," added Emily. She nodded. "I will . . ."

Without any warning sound of footsteps, the key rattled in the lock. Richard quickly joined Emily against the brick wall beside the door, pressing his back against it.

"Watch me," she whispered.

Before he could ask what she meant, the door swung open.

Lydia Farrell walked in. She was alone and unarmed, Richard saw incredulously.

A wail like a steam whistle reverberated through the little room, and Emily flung herself onto Lydia, wailing and pleading like the most volatile of hysterical women. The room was suddenly filled with flailing arms and frothing skirts. Richard, astonished, stood stock-still.

The melee ended with Emily sitting on top of his cousin, pinning her arms to the stone floor with both hands.

"What are you doing?" cried Lydia. "Have you lost your mind?"

"You think I should simply let you kill us?" demanded Emily. She threw Richard a harassed look, as if wondering why he did not help her.

"Kill you?" cried Lydia in horror.

The emotion was so obviously genuine that Emily eased her grip and sat back a little. "So you can get Lord Warrington's land and the coal on it."

Lydia looked ashamed. "You found out about that." She glanced at Richard and away.

"You hired thugs in London to murder him," accused Emily.

"No!" Lydia frowned. "Is that who they are? But . . ." She looked bewildered.

"I think you had better let her up," commented Richard.

Slowly, Emily released her captive and rose. Lydia sat up, making no move to flee.

"Tell us about the coal first," said Richard.

Again, she looked ashamed. "We discovered it about a year ago. The deposit is very large. I didn't see why you . . . that is, you had no connection with this place and you never . . ."

"You didn't think I deserved a share in it," finished Richard.

Lydia looked at him almost fearfully. "You are very different now."

"But what about the attacks, the men who shot at us?" asked Emily.

"There is a madman in the neighborhood," Lydia blurted out. "He's looking for Richard, and he has two very sinister individuals with him."

Richard and Emily stared at her.

"He had just been at the front door when you arrived last night. He threatened my family—my sons!"

Richard and Emily looked at each other.

"You have to go," insisted Lydia. "Your mother, too. I'm sorry, but I can't have my boys put in danger."

"A madman?" said Emily. "But who . . . ?"

"Can you describe him?" asked Richard.

Lydia shook her head. "He wore a hooded cloak, and he had a scarf swathed around his face. But his eyes . . ." She shivered.

"What about the men with him?"

"Large," she answered. "Scarred all about the face and hands. Not countrymen."

"Bob Jones and Ralph the Thumb," cried Emily. "It must be."

Lydia gaped at her. "You can see why you must go?" his cousin added pleadingly. "He said if I tried to help you, he would kill my sons."

"You will have to lend me a horse," responded Richard.

She bit her lower lip and clenched her hands together.

"Can't we just send for help?" objected Emily.

Lydia made a gesture of denial. "I doubt that a messenger would get through," replied Richard before she could protest. "I will draw them off, and then you can get word out."

Emily swung around to stand right in front of him, her hands on her hips. "You cannot mean to leave here alone?"

"It is the only answer. You and my mother will be safe, while I . . ."

"While you are shot as soon as you ride out of the stable!"

"I can evade . . ."

"This is not the jungle," she cried. "We are not talking of snakes and panthers. They're lying in wait for you out there."

"There is no other way."

Emily glared at him. "Oh yes, there is."

"You all have to go," interjected Lydia.

When they turned to look at her, she was scrambling up from the floor. Under their eyes, she took a step backward. "I'm sorry. But I will not risk my family."

"If I am gone," began Richard.

Emily turned to Lydia. "They can't be certain we're here. No one saw us come in. Unless your servants . . ."

"They wouldn't speak of it."

"You must lend us a carriage. Lord Warrington and I will conceal ourselves in the vehicle while it is still in the stables."

Richard started to object, but she waved him to silence.

"When it pulls up at the front door, only his mother will get in. It will appear that she is leaving. They will probably follow, but . . ."

"No," said Richard.

"It is a much better idea than yours," declared Emily.

"I'll tell Lady Fielding," said Lydia, and slipped out before anyone could speak again.

"This won't do," said Richard.

"It will have to."

The courage and sheer will in her blue gaze reached into the most guarded coverts of his spirit. "I cannot put you in danger," he murmured. "I can't bear it."

"So you ask me to bear it instead?" Emily demanded. "I am to endure what you cannot?"

Richard couldn't speak.

"Well, I won't," she added almost saucily. She smiled, and Richard's throat grew tight with unprecedented tears.

EMILY SAT SILENTLY in the Farrells' traveling carriage as the stablemen finished harnessing the team. The curtains had been fastened down at the windows, so no one could see inside the vehicle. In the dimness, she clasped her hands and made herself stay still. She was trembling, but it was exultation more than fear that shook her. The way Richard had spoken to her, and looked at her—he had to feel as she did. The emotion in his face had been unmistakable. He cared for her. Even the threat they faced couldn't outweigh that revelation.

The carriage door opened, and Richard joined her on the forward seat. "Ready?" he asked quietly.

"Yes."

The vehicle jerked and rolled out of the stables and around to the front of the house. Emily shrank back as the door was opened and first Lady Fielding, then her maid were handed in. They both looked irritated. "You are here," said the former as she sat. When Richard gestured sharply for silence, she glared at him.

The door was closed, and they started off at a brisk pace. "I do not understand this at all," continued Lady Fielding in a harsh whisper. "Everyone seems to have lost his wits. First Lydia tells me I must go—not very hospitable! And then she gives me some rigamarole about ruffians threatening her family. It made no sense whatsoever. And you!" She fixed Richard with an accusing stare. "Hiding in the stables? Really!"

"I'm afraid it was necessary, Mother. Things are rather serious." Quickly, Richard told her the whole story. When he had finished, Lady Fielding sat back in her seat, white and silent.

The carriage rocked as the team increased its gait. Richard raised a hand to the window, then let it drop, clenching it on his knee. Hoofbeats sounded off to the side. "Mother, would you look out and see what is happening?" he asked in a rigidly controlled voice.

Lady Fielding complied. "There is a rider coming in from the right," she said. "Check the other side, Jevers."

Her maid looked and said there was another horseman on the left.

Richard looked frightening. "If they hurt the coachman, I will . . ."

"Mrs. Farrell told him not to take any risks," responded Emily.

A shot rang out up ahead. A horse squealed. The carriage rocked on its springs, then started to slow.

"They will have to open the doors to kill us," Emily said. She was pleased to find her voice steady.

"That will be the time to move," agreed Richard.

"They will not expect me to do anything, so I should be first."

"What sort of woman are you?" wondered Richard's mother.

"The sort who does not sit back and let herself be killed," Emily replied.

Surprisingly, Lady Fielding took this in without hysterics. "So I will leap . . ." she began.

"You will not," Richard interrupted.

"But it makes sense for me to . . ."

"It's out of the question."

"They will be most wary of you," she argued. "If we are to take them by surprise, we must . . ."

"I should do it," put in Richard's mother.

Everyone turned to stare at her.

"They won't expect anything from me."

No one disputed this.

"Tell me what to do."

"Mother, I don't think . . ."

"I'm capable of more than you imagine."

"The danger . . ."

"You say they intend to kill us. What is more dangerous than that?"

"No," said Richard. "I will take care of the matter."

"So I expect," responded his mother. "But perhaps I can give you the opportunity."

"She should have her chance," said Emily.

"Thank you, dear."

"Perhaps you didn't hear me?" snapped Richard. "I said . . ."

"They will probably stand back when they open the door," said Emily.

"Emily! Mother!"

"If you stumble out weeping . . ."

"Stop this at once!"

"You could pretend to be disoriented and hysterical, and start to wander off. Then they would have to . . ."

"Shoot her?" finished Richard sarcastically.

"Yes, I see. Very clever, dear."

"I forbid it," said Richard.

The silence that followed didn't sound like the

silence of obedience, Emily thought. "What is your plan?" she asked him.

"As soon as the door is free, I'll burst through it and overcome them."

"All of them?"

"Yes."

Emily heard the doubt in his voice. "They'll kill you."

"You must sit on him while I get out first," answered his mother. "Jevers can help you."

The maid gave a little squeak.

"All right," said Emily, her voice a bit self-conscious. She was assailed by a vivid picture of her sitting on him to hold him down.

"You'll do nothing of the kind."

"Richard, it is settled," said his mother in the tone that brooked no argument. "Don't be difficult."

"Difficult? You are proposing to put yourself in . . ."

"I said, it is settled."

The carriage slid to a stop.

"I can defend my family," added his mother with such pride and dignity that no denial was possible.

Footsteps crunched on the road on both sides of the coach. Richard reached for the door handle, and found two small hands gripping his arm and tugging it away. He looked down, and what he saw in Emily's face held him motionless just a moment too long.

"Why have we stopped?" demanded his mother, pushing the door open and surging forward.

She was met by the barrel of a gun and thrust back. At the same moment, the opposite door was flung back and another gun aimed at Richard. "Here they are," called the huge man holding it. "Just like you said."

Another figure joined him, tall and heavily cloaked. Richard stared into the darkness of the hood, but all he could see was the folds of a scarf and the glitter of eyes.

The reflexes honed in the jungle took over, and he launched himself through the air at the man's throat.

He heard Emily scream as he struck. The man went down under him and thudded onto the road. Richard's hands closed on his throat.

Something struck Richard's head with stunning force. He reeled, but didn't let go. Then a voice snarled, "Get out of that or I'll shoot the girl."

Turning, he saw that the gunman had Emily. Red rage and the urge to kill flashed through him. If he dared to hurt her . . .

Shaking with fury, Richard let his hands ease. The man under him struggled. At least he would know one thing, Richard thought. As he sprang up, he grabbed the scarf that hid his assailant's face and pushed the hood aside. "Taft?"

The old man rose with some difficulty, ignoring Richard's incredulous gaze. "Put her back in the carriage," he said to his henchman. "And secure the other door."

"Taft?" repeated Richard.

"Get the servant and tie her up with the driver," said Elijah Taft, still paying him no heed. Lady Fielding's maid was dragged from the coach and led off.

"Why?" demanded Richard.

Finally, Taft turned to him, contempt clear in his

eyes. "You'll not be pulling down the house I've spent my life preserving. It'll go to a man with some money, and some sense. It'll be saved."

"But I didn't . . ." He had said something about razing the house in Somerset, he remembered, but he hadn't been serious.

"You'd say anything now, to save your worthless skin." Taft turned away. "Why the good Lord didn't drown you, I'll never understand."

"You sent me to that shipping agent," Richard exclaimed. Taft had recommended the firm, said they were friends and would give Richard a good price on passage to the Indies.

Taft merely turned to the gunman. "Take the reins and get rid of them once and for all. This time, make it look like an accident. Drive them over a cliff. No more shooting."

"We was just trying to flush 'im out of the house," the man murmured sullenly.

"Well, now I have handed them over to you. Don't blunder again."

The man glowered at him but turned to climb up on the box. Richard was shoved back inside. When he tried the doors, he found them secured from the outside.

THE CARRIAGE BOUNCED along a rough lane, throwing its passengers against the seats and one another. Emily fell against Richard. His arm curved warmly around her for a moment, supporting her, then was withdrawn as the vehicle swung back. Emily's throat tightened and her eyes stung. He had gotten her through so much. She wouldn't give up just yet.

The carriage slowed. Emily heard a voice call out. One of the men on the box above them answered. She couldn't tell what he said. The more distant voice replied. The carriage slowed further.

There was a shout. Two shots rang out as their vehicle jerked to a stop.

"You don't suppose it could be highwaymen?" Emily was shaken by a crazed desire to laugh.

"Whatever it is, we'd better try to take advantage of it." Richard shifted in the seat. "Move back."

Richard turned sideways and kicked the door with both feet, hard. It shuddered, and the carriage rocked on its springs.

"Stow that," bellowed one of the men on the box.

Another shot split the night. It seemed to Emily that it had not come from their guards.

Richard kicked the door again. It gave a little. Their captors pounded on the roof. He kicked again with all his strength, and the carriage door sprang open, the latch shattered.

"Stay back," he commanded.

Scrabbling sounds up above warned them.

"Down," said Richard.

They all crouched. The barrel of a gun appeared in the opening, then the distorted face of one of the London ruffians, hanging upside down. With a lunge, Richard took hold of the gun and twisted it. It fired, and the bullet tore through the carriage roof. There was a sharp cry from above.

Richard jerked savagely and the man hurtled off the carriage roof, landing with a thud on the ground. His gun remained with Richard, Emily saw. He tensed to leap. She put a hand on his arm. In that moment there was a roar of rage outside. The carriage dipped as if a great weight had hit it, then swayed as it was removed. "I'll put your lights out for good, Bob Jones," roared the voice.

"Is that . . . ?" began Emily.

"If you move, I will shoot you," someone else declared.

"Papa?" she exclaimed.

"If you've harmed one hair on my daughter's head, I'll shoot you anyway," he added.

The man who must be Ralph the Thumb moaned on the ground beneath the door.

"Emily? Are you there?"

"Yes, Papa," she called.

Richard climbed out of the vehicle, looked around, then turned to lift her over the recumbent form of Ralph. Emily's father materialized from the bushes at the side of the road. Simultaneously, the Bruiser appeared, frog-marching Bob Jones to join them.

"Jerry! How did you get here?"

"I brought him," replied Sarah Fitzgibbon, emerging beside Alasdair. "I had a feeling you were going to need some help, so I set him to watch Lord Warrington's house."

Astonished, Emily tried to take it all in. There was a post chaise blocking the road. Sarah also held a pistol. "Mama didn't come?"

"Of course I came," answered her mother, pushing out from between some branches on the other side of the road. She gestured with her gun. "Don't be ridiculous."

Lady Fielding emerged from the carriage. She surveyed Emily's parents with far more approval than before. "I see what you mean about the pistols," she said to Emily's mother. "Did you really learn to shoot when you were twelve?"

Olivia approached the group around the vehicle. "Oh no. My father would never have allowed such a thing. Alasdair taught me."

Lady Fielding nodded judiciously. "Richard, perhaps you could . . ."

"Yes, Mother. We can discuss it another time. Where is Taft?"

"Taft?" Alasdair Crane growled.

"A cloaked man rode off that way," said Sarah, pointing back the way they'd come.

Richard strode over and began unharnessing one of the horses.

"What are you doing?" asked Emily.

"I have to go after him." Richard threw off the last of the straps and mounted the restive horse bareback.

"Wait."

"I must find him," was all Richard said. Setting his heels to the horse's flanks, he pounded off.

Emily took two steps after him.

"You, young lady, are by no means out of trouble," declared her father. "How dare you go sneaking off alone from the inn, without a word? And you have spent days—*days*—in the company of . . ." He broke off as Olivia put a hand on his arm.

"I didn't mean to be gone for days, Papa." She watched Richard disappear around a bend.

"We should go back to the village," put in Olivia.

"He's taken one of the leaders," objected Alasdair. "How are we to drive without a full team?"

Emily's mother quieted him. They deposited Bob Jones and Ralph the Thumb in the carriage with the single horse, with the Bruiser to watch them. The rest of the party took the post chaise, which Emily's father drove. Once they were moving, Olivia took her daughter's hand. "Are you all right?"

Exhaustion was dragging at Emily now that the ordeal seemed over. It felt like a huge effort just to nod. "I'm tired and bruised and filthy. But I'll be fine once I can rest."

"This is all very inconvenient," complained Richard's mother.

"Very unsettling," said Olivia. And Emily acknowledged that Lady Fielding's amazing transformation earlier was not to be lasting.

"I want to go back to Lydia's. And someone must fetch Jevers."

"And the coachman," remembered Emily.

When this was explained, Olivia promised to send someone from the inn to retrieve them both.

"I don't understand how you found us," said Emily then.

"Jerry saw the attack on Lord Warrington's house," Sarah explained. "He tried to follow, but he's not very good in the countryside. So we started watching the Farrell place instead, and when he saw Bob Jones and Ralph call there, he kept an eye on them from then on."

"Sarah explained everything to us, and we were able to set up an ambush," Emily's mother finished. She gave Emily a reproachful look. "You really ought to have confided in us, you know. Your father was very hurt that you did not ask him to shoot those men."

"I'm sorry," Emily mumbled. She laid her head back against the seat and closed her eyes. She and Richard hadn't been separated for days, and now he seemed very far away. Events had been moving so quickly since the moment she found him lying bound in the field behind her house. She had been whirled off to London, made over by her aunt, and then embroiled in a murderous plot. There'd been no time to think.

The mystery was solved, she realized. They had discovered who was behind the attacks on Richard. Their agreement was at an end.

But things had changed since they set those terms. She rubbed her forehead with one hand. What had changed was not circumstances, but herself. She loved him, she admitted. She wanted to spend the rest of her life with him.

And what did he want?

Sometimes, she was certain he shared her attachment. At other times, he looked at her as if she were an irksome problem he had to solve. Was he thinking then of the engagement? Was he wondering whether she would keep her word?

Emily swallowed. He would come and speak to her once things were more settled. She would see in his eyes what he felt, and then she would know what to do.

"Emily."

She started violently.

"We've reached the inn." Her mother sounded quite concerned. "Are you burnt to the socket? Come inside and rest."

Slowly, she climbed down from the chaise. There was no sign of the other carriage, or of Richard. Weariness dragged at her. Nothing more could be done tonight. When she saw Richard again, she would decide what to say.

TWENTY-ONE

THE NEXT FEW DAYS passed in a flurry of activity. Messengers came and went from the inn. There were visits to and from a solemn magistrate. Richard appeared at unexpected moments, always preoccupied and hurrying, and left again without saying much of anything. People seemed to swirl around Emily with dizzying speed, but none of them appeared to want her opinion or her help.

Richard certainly made no effort to speak privately to her. He hardly seemed to notice her existence, and Emily grew more apprehensive with each hour. Perhaps she had been mistaken. Perhaps he was waiting for her to fulfill her promise and set him free.

"Warrington knows how to get things done," said her father approvingly at dinner two nights later. "He's even managed to get that poor excuse for a magistrate to move. I daresay he'll have the business wrapped up by the end of the week."

"What will happen to that man Taft?" asked Emily's mother.

Alasdair shook his head. "Warrington didn't want to prosecute. Said it was a misunderstanding. He's pensioning the man off." He seemed torn between outrage and admiration.

"I still don't understand what he thought he was doing," said Emily.

"He's a bit unbalanced," replied her mother. "Apparently he has devoted his life to preserving the Warrington estates in Somerset, and now that he is getting old, he became obsessed with leaving them in good hands. He seemed to think Lord Warrington's heir was the answer."

"So he decided to get rid of R . . . Lord Warrington?"

Olivia nodded. "And those close to him. Who might prevent the heir from inheriting."

Alasdair growled.

Emily tried to imagine being so attached to a place that you were willing to kill for it.

"The man's demented," said her father. A thought seemed to strike him. "Still, he'd make a splendid Mephistopheles." His hand moved as if it held a paintbrush.

"Too old," protested Olivia.

"Not necessarily."

Emily's thoughts drifted as they disputed the matter. They would go back to their painting, and Papa's bickering with the neighbors, and the love which sustained them through every difficulty. She had to see Richard. Why didn't he come to her? Just then, his name caught her wandering attention.

"Warrington will be here tomorrow at three," said her father.

Both her parents looked at her.

"It's all arranged," Alasdair added.

Was he coming to say good-bye? "Good. I need to speak to him," she said.

Alasdair raised his dark eyebrows. "You'll have plenty of time for that."

Emily rose from the table. "I'm going to walk a little."

"Emily," began her mother.

"I won't be long. I'll stay near the inn." Emily hurried out before they could object, leaving behind a concerned silence.

"I hope we're doing the right thing," said Olivia after a while.

"No question of that," answered her husband.

"I wish I could be as sure as you."

"How can you think of any other course of action?"

Olivia shook her head. "I don't understand what Emily feels about it."

Alasdair nodded. They contemplated this enigma for a while. "Never have understood her," he ventured finally.

"I know." Olivia sighed. "She's always been so self-contained. It's worrisome."

After another interval, Alasdair brightened.

"Been that way since she was a tiny creature," he pointed out.

"That's what I just said."

"No, I mean, perhaps she's very happy. Wouldn't show that either, would she?"

Olivia pondered this.

"Warrington hasn't been about much," he added. "Perhaps she pining for him."

"Do you think . . . ?"

"Dragged us all down here to save his neck."

"That's true," said Olivia, looking happier.

"Went haring off into the wilderness with him." Alasdair scowled. "Alone. When I think that *my* daughter . . ."

"Yes, yes. You must be right."

"I dashed well am right. Warrington sees it."

"I know."

"It's all settled. Let us say no more about it."

Setting aside her doubts, Olivia nodded.

EMILY ROSE EARLY the next morning and set off before anyone else was stirring. Finding a secluded spot not too far from the inn, she sat in the summer sunshine and tried to prepare herself for the afternoon. She moved her hand, making the ring glitter and throw rainbow reflections on the stones. It was an exquisite piece. But more than that, it was a symbol of what she wished for more than anything else in the world. Emily slipped it off and put it carefully in her pocket. She wouldn't put it on again until she was certain.

She didn't return to the inn until past noon, and when she got there she found her parents were out. "They said they had some things to do to get ready for this afternoon, miss," the landlady told her. She smiled broadly at Emily as if they shared some secret.

Mildly puzzled, Emily ate the luncheon set before her and then went up to her room and lay down. She hadn't slept well, and the walking had tired her a bit. After a while, she dozed.

It seemed only a moment before someone was shaking her awake again. She blinked sleepily up at her mother's face.

"It's time to dress. How can you be sleeping?"

Emily sat up, surprised by the urgency of her mother's tone.

"I found some flowers. One of the local land-owners let me take some from their cutting garden."

Emily rubbed her eyes. "What time is it?"

"Nearly two. We haven't much time."

Her gown was crumpled and her hair in disarray. "I must change."

"Well, of course. I thought the blue sprigged muslin. I had them press it."

Emily looked at the gown hanging on the door of the wardrobe, then at her mother. Why should she take such an interest in what Emily wore for Richard's visit?

Swinging her legs around on the bed, Emily stood. "I'll be down in a few minutes."

"Don't you want me to help you dress?"

Emily stared. Her mother hadn't helped with her clothes since she was four years old. "I can do it."

Olivia looked oddly disappointed. "Are you sure?"

"Yes, Mama."

"Well, all right." With obvious reluctance, she moved toward the door. "Your father and I will be waiting downstairs."

She would have to find a way to get rid of them, Emily thought.

Emily washed her face, dressed, and tidied her hair. She transferred the ring from the pocket of her crumpled gown to the sprigged muslin. All she wanted now was to get this over. She couldn't think clearly, or make any sensible decisions, until it was.

There was a tap on the door. "Emily?"

"Yes, Mama?"

Her mother came in. "I made you this." She held out a garland of summer flowers—blues and yellows with a touch of white. "I thought it would look so lovely with your dress."

She never grew accustomed to her parents' artistic fancies, Emily thought. They would suddenly take it into their heads to decorate all the china with eccentric designs, gather seaweed to make some sort of exotic paint—or to weave circlets of blossoms that their daughter was expected to wear.

"May I put it on?" asked Olivia. Her mother settled the flowers on her head, then stood back. "You look lovely," she said, her voice catching as if she might cry.

That was something. Perhaps Richard would think so, too? "Shall we go down?"

"We hadn't so much as a daisy when we married,"

said Olivia as they walked down the stairs. "Not even a bit of green."

Emily hardly listened. She had heard the details of her parents' runaway match so often that she could have told it herself.

In the private parlor on the ground floor, they found Emily's father talking with Richard. "Warrington came early," said Alasdair jovially when they walked in. "Couldn't contain his eagerness."

Emily scarcely heard him. She couldn't attend to anything except Richard, looking very handsome in a dark blue coat and buff pantaloons. She wondered fleetingly why he was so dressed up. But the thought evaporated as soon as she reached him.

"You look splendid," he said with a small bow.

He seemed stiff and strained, Emily thought. Perhaps he was worrying about what she meant to do. "I must speak to you," she said quietly.

One corner of his mouth quirked. "We will have ample time to talk later on."

Emily looked around. Had her parents planned some event?

"Where is your ring?" asked Richard abruptly.

"In my pocket. I . . ."

"Put it on at once."

He seemed angry. Meeting his eyes, Emily swallowed. They were hot with something she didn't understand at all. He frowned. She slipped the ring back on her finger, her heart pounding.

"There he is," said her father, who was gazing out the window. He took a folded sheet of paper from his pocket and left the room.

"Who?" asked Emily.

"The vicar," answered her mother.

Emily grimaced. Had her father already become embroiled in some dispute with the local parson? She wouldn't have thought he had time.

Her father returned, followed by a small, dark-haired man in clerical bands. Emily was relieved to see that the latter was smiling. "All in order," said Alasdair, rubbing his hands together.

To Emily's surprise, Sarah Fitzgibbon and Richard's mother came in behind them.

"And all present and accounted for," her father added. "We can get started."

Olivia took Emily's hand and squeezed it. Emily gave her a wild look.

Suddenly, Richard was standing beside her. The vicar came over and faced them both. He smiled benignly and opened the small book he was holding. "Dearly beloved . . ."

Emily's throat closed in astonishment. She gaped at Richard. His attention was on the parson. She stared at her parents. They looked serene. She turned to Sarah, who winked at her.

The vicar was speaking Richard's name, asking if he took this woman for his wife. His face solemn, Richard said, "I do." He looked down at Emily. His hazel eyes were clear, but unreadable. The parson turned to her.

How had this happened? Emily wondered in a panic. Her gaze flew over the faces again. Richard's mother looked resigned. They had all thought the engagement was real, Emily recalled. They would have no reason to question a marriage. But Richard . . .

She met his eyes again. He didn't look angry. He didn't look anything.

The parson was asking if she would take him for her husband.

Emily's throat was tight with tears. She wanted to, and she was afraid to. Had her father forced him to stand up with her?

"Miss Crane?" said the vicar. He started to frown.

Emily swallowed. "I . . ."

Richard took her hand and held it. His fingers were warm on her icy ones. He held her eyes—steady, serious. She tried to ask with her expression what he really wanted. But he simply waited.

"Emily?" said her mother.

She couldn't look away from Richard. Her senses swam a little as she lost herself in his gaze. It felt almost like being in his arms. She could think of nothing else. "I do," she said.

Several breaths sighed out in relief. The vicar eyed her for a moment, then went on with the ceremony. In another few moments, it was complete. Richard's lips brushed hers for an instant, then the others crowded forward with congratulations.

Emily put a hand to the flowers in her hair. Had she actually gotten married?

Her father was opening a bottle of champagne; Richard was opening another. Glasses were poured. Toasts were made. Through her turmoil, Emily gathered that Sarah and Lady Fielding were traveling back to London together the following day. Her parents would be leaving for home soon after. And she would be left here with her new husband, whose only words to her so far had been an apology for the lack of a wedding journey because there was "far too much to do here."

Perhaps she was dreaming, Emily thought as the party went on. Perhaps she was actually still asleep in her room at the inn, having a nightmare in anticipation of breaking things off with Richard forever.

But she didn't wake. The parson took his leave. A carriage with ribbons tied to the traces was brought round, and her trunk—which she had not packed—was fastened to the boot. Before she knew it, Richard was handing her in and the others were waving and tossing blossoms at them. He climbed in after her, and the horses started off. Emily watched out the window as her parents grew smaller and smaller and finally disappeared around a bend in the road.

"I managed to get a few more furnishings for Morne," Richard said. "Lydia was very helpful. And I've engaged some servants. I think you will be tolerably comfortable there."

His tone of voice was perfectly normal. He was looking at her as if there was nothing odd about the sudden change in their situation.

"I have some people coming to talk about development of the coal," he added.

Now he sounded apologetic. Emily couldn't imagine why.

"It's rather important. My other estates are heavily encumbered."

The tension in Emily was rising too high to ignore. "I was going to break the engagement," she blurted out.

Richard's head jerked slightly, as if taking a blow. "I was going to keep my word."

"That was no longer possible," he replied, his words clipped.

"I meant to tell you today, but there wasn't any time. I didn't know . . . everything happened so fast." Emily fell silent. It sounded as unreal as it had felt.

"Your father told you he was sending for a special license."

Richard sounded bewildered, and perhaps something more. Emily couldn't be sure. She remembered her father mentioning a bishop, and thinking it odd. But she hadn't been paying attention. "I didn't want a forced marriage," she murmured.

The carriage bounced in a rut. Emily grabbed one of the leather straps to stay upright, fighting a growing sense of panic. She longed to ask Richard if he had married her against his will, but she was afraid of the answer.

RICHARD STOOD on the bit of lawn in front of his house and watched the last streaks of sunset fade in the west. This land that his stepfather had left him, which he had once thought worthless, was going to redeem all the rest. With the funds the coal brought, he would be able to pay off mortgages, improve his estates. He appreciated the irony as much as he regretted the way he had made the discovery.

The sky dimmed. Stars were winking into view, and there was a hum of insects. One of the upstairs windows turned golden with lamplight. Richard stared up at it. His wife was there, in their bedchamber. It was his wedding night.

One corner of his mouth jerked. He had never imagined that Emily would feel forced into the marriage. He had been too occupied with his own struggle over the matter, and with all the business that had to be dealt with. But he shook his head, refusing the easy excuse. He could have found time to talk with her.

When she had said they had to marry, he had resented it. Why should he be so astonished, or angry, if she felt the same? He had known she wasn't like other women. His mouth jerked again. There was no one like her. If he hadn't been such a fool . . .

Above his head, the casement opened. Looking up, he saw Emily sitting in the window, the lamp throwing a golden aureole around her. Her hair was down, falling over her shoulders like liquid fire. She wore a pale nightdress that left her neck and arms bare. A mixture of desire and tenderness burned in his chest.

She was looking upward. Suddenly, she raised a hand as if startled. Following her gaze, Richard saw a shooting star hurtle across the sky. Turning back, he thought he saw her lips move. What was she wishing for? Was it anything he could give her?

He must have moved, because Emily looked down, putting a hand to the front of her gown. "Who's there?"

"It's all right," he said. "I was getting a breath of air."

"Did you see the shooting star?"

"Yes."

"They're a sign of good luck."

They could use a bit of luck, he thought.

Emily leaned out, a figure of copper and ivory and gold. She seemed to be gazing at him, but he couldn't make out her expression in the shadows.

Silence lengthened between them.

"Are you . . . coming up?" she said finally.

Richard had to close his eyes at the fierce longing that shot through him with the question. No qualms or doubts were going to keep him from her bed tonight. The feel of her was branded into his nerves; the mere memory could make him shudder with desire. "In a moment," he replied, his voice thick.

Emily hesitated, then withdrew from the window. Richard stared at the empty square of golden light, then turned and strode inside.

She was sitting on the bed, waiting for him, her legs curled under the silky folds of her nightdress. The lamplight was molten after the darkness outdoors, and Richard blinked at it, and at her delicate beauty.

"It's . . . getting cool," she said.

"I'll close the window." He started toward it.

"No!"

He stopped.

"I like hearing the crickets, and the wind."

He turned away from the casement.

"Unless you want it closed," Emily added hurriedly. "If you would rather . . ."

"I prefer it open."

"Oh." A smile trembled on her lips. "We . . . we will have to learn each other's habits."

Richard was finding it difficult to breathe. They had trekked for days in the wilderness without this awkwardness. Did marriage destroy all that? The idea weighed on his spirits intolerably. He stripped off his coat and put it over the back of a chair. Sitting down, he pulled off his boots.

When he looked up, Emily was gazing at him. Her eyes dropped at once, then rose again. A flush spread from her face down her neck and under the scooped neckline of her gown.

Richard felt a thrill of recklessness. Pulling his shirt free of his breeches, he jerked it over his head and let it fall to the floor. Holding Emily's eyes, he stepped closer to the bed. Her gaze strayed downward, then quickly back to his. Richard felt a wild desire to laugh.

He took another step. Putting a hand to the fastening of his breeches, he raised a questioning eyebrow. At first, Emily didn't react. He waited, watching her eyes flicker from his face to his hand and back again. Her cheeks were flaming now, but she was leaning forward with what certainly appeared to be eagerness.

He moved his hand a bit, but continued to wait. Emily's lips parted. Richard cocked his head. She nodded, then looked daunted by her own temerity.

He undid the fastenings and stripped off his final garment, standing before her in the light of the lamp. He had never done such a thing with any other woman. Wild laughter rose in him again, an exultation that he didn't begin to understand. It burned him. He felt as if his eyes were glowing with it.

He reached the bed in two steps, and swept Emily into his arms, molding her against him. Her lips were sweet and pliant, urging him on. Her arms slid around his neck. Richard smoothed the curves of her back. Her body was intoxicating, maddening.

Her knees slipped around him. He ran his hands up her thighs and cupped her hips to press her closer. Their kisses were incendiary now, rising to a pitch beyond anything he had experienced.

The nightdress was becoming a nuisance. He grasped the silky material and tugged it up. Emily released her arms, but not her legs. She leaned back a little and helped him pull the garment free. When he threw it across the room, she laughed.

Richard pushed her back onto the bed. He couldn't take much more. And he wanted to hear her gasp. He dropped kisses across her shoulders and down to tease first one rosy nipple, then the other. His fingertips found the warm liquid spot that brought him the gasps he wanted.

She moaned his name. He ached with wanting her. Her fingers brushing over him were sweet torment.

Feeling her muscles go rigid, he shifted and buried himself in her warmth, moving with her as she pulled him closer. When she cried out, he loosed the iron control that had bound him and let himself rise to ecstasy in her wake. The world fell away. Every secret part of him thundered with release. It left his heart pounding, his breath rasping, and an odd, unexpected ripple of happiness spreading through his chest.

Richard held his wife close as the sensation ebbed. He could feel her heart beating under his hands. He kissed her neck, her shoulder. When he rolled onto his back, he pulled her with him, drawing her close to his side.

The sounds of the night spread around them. A current of cool air from the window caressed their heated skin.

"I should have . . ." began Richard, then stopped. Emily had said the same words at the same moment.

"Go ahead," they both said.

Emily gave a nervous laugh.

"You . . ." each of them began.

Richard closed his eyes, shaking his head slightly. "I never meant to force you into this marriage," he blurted out. Then he rose on one elbow. Emily had said almost the same thing once again. "You didn't . . ." he started to answer. So did she.

"Stop this at once," Richard said.

Emily pressed her lips together. She looked apprehensive and hopeful at the same time. Silently, she waited.

Now that he had the opportunity, Richard couldn't think what to say. She looked so very beautiful, lying there with her hair spread over the pillow.

"*You* didn't force *me* to marry," she said at last. "It was my aunt, and then Papa, who made you . . ."

"No."

Emily celestial blue eyes were intent.

"I told your father to send for the special license."

"You did?"

"I've known for some time that you were the only woman for me."

She stared at him. "But you never said . . ."

"Until our adventure together, I had no right."

The delicate flush that showed her skin's translucence appeared again. "If you mean what happened by the pool . . ."

"You did say that I was obliged to marry you after that," he pointed out, gaining confidence now.

"It was a joke!"

"Was it?"

"Yes."

"Many women wouldn't think so."

"I am *not* 'many women.' "

Richard let himself smile. "I know. But I wasn't referring to that, er, interlude."

"What then?"

"Perhaps you don't realize that until we discovered that coal deposit, I was nearly penniless?"

She frowned as if he had said something confusing.

"I had no right to marry."

"Because of money?" She looked incredulous.

"Absolutely."

"You mean, if we had not found the coal . . ."

"I never would have touched you. I would have asked that you honor our bargain and break off our pretended engagement."

Emily shivered. Richard pulled the covers up.

"Even though you cared for me?" she whispered.

"Even though I have known for a long while that I would never love anyone else."

She gave a little gasp at the word *love*. "You would have left me alone—for money?"

"Honor," he corrected this time.

She sat up and glared down at him. "I would

never have forgiven you as long as I lived! I don't care anything about money."

He laughed a little. "I know you don't."

"But you still . . ."

"*I* cared. I wanted to give you the ease and comfort you've never had. I wanted you to have all the luxuries of the duchess's household *and* the passion of your parents'."

Emily gazed at him. Her blue eyes pooled with tears. "How did you . . . ?"

"I know you. How else could I love you?"

She threw herself into his arms. He thought she might weep, but she didn't. She held him fiercely, possessively, for a while. He enjoyed it.

"There's something you haven't said," he pointed out when she relaxed a little. "It's rather important."

She raised her coppery brows. There was a challenging glint in her eyes.

"I have told you that I love you," he pointed out.

She nodded regally, a smile tugging at the corners of her mouth.

"You haven't . . . reciprocated."

Emily tossed her head. "I don't believe I shall. I think I'll keep you wondering for, oh, a year or two. You'll have to cater to all my little whims and fancies and . . ."

Richard pulled her down against him and kissed her lingeringly. "I could keep you here until you admit it."

"Mmm," breathed Emily. "Oh," she said as his hand moved. "Yes, why don't you?"

Dizzy, intoxicating minutes passed. Richard was breathing hard, desire driving him further than he had believed possible before this night. It was like a molten wave carrying them both beyond ordinary realms of sensation, into the transcendent. It rose and rose until the demands of passion nearly over-whelmed him.

"Richard," murmured Emily. "Please," she pleaded. "Oh, please."

"Tell me," he demanded through gritted teeth. He resisted the wave with all his strength.

"I love you," Emily breathed. "I'll never love any-one else so much."

Gloriously, the wave broke.

EMILY NESTLED CLOSER into the curve of Richard's shoulder, her arm thrown across his muscular chest. They would sleep side by side in the night for the rest of their lives, she thought drowsily. She could hardly believe it even now. "So everything came right in the end," she murmured, mainly to herself.

"Very right," Richard agreed.

"When are they coming about the coal?"

"Tomorrow, I'm afraid."

Emily remembered something else. She rose on one elbow. "What did you mean that night, at the evening party, when you said I had cut through weeks of pondering and confusion?"

Richard looked up at her, his expression tender. "You said someone should make certain that the new inventions were used wisely."

She nodded.

"It was the hint I needed. The purpose I had been looking for in my life," he added simply.

The appreciation and respect in his gaze rendered her speechless for a moment.

"And with this coal deposit, I will have the funds to act as well."

"And you owe it all to me," she teased. "If I had not come down to Wales, you would not have been chased through the countryside and found the coal."

Richard frowned. "A method of discovery not to be repeated."

"I certainly hope not."

A thought struck Emily. "You know, I have a friend who might be very helpful about new inventions . . ."

Richard's expression stopped her. "Another friend?"

She nodded.

His hazel eyes danced. "A pickpocket? A singing teacher who used to smuggle brandy out of Napoleon's France?"

"No. He is quite respectable. Except . . ."

"Yes?" He was smiling. "Except?"

Emily gave him a look. "He has a sad habit of designing his own banknotes."

Emily's brand new husband dissolved in laughter as he pulled her close.

ABOUT THE AUTHOR

JANE ASHFORD grew up in a small town in south-western Ohio, where she discovered the romance of history at an early age in the public library. After extensive travel in Europe, she settled in Cambridge, Massachusetts. She has written novels of romantic suspense as well as numerous Regency romances. She has also taught literature and writing, and written speeches, book reviews, and newsletters.

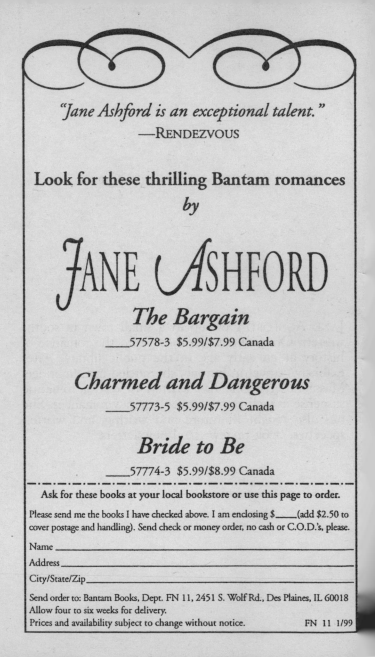